About the author

With twenty years' experience of Fleet Street behind him, William Moore brings a challenging and perceptive eye to bear on military history. His other novels in this series, still featuring the Mallindine family, deal with the Zulu war and a crucial campaign in World War I. Mr Moore's non-fiction titles are *See How They Ran – The British Retreat of 1918*, *Accidental Agent* – written for John Goldsmith, S.O.E. agent, *The Thin Yellow Line* and *The Durham Light Infantry* – for the 'Famous Regiments' series.

THE SOLDIERS

Bayonets in the Sun

WILLIAM MOORE

SPHERE BOOKS LIMITED
30/32 Gray's Inn Road, London WC1X 8JL

First published in Great Britain by Sphere Books Ltd 1974

Acknowledgements

I would like to place on record my gratitude to Miss Travis and the officials of the India House Library for their assistance.

W.M.

TRADE
MARK

Set in Intertype Plantin

Printed in Great Britain by
Hazell Watson & Viney Ltd
Aylesbury, Bucks

ISBN 0 7221 6152 2

MAPS

SIKH WAR 1848~49
Theatre of Operations

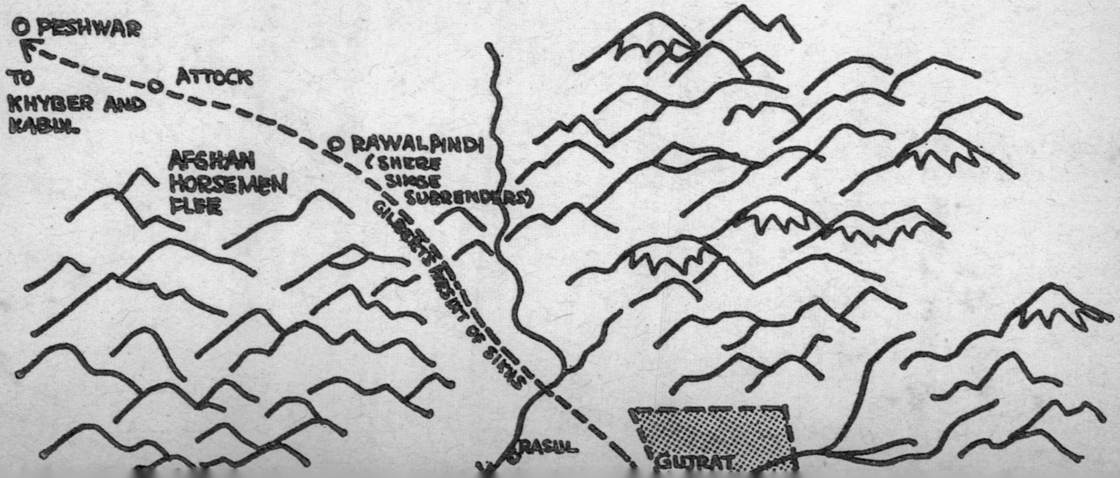

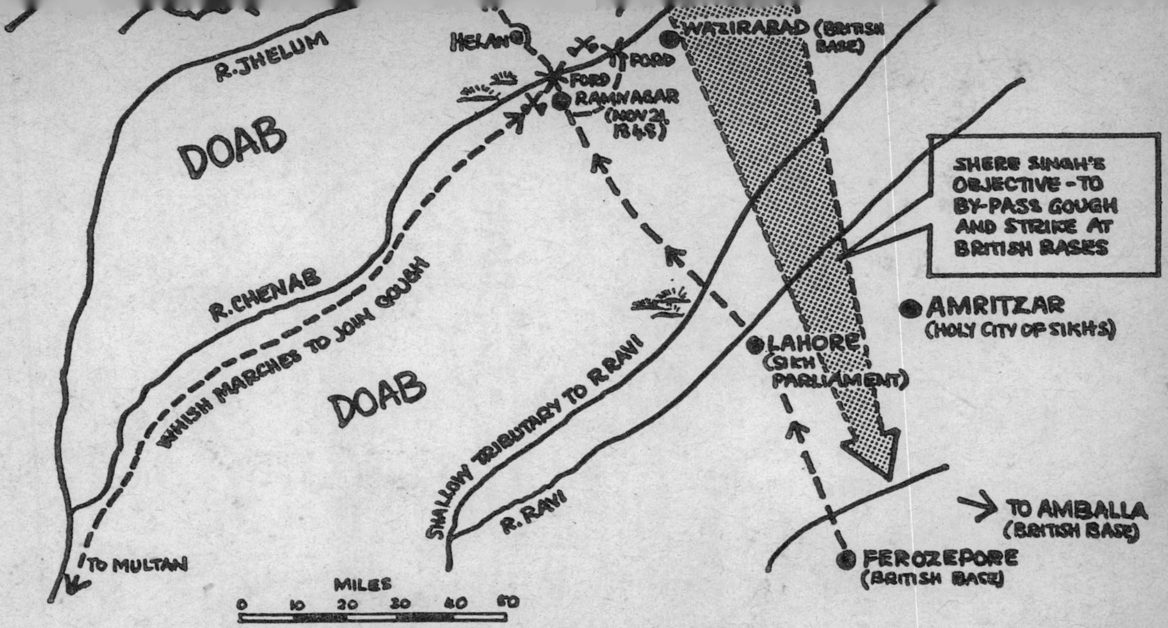

R.JHELUM
HELAN
FORD
FORD
RAMNAGAR
(NOV 21, 1848)
WAZIRABAD (BRITISH BASE)
DOAB
R.CHENAB
WHISH MARCHES TO JOIN GOUGH
DOAB
SHALLOW TRIBUTARY TO R.RAVI
R.RAVI
SHERE SINGH'S OBJECTIVE - TO BY-PASS GOUGH AND STRIKE AT BRITISH BASES
AMRITZAR
(HOLY CITY OF SIKHS)
LAHORE
(SIKH PARLIAMENT)
TO AMBALLA
(BRITISH BASE)
FEROZEPORE
(BRITISH BASE)
TO MULTAN
MILES
0 10 20 30 40 50

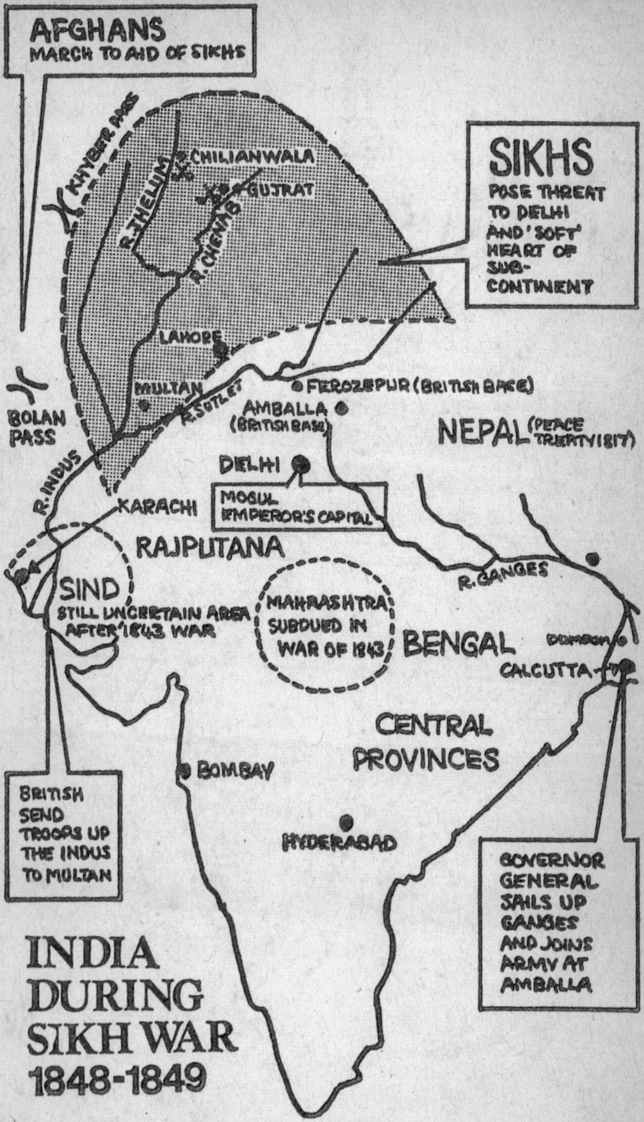
AFGHANS
MARCH TO AID OF SIKHS
KHYBER PASS
CHILIANWALA
GUJRAT
R. JHELUM
R. CHENAB
SIKHS
POSE THREAT TO DELHI AND 'SOFT' HEART OF SUB-CONTINENT
LAHORE
MULTAN
R. SUTLEJ
FEROZEPUR (BRITISH BASE)
AMBALLA (BRITISH BASE)
BOLAN PASS
NEPAL (PEACE TREATY 1817)
R. INDUS
DELHI
MOGUL EMPEROR'S CAPITAL
KARACHI
RAJPUTANA
R. GANGES
SIND
STILL UNCERTAIN AREA AFTER 1843 WAR
MAHRASHTRA SUBDUED IN WAR OF 1843
BENGAL
CALCUTTA
CENTRAL PROVINCES
BOMBAY
HYDERABAD
BRITISH SEND TROOPS UP THE INDUS TO MULTAN
GOVERNOR GENERAL SAILS UP GANGES AND JOINS ARMY AT AMBALLA
INDIA DURING SIKH WAR 1848-1849

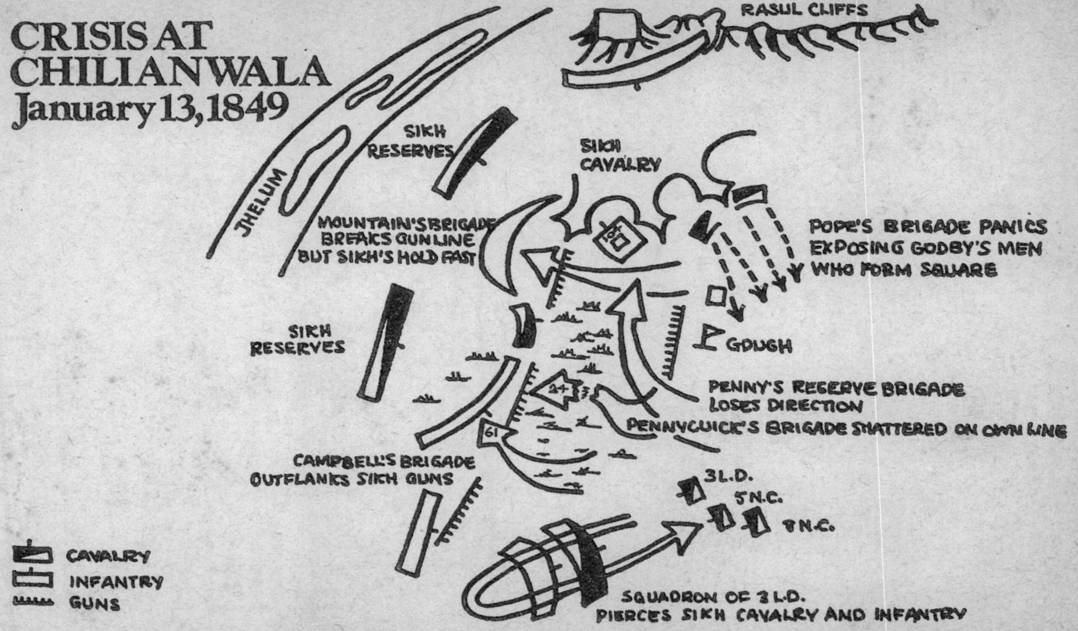
CRISIS AT
CHILIANWALA
January 13, 1849
RASUL CLIFFS
JHELUM
SIKH RESERVES
SIKH CAVALRY
MOUNTAIN'S BRIGADE BREAKS GUN LINE BUT SIKH'S HOLD FAST
POPE'S BRIGADE PANICS EXPOSING GODBY'S MEN WHO FORM SQUARE
SIKH RESERVES
GOUGH
24
61
PENNY'S RESERVE BRIGADE LOSES DIRECTION
PENNYCUICK'S BRIGADE SHATTERED ON OWN LINE
CAMPBELL'S BRIGADE OUTFLANKS SIKH GUNS
3 L.D.
5 N.C.
8 N.C.
SQUADRON OF 3 L.D. PIERCES SIKH CAVALRY AND INFANTRY
CAVALRY
INFANTRY
GUNS

CHAPTER ONE

Brigadier-General Charles Cureton, C.B., cocked a thick silver eyebrow and raised a rosy face to the sky.

'Annoying beggar, isn't he, Mallindine?'

A young officer in the uniform of Her Majesty's 14th Light Dragoons followed the direction of the glance and dutifully, if woodenly, studied the dot circling slowly overhead. Not knowing what he was expected to say he said nothing. He wished the general would get moving again and bring some relief from the swarm of flies which hung in a cloud over the stationary group of mounted officers.

'Yes, our feathered friend up there has probably got the answer to all our questions under his eyes right now. Shere Singh's guns, his reserves, his cavalry and trenches are as clear to that bird as if painted on one of the maps the Horse Guards are so fond of drawing up *after* a battle. Any soldier would give his right arm for such a view, and yet all that creature is concerned about is his next meal. Carrion! That is all we are to him, Mallindine. Shouldn't wonder if he isn't weighing us up for dinner at this very moment.'

The general, a lithe figure, despite middle age, stopped musing, touched his horse lightly with his spurs and trotted forward at an economic pace that spared men and animals and raised the least amount of dust.

The movement was noted by the vulture, one of the dung-eating variety known as Pharaoh's Chickens. Its cold, calculating gaze missed little as it wheeled on the thermals, but a sickly limping baggage camel was of more interest to it than Cureton's headquarters staff or the marching columns below. Vultures don't take sides. They make war only on the dead. And, for the moment, the living dominated the baked Punjaub plain.

To the north lay the grey-green foothills and, beyond, the white-tipped giants of Kashmir. There in the chill shadows of empty valleys rise the icy sources of the five rivers that bring life to the Doabs – the areas between the waterways which join with the Indus.

In spate, each river is an implacable, formidable force, writhing and gouging its own treacherous path. But in November, 1848, the waters were deceptively complacent. The snow-fed torrents had dwindled, leaving the land scarred with twisting, dried-out nullahs where burnished pebbles reflected the rays of a sun which, though strong, had lost the ferocity of mid-summer. It was, in military terms, good campaigning weather.

Eldred Mallindine regarded Cureton with a certain amount of displeasure. They had been on the move at snail's pace since dawn five hours earlier and the old man (Cureton was sixty years old) looked like going on for another five hours. There was not the slightest indication of him wearying of the excursion or of doing anything else except pause now and then to stare. Mallindine had been warned that being attached to Cureton as an extra A.D.C. would be uncomfortable and boring. Up to now the prophesy had been fulfilled.

They seemed to have been trailing backwards and forwards on the fringe of the Sikh host for a lifetime; most of it either in the saddle or lying fully-clothed alongside their horses with the reins fast to their belts as they tried to get some rest. Trumpets and bugles gave a brassy welcome to each dawn, sounding the 'stand to arms'; the squadrons mounted, the few companies of Foot fell in and the gunners stood by their cannon yawning and working up a glow on their matches. But nothing happened. After Cureton had emerged from his tent and aired his flowing white whiskers in the morning air, they would set off on one of his interminable slow-trot scouting expeditions. Mallindine's hope of being able to boast of having seen some action by the time the main army arrived had vanished very early in the campaign. Now the greater part of it was on the scene – and still Cureton was ambling about the plain staring around him.

If some of his staff were bored, Cureton was not. He had enjoyed the past few days, trying to tempt Shere Singh to stay south of the Chenab so that the Commander-in-Chief might fall upon the Sikh flank while he was absorbed with the smaller force. And for a time it looked as though the enemy might oblige by doing something violent. At any rate, Cureton had taken no chances and had posted a double cordon of vedettes around the camp each day, two horsemen every hundred yards and infantry forming an inner ring of sentries. But Shere Singh had obviously thought better of it and pulled back his troops from Ramnagar to a camp across the river. Now the enemy held four lines of deep, wide trenches on the high north bank of the Chenab with heavy batteries covering the shallow ford and all the approaches on the southern side. There were still Sikhs on the near side, but they were only detachments forming the rearguard and as the army advanced in what was tantamount to a huge reconnaissance in force, they were falling back, too.

'Shere Singh won't take any chances,' Cureton remarked confidently, rising in his stirrups to let his charger stale freely.

Mallindine noted absentmindedly that the urine dried on the hot sand almost before it had time to steam.

'Can't see him popping across to oblige us by getting stuck with a river at his back like they did at Sobraon,' Cureton continued. 'He's too fly for that. He'll squat behind his ramparts inviting us to try a rush across the water and bom!' (Cureton smacked his gauntlets together) '. . . he'll blast us with his heavy metal. He'll stretch his shot from that elevation all right. Stops us seeing what he's up to. That's why I wouldn't mind being a blasted bird – just for a minute or two mind you. I wouldn't want to be a vulture for long. Fancy having to eat a dead dragoon, eh?'

The little group of officers laughed dutifully, but Cureton knew what was really on their minds. They would rather be at the head of a squadron waving sabres than trotting about tamely at his coat tails. Well, it was all right for youngsters to think like that and they would have to do it when the time came. But they'd also have to realise that horse soldiering wasn't all done at the gallop and – even when it was – not everyone enjoyed it, or lived long enough to enjoy it, come to that. He hoped he'd managed to drum some commonsense into his son who was somewhere behind with his squadron of the 14th Light Dragoons. Ah, the old 14th. He turned to Mallindine and, brushing his sweeping moustaches with the back of his hand, remarked in what he thought was a sympathetic tone:

'I can't see the regiment cutting its teeth today, my boy. Ye'll have to be patient.'

'No, sir. I suppose not.'

It was funny to think that Cureton had served in the ranks of the 14th during the Peninsular War. He looked as though he'd been a general all his life, with his whiskers and his little paunch which the most cunning of cummerbunds could not conceal entirely. Even stranger to realise that Cureton had got himself so much into debt as a young blood that he'd tried to fake his death by drowning. What on earth was there in Shropshire for a man to spend money on, Mallindine wondered? Anyway, he'd got through a fortune, had Cureton, and when the creditors didn't altogether accept the idea that he was drowned he had changed his name and taken the King's Shilling. The old boy had actually become a sergeant by the time he was spotted by an old acquaintance on Wellington's staff – old Fitzroy Somerset it was said – and been given a commission in his own name. The Duke had said if all debtors fought like Cureton he'd form a regiment in the Fleet Prison. After the war Cureton had taken himself off to India and seen service against Mahrattas and Afghans and almost anything on horseback. They said he was the best cavalry commander in the army. But for the life of him Mallindine couldn't see why. More experienced warriors – Shere Singh included – were aware that what Charles Cureton did not know about handling large bodies of horsemen was not worth knowing.

If Cureton had spent a lifetime on active service, the 14th Light Dragoons had not. Since their distinguished service during the Napoleonic Wars they had not drawn their swords in anger; unless one counted a squalid affair at Bristol when they were called out to curb a riot. No one was more conscious of this than Mallindine.

The 14th had arrived in the theatre of operations too late to take part in the First Sikh War and had missed the medal and the prize-money. Mallindine, who felt he had been unfairly cheated of the glory, did not like being reminded of the fact and smiled a tight, diplomatic smile at Cureton's remark about drawing blood. He avoided the eye of a gaunt captain in the 3rd Light Dragoons, who had served through the campaign two years previously and had a finger missing to show for it. The Drunken Third! That was how Mallindine regarded them. He wished, sourly, that the uniforms of the two regiments were not so alike. Apart from the buttons and badges and odd pieces of equipment, the dark blue tunics and skin-tight trousers were almost identical. The drinking habits of the 3rd were quite distinctive, however. Whereas the 14th were restricted to three-quarters of a pint of rum a day, the 3rd were allowed to drink as much as they could hold – a formidable amount in some cases. Quite a few had gone so far as to kill themselves with liquor, although that was a common enough occurrence in India at the time. Mallindine reflected that, grog or no grog, the 3rd Light Dragoons had covered themselves with glory at Sobraon, riding through the Sikh camp and turning a defeat into a rout. If those drunkards could beat the Sikhs, a well-disciplined sober regiment like the 14th would eat them.

'Jesus, sergeant, what wouldn't I give to be back at Amballa. A month's pay for a dram. Yes, a month's pay for a dram. That's what I'd give.'

Private Hacken tried to smack his parched lips but succeeded only in looking like a stranded codfish.

The 3rd Light Dragoons had been drawn up in jingling, chinking squadrons, the horses tossing their heads restlessly, tails swishing continually as a protection against the attentions of swarms of industrious insects.

'Keep your mouth shut, Billy, and try chewing some of the booze out of that pickled tongue of yours,' said Sergeant Wood good-naturedly. He was fiddling with the sun curtain which hung over his neck from the quilted white cover on his shako. A button had come off and the flap hung crookedly.

'I knew something had gone when we jumped that bleeding nullah back there,' he said. 'And where am I going to get a button in this God-forsaken hole?'

'Yer won't need it if those gorchurras cut yer head off, will yer?' said a grizzled private nodding in the direction of the Chenab which glittered invitingly in the distance. A swarm of white-robed Sikh irregulars wheeled and cantered in loose formation, the legs of their horses hidden in a low haze so that they seemed to float over the ground. Here and there the gold-pointed kullah of a Pathan glinted in a blue turban. Lance points dancing above the dust flashed menacingly in the bright sun.

'You'll know all about it if one of those bastards sticks his spear up your arse,' said Hacken.

'Look to your front. Here comes the colonel,' snapped Wood.

Colonel Lockwood cantered past followed by another officer. He was pleased with his men. They had remained well in hand while skirmishing with the Sikhs and now they formed a picture to delight the eye of an artist as they waited for orders. Both troops of No. 1 Squadron were mounted on bays. No. 2 Squadron had a troop of chestnuts and one of dun horses. The mixture of skewbalds and piebalds in 'E' troop struck a discordant note but at least the rest of No. 3 Squadron had plain black mounts. No. 4, composed entirely of greys, looked coolly superior to their fellows.

So far there had been no casualties. The Sikhs had sent cavalry over the river to protect the last of their retreating columns as the British approached and these had been driven back without difficulty. The 3rd had encountered a particularly unpleasant dry watercourse running diagonally across their front and had halted some distance from it about half a mile from the river. The gorchurras were trying to lure them within range of the efficient Sikh artillery without success. To the right of the 3rd and the rest of the cavalry – the 14th Light Dragoons and two regiments of native cavalry in light blue – stood sweating lines of scarlet infantry under Sir Colin Campbell.

Between Cureton and the Chenab stood what would have been an island if the river had been in spate. Now it appeared as a long, low hillock, studded with withered trees. Beyond it, across the sluggish waters, the yellow turbans of the Sikh gunners dotted the earthworks crowning the bank.

'Well, I suppose we'd better find out what they're hiding, White.'

Cureton went into conference with the brigade commander, another Peninsular veteran.

'Wicked old bastards,' muttered Private Hacken darkly as an orderly detached himself from the little headquarters group and trotted smartly towards the 3rd.

'No. 1 Squadron . . . threes right. At a trot . . . *March!*'

Sergeant Wood stopped fiddling with his shako cover, kicked his horse into motion and swore. His red hair was soaked with perspiration.

'Now what?'

The plan was simple if cold-blooded. Cureton wanted a squadron of cavalry to gallop in open order at extended intervals round the other side of the 'island', exposing themselves to fire from the opposite bank. He reasoned that no gunners would be able to resist the target and that the Sikhs would open up. It was what professionals called getting the enemy to 'unmask' his batteries.

'You can count them aloud, Mallindine,' he said, 'and Thompson can write them down.'

A young officer fumbled in his sabretache and sat waiting with pencil poised. Cureton trotted a little way off 'to count for meself'. Captain Ouvery, commanding the leading actors in the plot, ordered No. 1 Squadron to break ranks and Mallindine watched as they raced off. The Drunken Third had three miles to go.

In the Sikh position the appearance round the side of the 'island' of first a solitary galloping horseman, then a trio followed by random groups, caused a flurry of excitement. With a crash and a hiss a twelve-pounder opened fire. A billow of saffron smoke marked its position. Far beyond the straggling riders a pillar of flame and dirt shot into the air. Another crash. Another cloud. This time the aim was better but the shell burst in a patch of soft sand with a muffled roar. Then the cannonade became general and orange-flecked dust geysers spurted among the horsemen.

Hunched over his mare's withers, Sergeant Wood dug in his spurs furiously and found himself saying 'Jesus!' at every near miss. To bolster his own spirits as much as anything he roared hoarsely: 'Keep going lads. They couldn't hit a bucket in a midden.'

At the same time, he told himself that if the gunners knew

their job they would start using solid shot at any moment instead of shells.

As if to compliment his judgment, a heavy battery started to drop cannon balls just short of the line taken by the scurrying dragoons. The missiles landed with clod-scattering thumps, hurtled into the air and bounded viciously among the legs of the horses. A crack like the sound of a boot kicking in the side of a tea chest was followed by an agonised squealing. Wood glanced back and saw a pathetic beast trying to drag itself up on its forelegs, its hind limbs having been severed below the hocks. His own mount startled him by plunging and heaving.

'Quicksands, be-Christ!'

He swung from the saddle and seized the reins. He could see now that what had appeared to be solid ground was actually dotted with irregular patches of soft sand.

'Come on there, gal, it's not too bad. Come on my beauty. Up now.'

The frightened animal snorted and plunged frantically, tongue hanging from the side of its mouth, neck covered in foam. Out of the corner of his eye Wood glimpsed a black object speeding towards him, growing larger and larger. He flinched and shut his eyes.

There was an obscene noise of simultaneous grinding and squelching; the reins went slack in his hands and he crashed on his back blinded and choking for air. A hot, stinking porridge-like slime filled his eyes and mouth and nostrils. Scraping desperately at his face he rose shakily to his feet and looked down. At his feet lay a glutinous mass of bright red flesh, hideous white bone splinters and oozing grey matter – the pulped remains of his horse's head.

The animal's hindquarters were still kicking violently in the sand. Wood vomited helplessly. He staggered away and tripped over his sword which had plunged into the ground as he fell. Gripping it in his trembling hand he began to run, a hatless, bloody apparition waving a shining blade.

The range was half a mile, in some places even less. So close that the dragoons could see the gunners applying their glowing matches. Even if they had been fresh the three-mile gauntlet would have been exhausting and all the horses were worn with constant patrol work. Some sank up to their bellies and struggled feebly. Their riders dismounted and scattered, pursued by shouting Sikhs who swarmed over the river once there was no danger of riding into the fire of their own guns. Sergeant Wood could hardly believe his good fortune when he was almost knocked down by a riderless gorchurra pony. Seizing its reins, he grabbed the unfamiliar native pommel and hoisted himself into the saddle. The little horse bucked and tossed its head for a moment before brutal use of spur and bridle drove it forward. A high-pitched yell behind made Wood look back. A yelling gorchurra on a great black horse was bearing down on him. The lance head with the cluster of bright ribbons was drawing nearer by the second. Automatically Wood threw back his sword to the right rear guard position in the forlorn hope that he would be able to deflect the point when the thrust came. He noticed that the man's teeth were showing a brilliant white in his dark beard. His pursuer was laughing at him.

The Sikh closing in for the kill could feel the power of his splendid gelding surging into his knees. A gentle pressure on the left rein and he would swing clear of the English soldier's feeble sword. Eleven feet of bamboo tipped with steel moved smoothly to align itself on a spot six inches below the hatless head of the fleeing dragoon. The Sikh's arm muscles tensed.

'Salaam, feringhee,' he yelled. Wood turned towards him, his face a ghastly mask of dried blood and horse-flesh.

The gorchurra heard a shrill voice shout a warning in Hindi. He glanced round in alarm but it was too late. A searing flame glowed white-hot between his shoulders and swept through his body. His elbows jerked convulsively into his ribs, his hands opened and rigidly splayed fingers let fall the lance which jolted quivering into the ground. With his head thrown back and his eyes glaring at a brassy sky he could not see, the Sikh rose bolt upright in his stirrups before toppling slowly over the rump of his horse which continued steadfastly to pursue the fleeing sergeant.

'That chap meant to have you, Joe,' Private Hacken told his comrade as he galloped alongside. 'If I hadn't put my sword through 'im you'd be making excuses at the bleedin' Pearly Gates by now.'

He added, with a flourish of his stained blade:

'With all that blood on yer face, I wasn't sure you was worth saving. What'd you do, Joe? Cut yourself shaving?'

But Joe Wood was too exhausted to reply. Terror had robbed him of all control of his bladder and he hoped that his trousers would dry before the men noticed.

Far in the rear another scream pierced the air. A tall Sikh in a scarlet turban cut down a running figure in blue, waved his tulwar and cantered away. On the smooth sand the fallen dragoon's spurs flashed like broken glass. He was one of seventeen who did not answer the roll call of the 3rd Light Dragoons that night. But the presence of some thirty Sikh guns was established by their sacrifice.

Paddy Gough, Commander-in-Chief of the Army of The Punjaub, was not the man to leave his soldiers in the lurch. When it was clear that the 3rd had run into trouble on the sandy bed of the river he sent forward two troops of the crack Bengal Horse Artillery to cover their retirement. Thick dun clouds rose behind each team as they swung across the plain. The chink of chains, creak of wheels and drumming of hoofs rippled over the arid landscape.

The horse gunners were big men. Black metal helmets, streaming plumes of scarlet horse-hair, made them look taller than they were. Their chests were covered with gold braid and they wore white breeches and thigh-length jackboots. Only the leopardskin band around their distinctive Roman-style helmet indicated their tropical service. The Afghans had respectfully christened them The Red Men during the disastrous war of 1839–42 when they were among the few troops to emerge with an enhanced reputation. Tough and adaptable, the Bengal Horse Artillery regarded themselves as an élite. And as they swept into action on the shores of the Chenab none was prouder than a little man who clung grimly to the muzzle of the 2nd Troop's No. 4 gun. Not for him or for Madho Dinnath, who hung on to the other side of the barrel, the gorgeous uniforms or the Red Manes. But even the humblest members of the crew could share in the glory. And Lala Rai's eyes were shining through the dust. He and his comrade were the lowly gun lascars. They did the tasks the

Gorah-log thought were beneath them. They had their own uniform and distinctive turban. They did not ride horses but perched precariously on seats built onto the gun axle-trees. Covered with dirt from the pounding hoofs of six horses, with every jolt threatening to propel them into the whirling spokes, they thrust their feet against wooden rests suspended on chains, tried to balance and trusted to luck. Dangerous though his position was, Lala Rai would not have changed it for the throne of Delhi itself. Woe betide any grasscutter or syce who went near his precious charge after Lala Rai had cleared the dust from its brazen throat at the end of a day's march.

'Action rear!' bellowed a voice.

Lala Rai leaped down. In a matter of seconds the horses were racing to the rear and the crew were sponging, loading, firing and running up the piece. But this time the running-up drill was not so smooth. As the third round sent a fountain of spray sparkling into the air well short of the Sikhs on the opposite bank, the gunners were aware that the six pounders were sinking. Some were almost axle deep in sand. Like the dragoons they were fast becoming helpless and immobile. What had been a demonstration to cover the cavalry now became an urgent operation to preserve the artillery.

Trumpets blared and the teams came racing back. Amid excited shouts and curses the traces were shackled. Whips cracked and horses heaved. Gunners strained at the wheels. Reluctantly the weapons of the 1st Troop yielded. By chance the troop had been experimenting with a system by which draught harness was worn by the horses of all members of the detachments. The extra power was put to good use immediately. Lala Rai's troop was not so fortunate. As Sikh shot whined overhead the struggle went on. The wheels of five guns were prised from the grip of the sand but the last remained well and truly rooted to the spot.

Lala Rai strained until his eyes started from his head and the veins bulged on his brown forehead.

'Narain!'

He spat and grunted.

'Oh, you cow, you double-dyed bastard cow,' swore Gunner O'Connor, ignoring the fact that he was blaspheming the sacred animal.

Old Sergeant Higgins made unintelligible grunting noises to his horse and Brown and Pender damned and blasted and panted and heaved while Mahdo Dinnath called on a score of gods.

The tall slender wheels of No. 4 gun sank lower and lower. Two wagons of No. 2 Troop remained equally obstinate.

As matchlock balls slapped into the ground in increasing numbers the order came to abandon the piece. An officer hastily hammered a shiny nail into the vent with the pommel of his sword and snapped it off at breech level. Sergeant Higgins methodically ripped up a cloak – not his own, O'Connor observed cynically – wrapped strips of the material round a cannon ball and rammed it firmly into the muzzle. If ever anyone did pull the gun free they would have other problems to cope with before they could use it. Other gunners dumped the contents of the waggons in the river and rode disconsolately to the rear. For a moment Lala Rai stood distraught over the obstinate brass barrel. He wept, realised his tears were smearing the polish, and instinctively rubbed it with his sleeve.

'Come on you bloody bhungi, it's time to go,' said O'Connor. 'We'll get you another gun, you little black bastard, don't worry. There are plenty more where that came from.'

A great white gauntlet seized Lala Rai's hand and he found himself clinging to the sweat-sodden blue back of Gunner O'Connor. He was still weeping into a torrent of scarlet horsehair as they rode back to the protection of a line of waiting cavalry. Behind them a swarm of jeering gorchurras splashed through the Chenab followed by a regiment of Sikh regular infantry.

Mallindine, who had watched the affair of the stranded gun with mounting rage, curled his lip in disgust as a gunner jogged past on a weary horse with a little Indian soldier hanging on behind. Like many other people, he was under the impression that the Duke of Wellington had never lost a gun throughout his illustrious career, and that to do so was shameful. It was entirely untrue – the Duke himself admitted to losing at least four but, as they were Portuguese, his admirers didn't really count them. Nevertheless the legend persisted and latterday generals found themselves judging and being judged by the number of guns they had won or lost. Surely, thought the young dragoon, Lord Gough is not going to leave a cannon in enemy hands. It was a matter of national pride.

Paddy Gough's fresh complexion deepened. He sank his chin on his famous fighting coat and demanded of the gunner officer concerned: 'Can't ye do anythin', Lane? Is it really stuck as fast as ye say?'

Lane, as red-faced and as angry as Gough, assured the General that it was.

Gough called for his telescope. An instrument bound in polished brown leather and measuring some three feet was produced. The man from Limerick put his fierce blue eye to it.

Mallindine, still in attendance on Cureton, watched expectantly. Old Paddy was a real fire-eater. Not much to go on as a gentleman in Mallindine's eyes; but then the Irish gentry weren't. As a fighting man, however, he had the reputation of having fought more battles than anyone serving in the British Army at that time. Even the Duke, it was said, hadn't fought as many actions, although no one had yet had the nerve to say so. Mallindine had heard people say that Paddy was not too bright but he had no time for such talk. Soldiers weren't expected to be clever. They were expected to fight. Paddy could do that. And would do. He looked at the stocky figure hunched up in the strange oatmeal-coloured coat with the big bone buttons and wondered what he was thinking.

General Lord Gough, in fact, was thinking that it was about time somebody did something. He was irritated and annoyed. He had risen at an unearthly hour in the morning and ridden through the night to see Cureton – and everything had gone wrong. Shere Singh had stuck himself behind his ramparts across the river and now that fool Lane had drowned one of his blasted cannon. Not since he joined the army as a boy of fifteen had he seen such a mess. Gough felt tired, and why shouldn't he? He was, after all, almost seventy. God in Heaven, he'd seen enough soldiering. Give him the old 87th and he'd have shown 'them Saikhs' a thing or two. The Sikh entrenchments were laughable compared with the places they had stormed in the Peninsula.

He always seemed to be storming places. Those forts in

China. And those mud ramparts in the Mahratta campaign. Those Sikh camps had been no easy matter either. Still, he'd taken them. And that was only two years ago. So he would take them again. If only he could get someone to do something. The trouble was that no one had any spirit any more. Look at Cureton. Didn't want to risk his cavalry because there was a dry river bed in front of them. And White was backing him up. Old Peninsular men, both of them. He couldn't understand what was holding them.

Gough put down his telescope and glowered at his assembled staff. Sir Colin Campbell returned his stare for a moment, then sniffed and looked away.

'It's no good, Campbell. It's not a job for the Foot. We'll need all we've got for better things later. So you needn't keep up that damn' sniffing. It's a job for the cavalry and they don't seem to think they're up to it.'

Cureton had heard it all before and ignored the remark and let Gough grumble on. That way old Paddy could let off steam. At that moment two officers approached and saluted Havelock, commanding the 14th Light Dragoons, and his adjutant. They were just in time to hear Gough exclaim in disgusted tones: 'Whoever heard of a dry nullah stopping cavalry before?'

Colonel William Havelock could hardly contain himself with excitement. In spite of his fifty-five years he felt like a young man again. It was the first time since the Napoleonic Wars that he had heard shots fired in anger. It was heady music. Back in 1813 when he had led his Spanish troops at Vera they had called him El Chico Blanco after he had leaped the abattis. Now he felt like the Little Blond Lad all over again. His hair might be grey but his figure was still trim. Today would be something to tell brother Henry about. Havelock's eyes were bright as he addressed himself to White and then Cureton.

Cureton remained some minutes in conversation and then walked his horse a pace or two nearer to explain that Havelock was requesting permission to drive back the enemy horsemen on his front.

Gough nodded. Good man, Havelock. No nonsense about him. Not one of these clever fellows. Get at 'em. That was what he'd do. Not quite catching the full gist of the conversation between the cavalrymen, Gough, now feeling decidedly better because something was going to happen, added a last-minute comment of his own.

'Don't forget if you see an opportunity for charging, Havelock, charge them.'

With a magnificent sweep of his sabre, Havelock saluted and galloped off, followed by his adjutant. His regiment saw him return radiant.

'All right, Apthorp.'

The adjutant turned in his saddle.

'14th Light Dragoons, walk-march . . . trot.'

Mallindine jogged anxiously up to Cureton.

'May I have permission to join my troop, sir?'

'No you may not. You can stand by your general. You'll not miss anything. They're only going to do what the 3rd did earlier. They'll hustle the gorchurras back and halt. It won't come to blows. Not yet.'

Mallindine bit his lip, saluted and walked his horse to a point behind Cureton where he could watch the squadrons move off in column, white shakos bobbing above the dust, swords glinting at the shoulder. It was thirty-six years since his regiment had gone into action and he was forced to look on.

There was nothing wrong with the men. There was nothing wrong with the horses. Although only a handful had seen active service before, the 14th Light Dragoons deployed immaculately into line and advanced on the taunting Sikhs who fled. At this point Havelock should have regarded his job as done. But from his saddle he could see more Sikh cavalry clustered in the shallows and on the dry bed of the river under their gleaming blue and yellow banners. He decided to charge them. According to the golden rule for mounted action he was well supported. The 5th Native Cavalry had followed him on to the field and his fourth squadron was in reserve.

'Trumpeter . . .'

Purposefully the 14th advanced over the plain. The enemy were a mile away. For half that distance the dragoons would keep up a trot. For two furlongs they would gallop. After that it would be hell for leather, howling like mad things.

To the watchers it became all too obvious what Havelock intended. It also became plain that he had not realised that the dry nullah now lay on his front; a situation brought about by an unconscious change of direction. The nullah was now full of Sikh regular infantry.

'My God, this isn't the way to use cavalry,' gasped Cureton.

'You'd better call him off immediately before he does some damn' fool thing,' added Gough irritably.

'You, sir . . .' he whirled on a staff officer. 'Ride to Colonel Havelock and tell him he is to take ground to the right and return at once to his former position.'

The officer vanished in a cloud of dust, and reappeared heading in a direction that patently would not enable him to deliver his message in time.

'Oh, my God, this is too much,' burst out Cureton. 'I shall go myself.'

The deed matched the word. Off he flew followed by his staff. Mallindine dug his spurs into his gelding with a force that made it snort with pain before it settled down to its stride. He kept his eyes on the silver whiskers of the erect figure in front. Obviously Cureton intended to cut off the charging regiment, or at least to attract the attention of its leader.

The veteran of a score of cavalry battles was beside himself with rage. For years he had tried to dissipate the headstrong legacy of the Peninsular War and Waterloo, when the cavalry had often destroyed itself through lack of discipline.

Havelock's action was almost criminally irresponsible. Did he not realise that the Sikh army was the only one on the Indian continent capable of challenging the British? He would have something to say to him, by God he would. And to the Commander-in-Chief. Why didn't old Paddy stick to his bayonets?

Mallindine was galloping slightly to the right rear of Cureton when he saw a solitary Sikh in a white uniform with black cross belts step out from behind a tree. The man raised his matchlock carefully, paused for a moment and fired. The shot was unheard in the general uproar but the puff of smoke told its tale. Immediately Cureton's head snapped back, his hat sailed away and with both hands clawing at the air he was gone. Unable to stop, the little cavalcade thundered past and then pulled up in confusion before cantering back to the crumpled figure. An officer dismounted and bent down. He heaved at the shoulders and then fell sprawling where a musket ball had flung him. Mallindine jumped down and saw that Cureton was dead. His sightless eyes still glared angrily but the shot had hit him in the heart and his chest was soaked in blood, now caking in the sand. The body was thrown across a horse and led hurriedly to the rear. Mallindine saw the officer who had been hit coughing bright scarlet gouts as he was propped up.

'Got him in the lungs,' the 3rd Light Dragoons captain said.

At the head of the 14th Light Dragoons, Havelock was totally unaware of the efforts being made to warn him of the menace in the nullah. His eyes were fixed on the banners of the Sikh cavalry. How glorious to be able to take one back to throw at Gough's feet. Thank heaven the Sikhs weren't moving. For troops who had been trained by French veterans like Allard and the Italian Avitabile, they hadn't learned much. Surely the rawest recruit knew that cavalry should be on the move to meet a charge, otherwise the shock would overwhelm them. The drumming behind him reached a crescendo and a roar burst from the lips of the dragoons. Unbelievably at that late moment a dense mass of scarlet and blue appeared as if out of the ground. Fierce eyes glared white out of dark faces behind levelled muskets. For one terrible moment Havelock thought he was charging a British regiment. The Sikh habit of clothing some of their regiments in red tunics and blue trousers had led to confusion on more than one occasion.

As Havelock's horse slithered over the edge of the dry river bed a jagged flash ripped the solid ranks of the enemy infantry who disappeared in a cloud of dirty white smoke.

The surprise for the young troopers of the 14th was no less than it had been for their colonel. But like him they kept going, hacking their way through a grey fog that smelled and tasted bitter, where demons in dark turbans fired at point blank range and tried to drag them from their horses. A man who fell to the ground lasted only seconds before Sikh bayonets and swords cut him to pieces.

Impetus carried most of the dragoons through the infantry and beyond into the Sikh cavalry who, fortunately, did not have the same determination as the foot soldiers, probably because of the confusion. Havelock, his shako gone, cut down one sowar and then another. Then a tulwar flashed out of the smoke and his bridle arm fell limply from the reins. Blood gushed down but there was no pain. Only a terrible numbness and helplessness. Wild with rage he flailed away with his sword at the snarling, cursing alien faces closing in on him. As his own blade bit home he tried to shout. But the noise would not come. There was no noise at all. The volleys, the screaming had ceased. In his throat something hard was expanding.

Jawahir Singh was laughing with the intoxicating joy of combat. How he loved these blue devils of the English. What a fight they gave a man. This old one had only one arm left but he had just cut the left ear off Mirza Khan, the Pathan. He reined back to watch the kill. The feringhee's horse was down now and still he was slashing with the stupid sword that was made for stabbing.

Havelock saw hate in the eyes of the man in the sheepskin surcoat. He saw hate in the eyes of the dead man on his sword. Then he saw fierce French faces and the abattis. The strength came back to his left arm, the noise returned and he leaped the barricade nimbly followed by his ragged Spaniards.

'El Chico Blanco' they were shouting. 'El Chico Blanco.'

His youth had returned.

Gough had been watching the 14th's charge when Cureton was killed. When his cavalry commander's death was reported he switched his glass to the little group bringing back the body. Gough's shoulders slumped. So many friends had been brought back in that way and yet he, who had seen more battles than any of them, had been spared. Why? Was it his fate to go on fighting for ever? His glass traversed the seething plain. An artillery colonel jumped as Gough's voice rapped out an order and obediently the gunner led forward his six-pounders to lash the Sikhs in the nullah with shrapnel at 1,000 yards. A solitary 12-pounder lobbed shells into the gully from a greater range. They exploded with ear-splitting crashes in the confined space and the Sikh infantry began to withdraw.

In the centre of a line of skirmishers sent out by the 29th Foot a tall sergeant watched riderless horses galloping aimlessly over the plain and spat thoughtfully.

'Donkey wallahs in trouble, by the look of it,' he commented to his right-hand man. Despite the uproar on the left, the infantry had been involved hardly at all that day and were duly grateful. They had spent most of their time staring dourly at a line of Sikh picquets three hundred yards away. Behind the thin British outpost line stood a solid red wall topped with white. The sergeant reflected that the Sikhs were not so easy to see because they wore blue turbans instead of bleached sun covers. He was glad that they were not Afghans with long jezails which could hit a man at five or six hundred yards. Cavalry calls drifted over the greying sand as the sun sank lower.

'Make ready to fire and retire,' he called to the straggling line. 'They'll be sounding "skirmishers in" at any moment,' he explained in a matter-of-fact way to a nervous young ensign. 'I shouldn't like the lads to let fly at the regiment accidentally as we run back.'

The ensign, who felt exhausted, dirty and thirsty, expressed his sincere hope that the sergeant was right. His ear caught a familiar note.

'There it is, Sergeant Leiston.'

A fusillade of shots left a ragged curtain of drifting smoke where the skirmishers had stood. The sergeant, a lean, tanned man with sharp eyes, loped along easily despite the handicap of the unexpired portion of 120 rounds of ball ammunition, weighing nearly twelve pounds, and a Brown Bess musket which was almost as heavy. Once back with his company he swiftly tore open the paper of the cartridge with his teeth, poured in the powder and rammed home the ball and wadding. Methodically replacing the ramrod he delved into a little pocket sewn into the front of his tunic and slipped a copper detonator over the nipple of the musket lock. Praise be the 29th were not armed with flintlocks like some of the native regiments!

He thought of the musket he had been issued with as a recruit – with a mutton bone in place of a proper flint to save government money. He wiped a crumb of powder from his blackened lips. What could you expect in a barracks in England anyway? What a bloody place. Give him India any day. India was the place. At least it had been until young Mallindine had shown up. Yes, he'd a lot to thank Mallindine for, Mallindine and his precious Uncle Ephraim.

CHAPTER TWO

The impetuosity of General Sir Ephraim Mallindine was no less than that of Eldred, his nephew and heir. If it differed in quality, it was because he had spent years commanding Portuguese troops. Cowed by his ferocious discipline and implacable will, his reluctant brigade had been terrorised into performing prodigious feats of valour during the Peninsular War. At Busaco, when the Portuguese militia ran away, Sir Ephraim's regular battalions cast an envious glance after their countrymen but stood firm, although common sense counselled instant flight. At Salamanca their comrades in other regiments had been driven into the attack by officers who beat them with the flat of their swords. Not so Mallindine's men. At the sight of him galloping up with the order to advance they had rushed headlong upon the French of their own accord.

The stern qualities which proved so admirable during the Peninsular campaigns were not to be wasted. After Waterloo a grateful government sent Sir Ephraim to stamp his inimitable mark upon the garrisons and people of a group of fever-ridden West Indian islands. To the disappointment of soldiers and civilians alike, he emerged from each mission unscathed. This knack of coercing peasants and negroes into making their due contribution to society he then applied to tenants on his extensive estates in the North of England. There, because of the intractability of the indigenous population, he found his efforts less rewarding. Nevertheless, as was his bounden duty, he devoted himself to the task unsparingly, finding relaxation only by indulging his passion for hunting. Robert Leiston was a mere footnote to a chapter in a full life.

'I have called ye here to tell ye that ye are to be married to Miss Howick,' he announced from behind a large writing table. And when the gangling figure before him replied with a scowl, he added in clipped tones:

'I have spoken with Leiston – with your father – and it is agreed.'

He slid out a drawer concealed in the gilded frieze of the

elegant Louis XV bureau plat – acquired for a song after Toulouse – and extracted a sheet of paper.

'The document is drawn up.'

Leiston stood glumly silent. He helped his father to run Sir Ephraim's home farm, three miles from Cleadon Grange, and although he had been schooled by the Rector he'd had little opportunity to develop conversation.

The silver buttons on the back of Sir Ephraim's plain blue coat rasped on the cane upholstery of his chair.

'Well, sir! What do ye have to say?'

Leiston stared at a thin white line running across the general's large, bony nose. What a pity the Frenchman hadn't hit him a bit harder.

'I don't rightly know what to say, sir.'

The words came out ponderously.

'Besides . . .'

'Yes?'

'I've heard tell she's . . . expecting.'

Sir Ephraim leaned forward and peered balefully at Leiston in silence for a moment.

'If you mean that the mare is in foal, you're right,' he said brutally. 'Why else do ye think she needs a husband?'

Leiston flushed.

'But why should I . . .' he began boldly.

A muscle bulged in Sir Ephraim's left cheek. He pursed his lips and pressed his thumbs together. It was a posture familiar to officers who had seen him sitting in judgment on looters about to be hanged. He sighed.

'I am not wont to account for my actions, Leiston,' he said. 'But I will explain why it is in your best interests to fall in with my wishes. Miss Howick, as ye know, is a companion to my nieces. Unfortunately some time ago she formed a certain attachment and abused my trust. If she were not the daughter of an old comrade, who died of the fever in Spain, I would dismiss her this moment. But I gave my word I would care for her. My nieces too, although aware that they cannot remain on such intimate terms, have begged me to be merciful and I have indulged them. I am determined that Miss Howick will live at Home Farm as a respectable married woman. If not as your wife, then as the wife of someone else.'

'But what about the father of her babe?'

'That is of no consequence. It is impossible for him to marry her.'

Sir Ephraim discerned a glow of rebellion in Leiston's eyes and dowsed it ruthlessly.

'Your father is a good bailiff and has a way with horses. I would be sorry to lose him but go he will, and your family with him, if I have to change these arrangements. Sign this document and Miss Howick will have £15 a year until the child is of age. Cross me and you may tell your father tonight that I want him out of the house within a week.'

General Mallindine pulled a slim gold half-hunter from his waistcoat and laid it on the desk. There was, he thought, little gratitude to be found in the labouring classes. He had found this lout a wife and guaranteed him an income and a home, and the booby was hesitating. His anger began to rise.

Leiston, sensing Sir Ephraim's irritation, cleared his throat. He was trapped and he knew it. If they had to quit Home Farm his father would never get another position in the area. People didn't take sides against Squire Mallindine. And his mother had made it quite clear before he set out where she thought his duty lay . . . but she didn't have to explain to Bessie Marchant.

'Well, Leiston. What have ye a mind to do?'

It was no good. Best get the thing over quickly. Miss Howick might not have Bessie's looks, but she was by no means ugly.

'Show me where to sign, sir.'

The general pushed the paper across the desk. His duty was done.

'The banns may be called as soon as you like,' were his last words on the subject.

A silent Portuguese manservant appeared in response to a tug on a plaited velvet cord. Leiston followed him to the back door and led his roan cob round to the front of the Grange; the general did not allow employees to mount until they reached the drive. As he crossed the gravelled carriage space in front of the portico, a window opened noisily.

'Tell your father to have Bonecracker saddled tomorrow. I expect him here at six o'clock sharp.' The general's voice sounded brisk and decisive. The window shut.

Robert Leiston mounted and looked back. Cleadon Grange stood confident amidst its rustling oaks and elms. Smoke from numerous chimneys on the snug slate roof drifted grey-blue against a lowering sky. He turned the cob into a stubble field and spurted up a wet furrow. Home Farm lay just over the hill.

Sophie Leiston sat upright in a plain wooden chair by the kitchen fire. Her bones, none too well padded, ached from the hard yew. She did not openly admit it was a woman's lot to suffer but accepted the creed passively. God, General Mallindine and her husband James – her submission to whom was spelled out in the row of socks on the brass rail under the mantelpiece – ordered her existence. She saw no point in defying them. Secretly she thought that Miss Howick was an excellent match for Robert, despite her 'misfortune'. So refined. Not at all like that great rosy-faced Bessie Marchant. She did hope that Robert would be sensible and not annoy the general. Sir Ephraim was so determined.

A barking and the slow clack of hoofs on cobbles told her that Robert was back. She thought of some of the bleak fell farms James had worked on when they were first married, and shuddered. Home Farm was a fine house and she had no desire to leave it. She listened to Martha and Jane chattering in the scullery as they washed the pots. Thumps and laughter told her the other girls were getting ready for bed. She pictured Robert rubbing down the cob and giving him his feed. Men were wondrous considerate to their horses. What a pity they did not show the same concern for their womenfolk.

'Well, I am to be wed. And by order of the great squire himself.'

Robert had taken off his boots in an outhouse and stood in his thick woollen stockings looking down at her. He seemed more disgusted than angry.

'This may prove to be a blessing,' said Sophie primly, her heart pounding with relief at the knowledge that she would not have to leave Home Farm.

'It is not given to mortals to order their lives, not ordinary humble folk, anyways. We must look on it as His will.'

Her eyes turned piously to the ceiling.

'Aye, Mother,' retorted her son drily. 'Sir Ephraim's will.'

The tall, spare figure of his father, who always looked ungainly off the back of a horse, appeared at the door.

'Well, lad?'

'Don't fret, Father. I'll be bringing back the brood mare just as soon as the parson can arrange things.'

His father approached the fire and warmed his bony red hands.

''Tis all agreed then?'

'Aye, and I get £15 a year as a stud fee.'

'Robert!'

His mother puckered her lips disapprovingly.

'Oh, there's something else, Father.'

'Aye?'

'Ye're to have Bonecracker ready for the meet tomorrow. Six sharp, says the General. And I hope he breaks his bloody neck.'

But all his father said was 'Reet.'

CHAPTER THREE

As cool shadows lengthened over the dust-covered corpses in the gully at Ramnagar, the guns ceased fire. Drums sounded and the Sikhs marched into their stronghold. The British withdrew for a distance and the glow of camp fires reddened the night sky. Most of the soldiers spent their time looking for something to fill their empty bellies. Sergeant Wood, wearing an ill-fitting tunic and the shako of a comrade who would have no further use for it, crept with Private Hacken towards a small bullock tethered near a cluster of huts on the outskirts of the town. A Jat farmer who appeared at his door began to shout but fell silent at the sight of the drawn swords.

'Nickle jao!' said Hacken cheerfully.

The farmer vanished.

'Sorry, old son,' Hacken murmured apologetically. 'We ain't 'ad no rooti issued. Not 'ad a bite all day.'

He led the beast to the rough bivouac where Wood took over the halter.

'Right.'

Hacken drew back his right arm, paused for a moment, then plunged his sword into the unsuspecting animal's heart. It grunted explosively and collapsed kicking feebly. Wood bent over and cut its throat with a swift movement. Other dragoons gathered round and as the fire blazed the carcass was dismembered with a speed that would have done credit to Smithfield. Half burned, half raw and without salt, the beef still served to ease the pangs that afflicted the hardened campaigners of the 3rd Light Dragoons and they lay down to sleep with their horses' reins over their arms.

In the lines of the Bengal Horse Artillery Lala Rai and Mohad Dinnath conjured up chapattis which they ate while earnestly debating fanciful schemes for recovering the lost cannon while at the same time speculating on their chances of obtaining a precarious perch on another gun. They came to the practical conclusion that as the war was in its early stages it would not be long before there would be room for them again.

According to their philosophy death or injury was bound to remove their comrades sooner rather than later. That they would expose themselves inevitably to a like fate was a matter of little importance compared to the need for restoring face lost with No. 4 gun.

Higgins and O'Connor and the remainder of the crew moodily munched a crude bread picturesquely described as 'elephants' lugs' not so much because the loaves resembled the ears of the animal but because they were concocted from coarse flour and bran baked with the chopped straw usually fed to the elephants. A liberal supply of arrack helped to wash it down and brought a certain fiery consolation.

Leiston waited patiently with a group of the 20th Foot at a fire tended by an industrious troll whose face shone in the firelight.

'What is it, Sergeant?' asked a hopeful youth.

The troll replied in a calm Cockney voice.

'Boiled beef. What else 'ud Old Julius give yer?'

He busied himself stirring the scraggy tail and a piece of the neck of an ox that had died of exhaustion pulling an ammunition wagon.

'It don't smell too 'ealthy, do it?'

'Fit for a king, me boy. Fit for a king.'

The troll's bulk loomed black as he waved his spoon enthusiastically.

''Ere, cut the jawing and give a hand wiv the bleedin' dixie.'

A camp kettle was juggled away from the flames amid clouds of smoke and steam. Eager hands fished into the scalding water and plucked at the flesh. The troll juggled with a piece in his fingers before popping it into his mouth. He smacked his fat lips and belched appreciatively.

'Ugh, it don't taste too fresh to me, Sergeant,' piped up a gangling private, chewing at a piece of gristle.

The troll answered in hurt but dignified tones.

'Didn't expect sojerin' to be all glory, lad, did ye? Not *orl* glory. I told you that when I 'listed you, Freeman, didn't I? No one ever heard Julius Begg say that it would be *orl* medals and batta and loot and rum and good vittles.'

Leiston smiled. He'd been ''listed' by Julius Begg himself.

Yes, Julius had said it would not be 'orl glory'. There were lots of things he said about the army on that first morning.

In his red and white silk tent, Jawahir Singh and his officers were celebrating. It had been a great day. The Khalsalji, the soldiers of the Khalsa, the army of the Sikhs, had once again met General Gough's army in battle. And this time they had thwarted it.

'Perhaps the days of Runjit are come again,' said a black-bearded warrior.

'It is written so in the san sakhi of the great Guru Gobind,' added a grizzled veteran. 'The prophecies say we shall have victory. We shall slay the feringhee soldiers and take our banners to the gates of Delhi.'

'Perhaps, old one, but it will not be easy,' replied Jawahir Singh. 'At Ferozeshah and Sobraon we killed and we killed but their pultons still came on.'

'Pah! We were fools to make our stand on the wrong side of the river at Sobraon. And beside, did not the Sutlej rise suddenly with the snow-water and sweep our bridge of boats away? This time there will be no mistakes. We are a nation of warriors. We will triumph.'

It was at about the time of the Spanish Armada – an event which made no impact on contemporary India – that the iron entered the soul of the Sikhs. Up to that time they had been a peaceful, devout Hindu sect following the teachings of devout gurus. But when the Muslim Emperor Jahangir tortured and executed their leader, his successor, Guru Hargobind, spurned the hereditary necklace symbol. In future, he announced, his sword belt would serve in its place. He proceeded to create a force resembling the Knights Templar and led them against the Mogul emperors until his death.

The great Guru Gobind completed the transformation of the warlike sect in the early part of the eighteenth century. Wine, tobacco and the smoking of hemp were abjured. The Sikhs disavowed caste, worshipped one god and ate meat to keep up their strength as befitted warriors. Every man had to take the name Singh – meaning lion or champion.

True devotees wore the five Ks. There was the kesh, the unshorn beard and hair. There was the kungha, the comb;

kara, the steel or iron bangle on the right wrist; the kuchcha, or shorts, and most important of all, the kirpan, the sword. Such a powerful and dedicated minority soon attracted the attention of authority. The Emperor Abdul Samad Khan suppressed them ruthlessly and they fled to the hills.

Years later, as the power of the Moguls declined, they emerged from their hill forts lean and hard. Their grip tightened on the Land of the Five Rivers. For a period they warred with each other. Then Ranjit Singh, a cunning, one-eyed, war-scarred genius, welded the opposing factions into a nation. Under him the Khalsa became the only army in India capable of facing the forces of the East India Company. With great diplomatic skill, the wily Sikh held the lands between the British-dominated country to the south and east and the Afghans in the west. His writ ran from Peshawar to Kashmir. With an appetite for military learning equalled only by his insatiable demand for women he hired the disbanded veterans of the Napoleonic Wars to train his troops on the great parade ground at Meen Meer. The grim Italian Paolo Avitabile, who had served Murat as a gunner, and Alexander Gardner, a soldier of fortune from Wisconsin, perfected the artillery. General Jean François Allard took over the cavalry and Jean Baptiste Ventura, another Napoleonic veteran, reorganised the infantry into a formidable army including Ghurkas, Pathans, Biharis and Ooriyas. And yet, carefully, Runjit avoided war with the British. They in their turn did all they could to maintain good relations with the man who held the North-West frontier and thereby saved them the expense of so doing.

Then, in 1839, the strong man died. And despite his many women, there was no son fit enough to fill his place. The Sikh state sank into anarchy and murder. In its regimental committees lay the real sources of power. Under the oppression of this unruly brotherhood the Sikh Durbar solved its problems by encouraging the invasion of British India in December 1845. After ten weeks of costly battles, in which the British were hurled recklessly at the Sikh entrenchments and squares, the Khalsa was defeated but not broken. A portion of the Punjaub was taken over while a Sikh council of chiefs with a British Resident ruled the rest of the country from Lahore.

Many of the Khalsa regiments were disbanded, but a considerable force remained in being.

It was a situation which could not last. Inspired by the dedicated British Resident at Lahore, Sir Henry Lawrence, the political agents went about their task with excessive zeal. Taxes which they considered unjust were suppressed along with unpleasant native customs. The feudal powers of the Sikh chiefs dwindled. Unrest and disaffection spread. At least beneath the surface. The signs went unnoticed elsewhere.

'The perfect tranquillity which prevails in the Punjaub is enabling the Durbar, with the assistance of the Resident, to promote reforms in the administration of the Lahore State, calculated to relieve its finances, and to ameliorate the condition of the people,' the Board of the East India Company was informed in March 1848. The following month the spark was struck which lit the torch of war.

Mulraj, the Sikh governor of the great fortress city of Multan, being unable to pay the revenues required of him, was told that he would be replaced by a new Sirdar chosen by the British. Mr. Vans Agnew, one of the most experienced political officers on the frontier, and Lieutenant Anderson of the 2nd Bombay European Fusiliers, a brilliant Oriental scholar, arrived with Sirdar Khan Singh and an escort of Sikhs and Ghurkas. Mulraj had been preparing to hand over the keys to his citadel when a truculent native soldier struck and wounded the Britons. Mulraj fled to his own quarters and the two officers took refuge in the Idgah, a muslim temple outside Multan. The following day their escort deserted them and a mob of fanatics dragged out both men, butchered them and hung their bodies from the walls of the town. Sikh officers fastened the iron war bracelet around Mulraj's wrist and the first steps on the road to war were taken. The inaction of the British merely served as an incitement.

The fact that the new Governor General of India, Lord Dalhousie, had been in the country only three months and was a mere thirty-five years old, and that Lord Gough, the Commander-in-Chief, had long experience of the country but was a septuagenarian, did not help matters. Both had inherited unfortunate problems from the previous Governor General, Lord Hardinge. At his instigation, the East India Company's

Sepoy regiments had been reduced in size and the army's extensive baggage train dispersed after the previous Sikh war.

Dalhousie, fresh from serving the penny-pinching British government at home, was reluctant to sanction increases in the army establishment. To make matters worse, it was not clear at first with whom the British might have to fight. The Sikh Durbar at Lahore was looked on as the lawful government and Mulraj as a petty rebel. It seemed, therefore, that the British were bound to help to quell a revolt. But while they dithered, the old soldiers of the Khalsa flocked back to their colours. No one could be certain which way they would move. Some Sikhs actually joined forces with a British force marching under General Whish to besiege Multan. Lord Gough complained bitterly that he did not know who were his enemies and remained immobile at his headquarters in the south. He pointed out gruffly that in any case it would be stupid to take the field in the middle of the hot season.

'As if,' wrote Lieutenant Herbert Edwardes, who had given up tax collecting to conduct his own private war against Mulraj, 'the rebellion could be put off like a champagne tiffin with a three-cornered note to Mulraj to name a date more agreeable.'

With the desertion of a 'friendly' Sikh force from Whish's army outside Multan, the movement of hostile Khalsa forces to threaten British posts and the advance of the Afghan allies of the Sikhs, all doubts vanished. A major war was obvious. And by the time Dalhousie had sanctioned the easing of the purse strings it became equally obvious that a familiar figure was going to be left to pay the bill. He wore a British uniform and the currency he used was blood. The affair at Ramnagar was merely one instalment.

The British troops passed an uneasy, disturbed night. Stray horses, cattle and camels blundered through the sleeping regiments. Snoring humans, snuffling animals, clinking chains and occasional shouts merged in a seething, low moan.

With the dawn, dying fires were rekindled and the main army and its horde of camp followers started to arrive at Ramnagar. Gough had left them ten miles away when he slipped quietly out of his splendid glass-windowed tent at

Noelwalla in the early hours of the previous morning. Now a vast pillar of dust announced their approach. Trumpeting elephants dragging 24-pounders, camels carrying chests for the officers, spindly legged bhistis staggering under their water-skins and teams of placid oxen hauling ammunition, stretched for miles along the sandy road. Ahead of them, engineer officers superintended the hammering in of gaily coloured flags and marker posts to indicate where the city of tents should arise. Horsemen hurried everywhere.

In the midst of this bustle Cureton and the colonel of the 1st Native Cavalry, who had also been killed on the previous day, were buried in the same grave wrapped in their cloaks. Havelock's body was still missing. It lay somewhere along the banks of the river where the crows and vultures hopped and squawked and stole unspeakable fragments from each other.

After the funeral, Gough and his staff trotted out to gaze at the impressive Sikh fortifications where Shere Singh sat waiting.

Mallindine, who had been released to rejoin his regiment because of the heavy loss in officers, guided his horse carefully over the tent ropes and picket lines and handed his mount to a syce. The lines of the 14th were full of Indian servants fussing over the horses which they had not seen for thirty-six hours. As he sought the mess tent he noticed a bay flatten its ears and stepped back quickly as it lunged forward with bared teeth. He made a note to have the animal sent to haul a baggage load. That should take the brute's temper away. Savage horses needed plenty of work. He knew that from experience.

CHAPTER FOUR

If Bonecracker had been a less headstrong animal Miss Howick might have kept her virginity, General Mallindine would have saved £15 a year, and Robert Leiston could have taken Bessie Marchant to the altar. Bonecracker, a powerful bay, could carry fourteen stone all day and never shorten his stride. But all the virtues he possessed as a heavyweight hunter were discounted by his temper. Like most rigs, having the inclinations of a stallion without the means of fulfilling them, he was savage. Stable lads, passers-by, donkeys and dogs suffered severely from his attentions during the hunting season. With ears laid back, yellow teeth bared and eyes rolling, he was given a wide berth at meets, although the general insisted that his mount's disposition was due to 'a bit of blood in its pedigree'. Bonecracker had felt the sting of the general's whip and the jab of his spurs too often to try conclusions with that gentleman. But when young Eldred had him saddled for the meet at the King's Head he did his brute best to unseat him. The battle lasted most of the day, during which Eldred did his best too, threatening at times to surpass the general in the use of the crop and spur. Bonecracker, although conceding his rider a certain amount of respect, was not deceived. As they rode homeward over Gallows Common he made a sudden dash at a narrow gate, cracking his rider's right knee against the post and depositing him in the mud. The result, for Eldred, was a painful bruise and mild concussion which forced him to take to his bed for several days.

Boredom, more than anything, induced him to take an interest in Miss Susannah Howick. She was the only person he could talk with. His cousins were mere children. His uncle spent every day in the hunting field or inspecting his estates. And the servants were for the main part Portuguese. Not that he would have dreamed of holding long conversations with a servant.

Miss Howick was 27 years old – nine years older than Eldred – and even more bored. Dark and pale, she was nevertheless sturdy with a full bosom and a waist which, if not exactly waspish, she kept tolerably trim by dint of severe lacing. Before the Bonecracker incident she had had little contact with the general's nephew. He dined with the old man. She ate with the children. He hunted and disported himself with other rich young men in the district. She struggled to teach Emily and Eunice a little French and arithmetic. Men, young men in particular, were an intriguing mystery to her. Once young Mr. Mallindine was confined to the house she determined to find out more about them – and him. At first she behaved with great circumspection, taking the children with her during visits. Later she permitted herself brief solo visits to borrow books from the general's extensive library. Finally she began to intercept the maids at the door of his room and insisted on taking in trays herself.

Eldred did nothing to discourage these attentions. He was amused at the attentions of this dumpy school ma'am with pretensions of a gentleman's daughter but the instincts of a whore. She hardly compared favourably with some of the colourful ladies who had helped to break the monotony of his short stay at Oxford. But no doubt she would learn. It was a pity she was so obvious.

Miss Howick could not help being obvious. To have a man had become an obsession with her. She had to know the secret. General Mallindine's library had not disclosed it, although she had surreptitiously scoured the shelves. The antics of Farmer Marchant's prize ram had been much more revealing. But ladies were not allowed to look on and she had to hurry her charges away. It seemed that she was doomed to eke out her existence in ignorance, marooned in the heart of the country, shrivelling on the arid charity of Sir Ephraim.

Her mind was made up one grey afternoon when Fonseca, General Mallindine's personal servant, took the children to visit a distant farm to inspect two ponies. The general was away, attending to his duties as a magistrate. Miss Howick watched the trap rattle out of sight and turned to her mirror. Determined eyes stared back at her as she removed the pins and let her long black tresses fall. Deliberately she loosened her bodice, took off her stockings and shed her underskirts. Her figure lost some of its shape but her body felt taut despite the loss of the restraining strings and ribbons. She opened her door carefully, then moved swiftly and purposefully down the corridor and crossed the landing. Brushing her hair from her eyes she paused for one second before closing her plump fingers round the cool white china of the door handle.

Eldred was lying back on a pile of pillows when the door opened and Miss Howick glided in. A fire crackled in the grate.

'Why, Miss Howick, is it tea already?'

He reached for his watch on a bedside table.

'No, Mr. Mallindine, it is not.'

He noticed that her voice was quite husky. There was a dull flush on her cheek bones and her eyes were big and bright.

'What have you brought me then. Is it a book?'

'No, not a book,' she replied in a low voice.

As she walked over to the bedside he realised she was somewhat dishevelled; in an attractive, interesting way. A curious little smile flickered over her face. He raised his hand in sudden alarm as she made as if to sit on the coverlet.

'Mind my leg,' he said hastily. 'It's still a mite tender.'

'Let me see,' she replied softly. Her hand slipped swiftly between the sheets. She fumbled for a moment, then impatiently turned back the bed clothes. Coolly she raised his nightshirt and began to knead an ugly yellow mark on his thigh.

'There. Is that any better?'

She bent her head suddenly and began to kiss the spot, taking him by surprise. Eldred ran his fingers through her hair.

'Why I'll be . . . You little devil. Come round to this side of the bed. I can't lie too well on that side.'

Miss Howick stopped her kissing and obediently and anxiously did as she was told. Conscious of his injured leg she lay still and watched absorbed as he gingerly eased himself round. So that was it. His hand slid inside her bodice and she felt a moment of panic.

'I'm afraid I've never . . .' she began apologetically.

The sentence went unfinished. Miss Howick drew a sharp breath.

'Oh, Mr. Mallindine,' she panted as he began to thrust slowly, carefully and mindful of his limb. 'Oh, Mr. Mallindine.'

Weeks later in London, when he received her letter saying she thought she was pregnant, Eldred felt an uncharacteristic twinge of sympathy. But he threw the letter away all the same. It didn't surprise Miss Howick that there was no reply. She did not expect one. Now she knew the secret she was content. For the moment. Wild horses would not have dragged from her the name of the father of her child. If Rosa, the little maid from Lisbon, who normally catered for the passionate side of Eldred's nature, had not seen Miss Howick leaving the bedroom the general might never have found out that Eldred was the father of Miss Howick's child. The bastards of rich men, especially one born under the roof of the ancestral home, are troublesome creatures. Which is why Sir Ephraim decided to foster this one in his peculiar way.

CHAPTER FIVE

Apart from his temper, Lord Gough's native island had given him a splendid touch of 'The Blarney'. As an Irish private in the 2nd Bengal Europeans put it: 'He's a lovely ould man but he's the divil wit de truth. Sure doesn't he love ivvery regiment just a little bit better than the last one he inspected.'

As Gough rode along the ranks of the 24th Foot he radiated a rosy charm. They looked, he told them in his address, as fine a regiment as he had seen and he knew he could rely on them to do their duty. He'd noticed how steady they had been at Ramnagar; he'd been proud to see the Colours, embroidered with so many famous victories, waving over part of his line of battle.

'You remind me of my own brave lads of the 87th . . . the men I led during the Peninsular War, under our great Chief,' he told them. 'I saw your regiment in action there forty years ago. Do as the 24th did then and you won't go wrong. When it comes to the charge . . . give them the cold steel, my boys.'

And because they were a regiment of strong, young men, yet to fight a major battle, they cheered him to the echo. They had marched 350 miles to join the army of the Punjaub and were lean, hard and fit. If they were green they were also enthusiastic. Give them cold steel is what the general had said. And cold steel they'd give. Didn't people sing of Gough after the First Sikh War:

> 'Sabres drawn and bayonets fixed
> Fight where fought Alexander,
> Oh, Paddy Gough's a cross betwixt
> A bulldog and a salamander.'

'Isn't he splendid, Lloyd Williams?' burst out Junior Ensign Pennycuick, who had just joined the regiment from Sandhurst. His eyes shone as he watched the Commander-in-Chief ride past followed by Pennycuick Senior, who was commanding the brigade. Lloyd Williams agreed that it was a stirring sight and they both listened approvingly to the cheers of the 25th and 45th Bengal Infantry as Gough went on to flatter the Sepoys.

A few days later when it was his turn to inspect the 29th Foot, Gough's patter was more subtle. He knew he was looking at a regiment which had lost a third of its number at Ferozeshah and which three times had obeyed his command to storm the Sikh field works at Sobraon.

'Ready to show thim Saikhs what ye've got in your scabbards?' he bellowed, tossing his head towards the Chenab.

He grinned at the roar of appreciation.

'Can't wait to get at them, eh, Mountain?'

The brigadier grinned back and the staff rode away happily, a colourful mixture of scarlet and dark blue and white, with a handful of turbaned attendants.

'Bloodthirsty old bastard, that's wot 'e is,' said Sergeant Begg later, lolling back thoughtfully on a battered charpoy in the guard tent of the 29th.

'Wot's 'e want to be fightin' battles for anyway at 'is age? Ever since God was a little boy old Paddy's been urgin' sojers to run someone through the guts. All right for 'im. 'E got a ruddy fortune in batta after the last little do with the Siks. Poor old Begg collected £7 12s. 6d. and damn' near got 'is 'ead shot off when 'e poked it over the top of that redoubt at Sobrayo-on. 'Sright. Isn't it Bob?'

Leiston nodded placidly and wondered how much silver would encircle Begg's vast girth by the time the campaign was over.

'If ever we do have to cross the Chenab, you'll drown, Julius,' he said with a yawn. 'That money belt of yours will need an elephant to carry it. How much have you made out of your lady-friends so far?'

Begg's piggy little eyes blinked rapidly. His face assumed a scandalised expression.

'For Gawd's sake 'ush, Robert,' he whispered sternly. 'Anyone might be listenin'. Them girls are doin' no 'arm at all. You know as well as I do it's all for the 'ealth of the rigiment. You wouldn't want your comrades to go with some 'orrid sandrat, would yer? The pox was bad enough in England, but 'ere . . .'

His bulky figure shook dramatically.

Ever since he had joined the regiment in India in 1842, Leiston had never known a time when Julius was not running a thriving brothel. Even when they were on the march three or four swaying dhoolis would be found somewhere in the vast concourse of camp followers, carried by match-stick legged natives from the plains. Any surgeon expecting to find a wounded man behind the cotton curtains would be disappointed. There would be no fever-ridden soldier in the litter but a dusky child of thirteen or fourteen with a glittering ornament in her nose. 'One of Begg Sahib's little bints' as a purple-faced major described them after spending an interesting afternoon during a previous campaign.

'It's not the girls I'm worried about, Julius, or the pox. It's you,' Leiston continued in mock solicitude. 'You've got so much tucked away that if you fall over we'll never be able to get you up again.'

Begg smirked appreciatively.

'I reckon Paddy ought to send you against the Sikh trenches all by yourself with your pockets full of gunpowder. When they shoot you, you'll explode and the rupees from that belt will mow them down. Then we'll rush through the hole you've made and settle them with the bayonet.'

Begg's smirk was replaced by a frown.

'Baynits, baynits, baynits . . . the 'ole army is baynit-mad from Paddy downwards. Wot did the good Lord give us powder and shot for if it weren't for pepperin' the 'eathen savages at a safe distance?' Begg was indignant. 'I swear if I 'ad my time again I'd join the Rifles or the hartillery.'

After a moment's thought he added crushingly: 'Baynits is old-fashioned.'

Leiston's hands moved in a flowing motion. Eighteen inches of burnished steel slithered from the scabbard. He let his thumb glide along the smooth shallow grooves which prevented the triangular blade being trapped by the suction of the victim's flesh and blood. Tightening his grip on the swan neck of the haft he poked playfully at his fat companion. Julius sniffed meaningfully.

'And wot d'ye think that is. I arsk yer. Wot is it? Two bleedin' pounds of scrap iron, that's what it is; two extra bleedin' pounds to go on the end of a musket what is cruel heavy as it is.'

Leiston, who knew that Julius could use the eleven pound musket as if it were a feather, smiled.

'Ho! It's a good joke, is it? Well, I tell yer it's useless, is that baynit. Wot can yer do with it? I mean . . . It's good for bleedin' nothing. Look at its shape – it's a terr-iangle. Now if we was in the Rifles we'd have something to brag about. Yer can cobble yer boots with a sword baynit. Yer can cut a steak from a dead horse. Yer can bleedin' well cut yer throat with it if yer gets fed up. But wot can yer do with our bleeding knitting needle? Nought that matters. Yer can stick it through some pore black bastard's guts, that's all. If it don't bend or break.'

He looked suspiciously at the gleaming steel in Leiston's fist.

'I only 'opes for your sake it ain't one of them sham jobs the Dutchmen are sellin' to 'er Majesty. They're like bits of tin, them Proosian blades. Old Fayres of the dragoons told me they've bin 'avin the same trouble with some of their swords. Don't temper them proper in water but sticks 'em in oil. If you polish 'em really 'ard you goes right through to dark metal. One of the 50th had a bad bayonet back in '46 and he showed me it twisted like a corkscrew after 'e got it out of some black devil wot was 'owling blue murder.'

Leiston inspected his own bayonet curiously while Begg rumbled on.

'Baynits! I wonder old Paddy don't make us dance round them like Scotchmen. We'll finish up worshippin' em, you'll see, bowin' three times towards Woolwich arsenal.'

Private Freeman whose angular figure was draped around a tent pole, shifted his weight from one foot to the other.

'Wouldn't be much good as soldiers without 'em, would we sergeant?'

Begg regarded him with scorn.

'Course YOU wouldn't, Freeman. Poking a soddin' nigger in the eye with a baynit is just about all you're good for. They gives 'em to the likes of you because yer too stoopid to be trusted with a decent gun like a rifle. Ye know what you are Freeman? Yer a spear carrier. We orl are. Dunno why they bother to give us muskets at all. Yer not allowed to fire 'em most times. May as well give us burnt sticks with a sharp end for all the use we make of powder and ball.'

A look of enlightenment crossed Leiston's face.

'I've just twigged.'

'Twigged wot?' said Julius irritably, pausing in full flow.

'Why you're running down the bayonet. The ramparts . . .'

'Yerse, Robert, the bloody ramparts at Feroosie-shower. I got your baynit up me own ramparts when we tried to get up them ladders and I don't 'ope to do it again in a hurry.'

He adopted a hurt expression.

'Well, you always said it wouldn't be all glory, didn't you, old lad?' replied Leiston retreating under a torrent of abuse.

Lord Gough dined that night with the officers of the 24th, seated at the regiment's great mess table which followed them wherever they went. Candlelight danced off silverware worth a king's ransom.

The general's face was rosier than usual and he was obviously enjoying the port.

'Damn' long table for a short campaign, eh Pennycuick? Dontcher expect to be back in your cantonments before next summer? Why them Saikh friends of ours will be off at the next flash of cold steel. Tasted too much of it in their time. Plenty of point, that's the best medicine for 'em. Put in a volley or two to warm things up a bit, then . . .' he carved the air with his arm '. . . sweep 'em away.'

A wine bottle went over with a crash and a red pool spread over the clean white cloth.

'There what did I tell you?' he laughed boisterously. 'I've tapped claret already. And we'll be drawing a damn' sight more blood before we've finished with the Khalsa.'

Brigadier Pennycuick joined in the general laughter but felt suddenly cold. He stared at the crimson stain for a second and shuddered. At the lower end of the table they were telling the story of Paddy Gough's remark at Sobraon when they brought him the news that the heavy artillery would have to cease fire as it had run out of ammunition.

'Thank God,' he had said, 'now I'll be at them with the bayonet.'

In the gory assault which followed enough blood had been spilled to satiate even Durga the dark Hindu war goddess. The ugly red blotch on the bleached linen seemed to betoken greater sacrifices to come.

CHAPTER SIX

It wasn't so much her taunts that made Leiston decide to leave Home Farm. It was the thought that there was something in what Susannah Howick said.

Leiston was not a complete innocent on their wedding night. He knew about as much as an observant country lad might be expected to and might have known a deal more if Farmer Marchant had not caught him in the hay loft with Bessie. The Marchants had kept a sharp eye on them after that. The fact remained, however, that he had never seen a girl in her shift before. So he looked on uneasily as Miss Howick (for so he still thought of her) undressed in the big back bedroom of Home Farm. Getting into his nightshirt without catching her eye had been a trying operation. Now he sat awkwardly on the edge of the bed as petticoats fell, pins clattered on the old dressing table and ribbons and laces hung aimlessly about this strange woman. What was going on behind that pale face and those evasive eyes?

She turned away from him, keeping the lower half of her body covered while she slipped her nightdress over her head. Then, to his surprise, she walked over to the mirror and stood there, her body silhouetted in the candlelight. Gently she placed her outstretched fingers on her stomach and frowned slightly. For a moment she paused. Without warning she whirled on him and burst out fiercely:

'Oh, Robert Leiston, what sort of a man are you?'

His heart jumped. His throat went dry. It was the first time she had spoken to him, other than formally, all day. Ever since Sir Ephraim had sent word that he might call on Miss Howick she had been reserved and polite. He assumed that like himself, she accepted the position. He had even tried to please her by smartening himself up. There had been no tantrums during the reading of the banns, although Bessie had nearly made a scene as the congregation left the church afterwards. The marriage ceremony had gone quietly – and the wedding breakfast, despite Uncle Reuben's crude humour and the good-natured banter of his cousins. Why shouldn't the match work out for the best, after all, he had thought. Only the Mallindines and his parents knew the truth. And Miss Howick, of course. He looked at the distraught figure, her full breasts heaving under the white cotton.

'How could you go through with it all?' she sobbed angrily. Then the tears came, large and glistening. She threw herself on the bed and beat her clenched fists on the counterpane.

'How could you? How could you? How could you?'

She buried her face for a moment. When she raised it she turned her head towards him defiantly.

'Have you no courage? No pride? At least you could have argued with him. You could have tried to talk him out of it. Instead you let him buy you and sell me in just twenty minutes. I saw you come. I watched you go. If you had refused, I would be free. I could have this baby all to myself. What harm can it do? I told him I didn't want to marry his precious nephew if it meant disowning him.'

So young Eldred was the father. Leiston had suspected as much. He reached out a conciliatory hand but Miss Howick shrank from it.

'Don't touch me,' she cried wildly. 'Do you know what you are? You're a coward. You're afraid of that horrid old man. He bought you. You're his. Go on . . . ask him if you may touch me. Bring me his authority to serve me. You'll make a fine entry in his stud book. Surely you have a licence to bed me? Has Sir Ephraim signed it?'

She leaned forward in a frenzy and pulled up his nightshirt.

'Oh, that won't do,' she shrilled. 'It doesn't bear the Mallindine arms . . .'

Her words ceased suddenly. A hand hardened by the constant use of farm tools clamped across her mouth. A lean body pressed her into the bed. Leiston's face came to within an inch of her own. The eyes were cold, glittering with rage. A genuine fear seized her. She struggled and moaned, stifled by the hard, unyielding palm.

'Hold your tongue, woman. Hold your tongue or it will be the worse for you. Lie still or by God . . .'

Susannah let her body sag and lay still. Leiston took his

fingers from her mouth. White and red marks showed plainly where they had been. The woman whimpered but said nothing.

'Don't whine. Thou's safe enough; at least as long as you keep that tongue still and hold your peace.'

He had dropped his respectful manner and his country accent became more pronounced. The bed creaked as he raised himself and walked to fetch the candle from the dressing table. He raised it and looked down at a frightened face, wet with tears.

'Here,' he said gruffly, 'I'll show you what we'll do. You get between the sheets. I'll lie under the coverlet. That way you will come to no harm. How do you say, eh?'

Miss Howick nodded doubtfully. Gingerly she curled up her legs, turned back the bedclothes and almost scurried between them. As Leiston pinched out the candle she lay rigid in the dark. The bed groaned. Something touched her and she flinched. Leiston said nothing. Through the sheets she could feel his muscular back, warm and hard. He had kept his word.

A week later when Leiston announced he was leaving home to seek his fortune and that she would not be going with him, she was glad. Her father-in-law had tried to persuade him against quitting the farm but to no avail. She understood that when Sir Ephraim heard the news he had just laughed. Actually he had said: 'Won't the wench have him then? No doubt he'll come back when she's in season again.'

Sophie Leiston went to church the night her son left home. She believed praying helped to build character. With its unyielding hassocks and icy flagstones, St. Aidan on the Cliff certainly made an excellent mould for cast-iron Christians.

CHAPTER SEVEN

At one o'clock in the morning of December 1, the 3rd Light Dragoons rose from their camp fires and settled themselves in their saddles for a long march, wrapped in cloaks against the cold. Near them jogged shadowy squadrons of native and irregular horse. Behind, on calloused feet and muscular legs, tramped the 24th and 61st Foot and dark masses of sepoys. A powerful artillery detachment raised a cloud of stinging grey dust which turned the columns into an army of phantoms. Gough having spent days trying to tempt Shere Singh to put his head into the noose, was now trying to outflank him with a secret march. Sir Joseph Thackwell, who had replaced Cureton at the head of the cavalry, had been given an independent force to ford the Chenab some miles up river and attack the Sikh flank. In the meantime Gough would demonstrate in front of the position near Ramnagar.

Ahead of Thackwell rose a fast-moving advance guard led by a black-bearded dark-eyed giant whom the Indian soldiers called Nikalsain. When the head of the column appeared he was waiting with fifteen large boats he had seized and the fords were staked out. The 24th clambered aboard and the crossing began. For the cavalry the passage of the Chenab was not so comfortable.

'Right lads, off with your boots, trousers and drawers,' said Sergeant Wood, proceeding to obey his own order. A groan of protest greeted him.

'Oh, no Joe,' roared Hacken. 'It'll freeze our balls off. That's snow water, that is. I'm not risking frost bite . . .'

'Come on, move, or you'll get my boot up your arse. We'll be lucky if the horses don't have to swim.'

Two long rows of camels had been driven protesting into the water and stood grunting and bellowing while their shivering attendants struggled to keep them in position. The animals acted as a living breakwater on one side of the dragoons and as a safety cordon on the other. Hacken crossed his stirrups and splashed into the water alongside Wood. The dragoons were crossing in a double file with their clothing tied around their necks.

'It'll be lovely if we have to go into action like this,' he shouted. 'They'll call us the bare-arse brigade for ever more.'

'Every whore in Amballa calls us that in any case, so what are you worried about?'

The Third Light Dragoons assembled on the banks in their shirt tails ready to assault Her Majesty's enemies then and there if necessary. But the Sikh vedettes were content to watch from a distance.

'I think they fancy your hairy legs,' said Sergeant Wood to Hacken through his chattering teeth.

General Thackwell watched his force assemble on the northern bank of the Chenab with considerable satisfaction. He despatched Nicholson to scout out the land and sent a report to Gough at Ramnagar that he was now in a position to move against Shere Singh's flank.

His Excellency, the Commander-in-Chief, was beginning to feel distinctly uneasy however. For two days he had kept up a steady bombardment of the Sikh entrenchments and gradually the opposing guns had fallen silent. All bar half a dozen which were well hidden and apparently supplied with unlimited ammunition. It was some time before Gough realised that, in the words of the Duke of Wellington, he had been humbugged. Shere Singh had been demonstrating to hold *his* attention while withdrawing troops to concentrate against Thackwell. Within an hour of awareness dawning cavalry and infantry reinforcements were on their way to Thackwell, now exposed on the far bank of the Chenab. A staff officer with an escort clattered out of camp carrying a message ordering Thackwell not to move farther until support arrived.

Soon after mid-day Sergeant Wood was lying sound asleep with his red head on his shako and his horse's reins secured to the swivel clip on his belt, when an urgent hand shook him awake.

'For God's sake rouse yourself, Sergeant,' said a young private. 'The enemy are on their way.'

Wood yawned and took in the scene. The 3rd, who had been resting after a steady march, were forming up while an advanced squadron retreated towards the position. Single ranging cannon shots whistled overhead.

Thackwell had been moving through sugar cane fields when Gough's courier arrived and had cautiously pulled back to more open ground. He and Gough did not get on. They had clashed after the Mahrattas had been beaten at Maharajpore and Gough had as good as accused him of not wanting to pursue the fleeing enemy. But the silly old fool wouldn't have thanked anyone for leading the cavalry into a ravine. That was Gough's trouble. He wanted everyone to leap before they looked. For him to urge caution meant that something must be wrong somewhere.

From a house in one of the villages dotting the area Shere Singh himself directed the operations, throwing troops into the cane fields and sending cavalry to find the British flank. He hoped they would assault his front. Thackwell hoped for just the opposite. The day was marked by vigorous artillery fire. A charge by Sikh cavalry was driven back by rapid rounds of case shot.

A mock retirement by the 24th merely brought them into the line of fire of some of the enemy's longer-range guns which inflicted a few casualties. A major found himself rolling on the ground as his dying horse collapsed under him. The hungry 24th watched the carcass closely until the fighting died down. Late in the afternoon, as the first of Gough's reinforcements appeared on the scene, a message arrived permitting Thackwell to attack if he felt it practical. But after a consultation with Colin Campbell, commanding the infantry, he decided not to. Campbell didn't seem to know his own mind. As Shere Singh was also hesitant, the affair at Saddulapore fizzled out. The British bivouacked and the 24th ate their major's horse. The young soldiers were learning.

A greater variety of fare was available in the ranks of the 3rd Light Dragoons who had stolen and slaughtered a goat, a sheep and a stringy cow, as well as sundry chickens surrendered by terrified villagers. After an issue of rum, they slept once more with full bellies and light hearts, their horses' reins secured to their equipment.

In the main army near Ramnagar, Sergeant Begg swore that this was the life as the 29th ended a day of bloodless marching and demonstrating. Sounds of battle to the north had filtered through during the day and there had been a considerable amount of excitement.

'I only 'opes we fights all the rest of the battles in this war the same as we fought this one,' he declared.

Mallindine, whose regiment had spent a frustrating day trotting this way and that, watched with a look of scorn as the 29th marched cheerfully back to camp.

'Look at them,' he remarked to a brother officer. 'If I'd had my way, I'd have thrown them across the ford and let them fight it out while we dashed up river to put some life into Thackwell's force.'

The officer sniffed thoughtfully.

'What? Sacrifice a regiment just as a demonstration?'

'Why not? Infantry are expendable, aren't they? You don't have to spend weeks training them to look after their horses. I mean, they aren't even mechanics like the gunners. You only get the dregs in the infantry. Look at 'em. Don't know where they get such scum.'

CHAPTER EIGHT

Boom! Bang! Thud! Noises through a mist. Drums? No. They couldn't be. Julius Begg had been a drummer boy himself once. Couldn't be drums.

The sergeant had fallen forward across the table, his cropped head flanked by massive arms, a carmine volcano ominous with rumblings. Presently the noise abated and a rosy cloud appeared. Piggy eyes pierced this phenomenon which melted into the shape of a face. The eyes blinked. Sergeant Begg carried out a methodical survey of the Anchor tap. The banging resumed. Screwing up a fearsome scowl, Begg yawned and stretched his arms straight in front of his chest. A mighty convulsion sent the table flying. The grey light, filtering reluctantly through the dirty windows revealed a soldier as broad as he was long. Five feet six inches tall and a solid fifteen stone, name of Julius Aloysius Begg. Unsteadily he marched into the tavern yard and thrust his pate under the pump. A ragged child jerked the handle two or three times and after a protesting gurgle a thin trickle of pale green water gushed into a broad stream. Sergeant Begg spluttered and stamped and shook his jowls. The shock jolted his cumbersome brain into motion. He began to remember. Somewhere . . . he hadn't dreamed it . . . he had a squad of four recruits. Gulping in the raw morning air he went in search of stimulation. The ragamuffin from the yard reappeared with a tankard. Begg sniffed its contents, threw back his head, shuddered and pronounced himself fit for duty. Picking up his shako from under the table he gave the badge a perfunctory rub with a none-too-clean sleeve, fastened the buttons of his coatee and strode erectly through the door.

'Come fer yer sojers, 'ave yer?' said a grinning dwarf in shirt sleeves and breeches. 'Whoa, there!' The little man was backing an unwilling, bony chestnut between the shafts of a cart. 'They've been settin' up a holler this past hour.'

Sergeant Begg walked purposefully in the direction of a tumbledown lean-to.

'I knowed it wasn't drums,' he muttered, lifting a hook and thrusting his expansive stomach against the door. It opened violently hurling a tall, thin corporal to the ground.

'Oi thought you was never comin', Sergeant,' said the recumbent warrior, showing no inclination to rise. 'We might have starved to death in 'ere. Fair famished we are.'

Begg regarded his comrade bleakly for a moment. If Baggott were not such a clodhopper he would not have to be locked up with their foundlings at night to stop them running away.

Never mind. He would humour him.

'What, have ye no faith in your sooperior orfficers, Jasper?' he intoned piously. 'Has old Julius, what 'as served 'is country since 'e was a drummer boy, lost your respeck? Then go in and tell Mistress Myers she is to sarve us breakfast as soon as she pleases.'

He gave the corporal a well-aimed kick from an iron boot to sharpen his appetite before switching a benign smile upon the bedraggled crew emerging from the shed. They still had money. He knew for certain. He would see they spent it like soldiers.

'Now, me lads. What say you to cold pork pie and a nice jug of ale?'

A pale young man in a dirty blue tail coat two sizes too small for him was promptly sick over his boots.

Leiston felt his stomach cringe at the thought of food and made for the tavern yard to sluice himself down. How in heaven's name had he fallen into the clutches of this monster? He had been all set to go to sea. Drink! That had been his downfall. He thought dolefully of his mother's warnings, delivered after his excursions to the Limeburner's Arms. Something about strong drink being a mocker. This was certainly no joke. He wished he had never allowed Tam Duncan and the crew of the *Grace Toomey* to talk him into joining them in that gin palace. A whore had tried to steal his bundle, a foreign seaman had hit him with a bottle and he'd had to knock down two foul-mouthed old hags who were obviously going to go through his possessions while the fight developed. A mob of howling riverside layabouts and jeering urchins had pursued them through the streets. It had been almost up with them when he and Tam took refuge in another tavern in a lane. They dashed in and pressed their backs against the wall, hoping the crowd would rush past without noticing. As they stood there with bursting lungs, Leiston found himself being studied by the fattest, pinkest man he'd ever seen. The apparition was earnestly carving slices of bread from a wheaten loaf and matching them with equal portions of a rock-like cheese. The fat man pointed to the door with a huge clasp knife.

'What's this then? A riot? Hev ye murdered someone?'

Leiston explained as best he could while the pursuers gathered outside shouting, gathering their breath and summoning up their courage to rush in. Instinctively as he described the theft of his baggage he put his hand to his money belt. He did not notice how the fat man's eyes lit up at this gesture.

'Me poor lads,' sighed the sergeant, 'this is a rebellion. A breach of the peace. An inn-surrection.'

Realising he had made a joke he beamed broadly and with amazing speed thrust his bulk into the narrow door. A howl went up from the rabble but Begg merely finished flicking the crumbs from his coat with the clasp knife until the noise had subsided.

'In the Queen's name . . .'

A volley of appalling oaths and blasphemies reduced the mob to complete and respectful silence. A prodigious belch brought mutters of admiration. Sergeant Begg acknowledged this with a fractional motion of his massive body which was meant to be a bow.

'Now, you whores' melts,' he said jovially, 'share this among you.' And turning his back he lifted his coat tails, exposed an acre of white duck trousers and thundered forth a contemptuous salute.

'Hurrah for old brass breeches,' cried an exceptionally dirty little girl. The crowd, greatly impressed by the sergeant's display, drifted off.

'That's what comes of 'andlin' men, mi lads,' he said, resuming his place on the settle. 'Discipline. That's what it is. Nothink can beat it.'

Sternly he added: 'Ye might have been lynched.'

Then the drinking began, paid for in gratitude by Leiston

and Duncan. With the drinking came the talking.

The inn was a mean place, low and grimy, with a yellow ceiling held by worm-eaten beams filched from a prison hulk gone aground fifty years earlier. A crumbling brick fireplace, cluttered with rusty ironmongery, took up most of one wall. In the hearth a paltry heap of ash gave off occasional wisps of smoke and flickers of green-blue flame when provoked by fragments of driftwood. Outside blue-grey clouds were overrunning a lemon sky and loosing stinging showers on the tangled alleys. Inside, Julius Begg's beady eyes were mesmerising a shabby audience. Education he might lack, imagination none.

Perspiration gleamed on his bull neck. Liquor dripped from his shiny red lips onto his greasy chin. But as he talked squadrons of cavalry, horses neighing and wild-eyed, thundered through the dingy room. Hogsheads roared and unleashed stinking sulphurous clouds. The blackened fireplace became a reeking, deadly breach where a frightened drummer boy beat a requiem for a vanished regiment. Flesh returned to bones long bleached on alien plains and phantom fusiliers paraded to be killed all over again.

'To the Duke. A toast to the Duke. No man sits while we drinks to old Wellington.'

Begg bellowed so suddenly that the ghosts fled and Corporal Baggott, who had been listening to the discourse with gaping jaws, crashed to the floor from the end of a bench and bit his tongue.

The company rose unsteadily to its feet.

Leiston tried to insist that he had enough in his pot to do justice to the toast but Begg would not hear of it.

'I'll have no flinchers here; no heel taps either. Fill 'em up, Mistress Myers, and give us a kiss while ye're about it.'

Mistress Myers bore a remarkable resemblance to Sergeant Begg. Her torn lace cap was as jaunty as any shako and the crimson shawl, criss-crossed over her immense bosom, was as warlike as a guardsman's tunic. A neat ankle gave her an impressive turn of speed, despite her size, which was just as well.

'You behave yourself, Julius,' she retorted. 'I'm not one of yer free and easy blackamoor gels.'

But Julius wasn't listening. He was drinking to the Duke. There were few soldiers he did not drink to that night.

After each toast Leiston found it more difficult to rise. Someone kept moving the tables and seats. Damned if they weren't moving of their own accord. But the sergeant was a grand fellow, one of the best, although he'd never heard of the soldiers he talked about.

In the middle of a graphic monologue about his service Julius reached a dramatic climax.

'There was the fort, me lads. And as full of heathens as a mattress is stuffed with feathers. They was gnashin' their teeth with rage and shakin' their 'orrid big knives at us. Our own blackies was fair terrorised and the rigiment was called on to show 'em 'ow to do the job. Well, I could see the lads needed a bit of cheerin' up, so I ups with me drum and strikes a tattoo until me wrists 'urt. Tarrum, tarrum, tarrumpity tum . . .'

The horn clasp-knife hammered on the table top.

'"Well done, my boy," says the colonel, and the rigiment rushes into the dreadful breach. *Like this!*

Sergeant Begg leaped onto a bench and put a massive boot on a table. Brandishing a bent poker he cried in a voice of thunder:

'Who's for glory ternight? Who's followin' me inter the breach? Wot? Are y'all cowards? Then I'll die alone.'

Tam Duncan looked up at the posturing figure. Tears were streaming down his face.

'I'm with ye, Sergeant,' he said. 'No Duncan can ever turn his back on the foe.'

He seized the sergeant's shako and thrust his head into its depths.

'Come on, you,' roared Begg to Leiston. 'Are yer goin' ter let me fight the soddin' niggers on me own?'

Leiston felt his blood stirring.

'Where Tam goes, I go,' he said. 'Lead on . . . down with the French . . .'

'Give him his musket,' bellowed the intrepid sergeant and Corporal Baggott thrust a broom into Leiston's hands. At this, an underfed tailor's lad seized an empty bottle and shouting 'Ta-ta-ta-tara' proclaimed himself a bugler. While his companion, a clumsy young labourer, stuck a dish-clout on a cudgel-cum-walking stick and insisted it was a flag.

'Right, Nell, you can sound the charge.'

And with Mistress Myers banging two spoons on an empty brandy cask, he leaped nimbly on top of the table and jumped down on the other side, slashing about him furiously with the rusty poker. Suddenly with a yell he collapsed on one knee.

'Me sabre arm's gone.'

Leiston and Duncan, balanced precariously on the table top where they had followed him, peered down in bewilderment.

'What? Have ye abandoned me? Yer own comrade!'

The would-be warriors clambered down unsteadily followed by the boy blowing the bottle and the standard bearer.

'Don't leave me, boys,' he said. 'Them niggers cuts up the wounded. They hacks off yer goolies and sticks 'em in yer mouth.'

Mistress Myers hurled a pot and told him to hold his vile tongue, but the missile bounced off his bulk like a cannon ball off the rock of Gibraltar.

'Ye'll never leave old Julius . . . promise.' His voice was quite pitiful.

'Never, Sergeant, never,' swore Tam Duncan solemnly.

'S'right,' scowled Leiston, thrusting his broom into space with a military gesture.

'Help me back.'

The motley quartet pushed and pulled the sweating sergeant back over the table and settles to a chair, where he collapsed.

'Water, for Gawd's sake.'

He seized the labourer's pot of ale and drained it.

'De y'know somethin', boys! I'm proud of yer. Yer stuck to me like good 'uns, otherwise I'd ha' bin a gonner. Swear you'll never desert me for some other rigiment.'

The response was a drunken chorus of 'Never.'

'The Twenny-ninth . . . f'rever.'

Sergeant Begg fumbled in his pocket.

'Fill us a bumper, Nell, we've four more heroes for the 29th. Drink up me gallant lads. Here's the Queen's shilling for each of you. You earned it nobly. I salutes you.'

Whereupon, grinning amiably, Tam Duncan slid to the floor.

Leiston, who was only dimly aware of who he was, never mind where he was, put down his broom and helped the others to carry Tam to what the sergeant called their 'quarters'. Duncan was still clutching his shilling tightly in his hand next morning, otherwise they might never have believed the corporal who told them they had joined the army and would be flogged if they tried to desert.

As they nursed their aching heads and moaned, Begg regarded them unsympathetically.

'Soldierin' ain't orl glory,' he said.

CHAPTER NINE

The neat figure of James Andrew Broun Ramsay, Tenth Earl of Dalhousie, had been at his desk in Amballa since ten in the morning and was certain to be there until six in the evening. He had left Calcutta some weeks earlier with the declared intention 'to regulate our proceedings with reference to the Punjaub' and would do precisely that. It did not trouble him that he had no military training. Nor did it concern him that his first-hand knowledge of the sub-continent dated from his arrival the previous January. He had been appointed Governor-General of India and Governor of Bengal by Her Majesty's government, and thanks to the qualities bequeathed to him by his Scottish ancestors, govern he would. Master-minding a campaign was hardly the employment one would have expected to come naturally to a man who had succeeded Mr. Gladstone as Secretary of the Board of Trade. Or one who had made his maiden speech in the House of Lords on the Church of Scotland's Benefice Bill. And who had been in his element bringing order to the railway mania which seized Britain in the 1840s. Nevertheless, before leaving England he had extracted a promise that as far as party politics were concerned he would be left in 'entire and unquestioned possession' of his 'personal independence'. Few men in modern history have been given such a blank cheque. With unlimited self-assurance he applied himself to the prosecution of the 'regulation' of the Punjaub and did not forget that his father had been one of Wellington's generals. It was his duty, he considered, as a Christian and as a product of Harrow and Oxford, to bring the benefits of Western civilisation to the multitudes of India. Despite his indifferent health, he was a hard man, a typical son of an aristocratic and wealthy Lowland family.

Calcutta had been somewhat shaken by his arrival at Government House. He had kicked out a lot of the decrepit furniture – the bed of one of his A.D.C.'s had collapsed the first night – and actually invited native officers to functions, grey-bearded subadars and wordi-majors. It hadn't gone down at all well with some of the old army clique.

That had not bothered Dalhousie once he had rid himself of old Hardinge – and the so-called sacred tiger which he took home as a gift for Queen Victoria. Dalhousie had been particularly happy to see the back of the beast, which was reputed to have eaten six men and seven women and children.

'I breathe a fervent and loyal prayer not only for H.M.'s safety but that Her Majesty may not catch so many fleas from him as my wife did,' he wrote to a friend. 'She was so bitten as to be able to appreciate in some degree the suffering of those whom the tiger had actually torn.'

Now his generals were being as irritating as the wife-eating fleas.

Dalhousie's finely chiselled features wrinkled in disdain as he studied the copperplate writing on the paper before him. The secretary who had brought in the despatch waited anxiously, sweltering in a serge suit and waistcoat, complete with watch-chain. Although it was the 'cool' season he could feel the perspiration soaking into his cravat. Why, he wondered, did His Excellency never sweat?

'Did you ever hear such a thing? The Commander-in-Chief really is a vain old fellow. He requests that I fire a royal salute to mark the fact that he and his army have crossed the river they have been encamped on for so long. As he describes it "the passage of the Chenab". It sounds like a veritable Battle of Nations from his words. He says we have taken eight guns. Well, maybe so, but we've missed many more. Had the old Duke been there we would have had every one. As it is, Shere Singh and his army have escaped and if anything we are in more danger than before, having another river between us and the Commander-in-Chief's hot head. No. There will be no salute for this wading expedition.'

Dalhousie shook his head.

'These generals are strange fellows, indeed. First Whish fumbles over the siege of Multan; the affair at Ramnagar was anything but satisfactory, and now this.'

The Governor-General left his desk and paced the floor with his hands clasped behind his back.

'I will write to him telling him that instead of worrying us with details of ceremonial I would be relieved to hear that he has sent away his surplus baggage, for he has taken the whole of the records of the headquarters with him, printing presses and all. And he has encumbered his army with twice as many tents as it needs. They are carrying what he calls a spare set. No wonder the Company has little money for necessities when the military are so extravagant.'

And Dalhousie proceeded to dictate.

Lord Gough was no happier than the Governor-General.

'Divil take us, Mackeson,' he declared, addressing his political officer, 'what does Dalzie want? He complains that my communications are insecure, my supplies are insufficient and that I have no reserves. But who was it who sanctioned the marooning of Whish in front of Multan? I doubt if Mulraj has more than five thousand men with him. Shere Singh left him to come down into the Doab in front of me, so he cannot be strong. Multan is not worth the powder and shot being wasted on it.'

The decision not to mark the crossing of the Chenab had hurt the old man.

'I suppose he would have been content if I had lost a packet of men crossing the Chenab. You know as well as I do that if Thackwell had done his job we would have taken the Sikhs in the flank. I've said it before and I say it again. I placed the ball at Thackwell's feet and he neglected to kick it. A single hurrah would have taken every Sikh gun in the field.'

The general stared at the map stretched on the table in his tent, held flat by a jewelled sabre. From the brown ink, which denoted the mountains of Kashmir, thin blue lines indicated the rivers of the Punjaub. He pointed a finger at one of them.

'We shall have to follow him there eventually, Governor-General or no Governor-General,' he muttered peevishly.

After Thackwell's inconclusive affair at Saddulapore which, despite all criticism, had left the cane fields full of Sikh corpses and the wells blocked with their dead, Shere Singh had slipped back to the Jhelum. There he had been reinforced by a strong detachment from Peshawar, and had settled with his left flank on the cliff-top town of Rasul. More allies, in the shape of an army under his father, Chattar Singh, plus a contingent of Afghan horse, were on their way to him. Gough, who had followed Shere Singh, was now encamped at Helan, fourteen miles from his enemy.

'Goddam, how long are we to sit here?'

Gough was genuinely puzzled.

'Men eat just as much in camp as they do on the march. More! And they've plenty of work to do. Does Dalzie think it's a picnic? Well, there's nothing for it but to wait for orders. Unless Shere Singh comes out, then I'll go for him. Eh, Mackeson?'

He turned to the political officer. This was a different type of man from the blunt veteran soldier. In Gough's eyes some of the old Sikh chiefs were preferable to these fanatical politicos. From the beginning of the campaign they'd done everything they could to look after their own little patches. If they'd had their way his force would have been split up into fragments chasing shadows. He'd put a stop to it by authorising his officers to clap the political agents in irons if they interfered with troop movements.

Mackeson, in his turn, studied Gough. A decent, brave old man, he thought but out of his time. The Commander-in-Chief was a relic of the society which took its style from the libertine Prince Regent. The reckless gambling, lechery and extravagance of that age might have produced some rich characters, but they had seen their day. Gough, after all, had been in the army when the men had to wear pigtails and powder; when duels were commonplace. He was an antique.

Mackeson could not visualise the General or any of his Peninsular cronies setting out with two or three Hindu clerks to hold court under a tree in a mudhut village. Or to work fifteen hours a day collecting levies, directing agricultural works, or improving roads.

'I have ruled this district for three years by the sole agency of the pen and if necessary I will rule it by the sword,' John Lawrence had written to the chiefs of Kangra when it appeared that they would throw in their lot with the Sikhs. 'Tell those who have joined the rebellion to return to me, as children who have committed a fault return to their fathers, and their faults will be forgiven them . . .'

Mackeson approved of the attitude heartily, but he doubted

whether Gough would have cared for the patriarchal sentiments or the way they were expressed. He felt obliged to give some opinion.

'Certainly I think we must be ready to strike Shere Singh, sir, before he is supported by that rascally father of his,' he said. 'And those thieving Afghans. They need a lesson.'

Gough agreed. Maybe he'd misjudged Mackeson.

As the political agent left Gough's headquarters he studied the sea of tents and hoped that the army would not fall a prey to any of the many diseases which plagued India. At the sight of the 24th formed into a hollow square, he frowned and touched his pony with his spurs. Floggings might be needed to maintain discipline during the enforced idleness of a fixed camp, but they were not an edifying sight to a man trying to impress the Indians with the superiority of the European.

CHAPTER TEN

Private Connelly pressed his bare chest against his tunic which had been folded over the iron tyre of the limber wheel. It had been placed there to stop the metal cutting into him. That was a laugh. He tugged resentfully at the cords which secured his wrists to the spokes. The colonel had said it was a good job the Duke had limited the number of lashes which could be awarded to fifty, otherwise he would have had more. The stupid old git. Didn't he know that a private in the dragoons had been given a hundred only a few days previously for the same offence – being drunk in the lines. Who the hell was going to complain on behalf of a private soldier anyway? All officers were bastards and all N.C.O.s were pig-bastards. He glared out of the corner of his eye at the surgeon standing smoking a cheroot beside an orderly who was waiting with a towel and a bucket of water. They wouldn't be needed, Connelly told himself.

A command rang out and the assembled troops came to attention with the sorry compromise that betokens boots stamping on earth rather than the crash of hobnails on a barrack square. Connelly braced himself and fixed his sidelong glance on his partner in crime, Private Perry, who had avoided arrest somehow, drunk as he had been.

'Right. Lay on!'

With a malignant hiss, nine knotted cords, each two feet-long, ripped his flesh. Connelly braced his stocky legs and emitted a low snarl. His mouth became a rigid slit and his chin thrust at the sky as the lash continued to fall. Now was the numbness. It would hurt soon. Burning, like sharp rocks, pressed into the flesh. Later, though, would be worse. At ten Connelly had been doing the work of a horse down the pit, in low stifling tunnels where there was no room for a pony. Although he was only five feet five inches tall he had shoulders like a wrestler. He took twelve lashes before the skin was broken enough for the blood to flow freely.

'Have to transfer the rogue to the 58th,' said an elderly

captain with a boiled face. 'He'd go down well in the Steelbacks.'

The flogging was done in the old style. Behind the drummer with the cat stood the drum major with a rattan cane. Officially that was to cut the drummer if he did not strike hard enough. Behind the drum major stood the adjutant with another rattan to make sure the drum major did his duty. The canes were not used but they served as a useful reminder that discipline was impartially applied. Or at least that it was supposed to be.

'What are those blue marks on Connelly's back?' whispered Junior Ensign Pennycuick. It was the first time he had seen a man flogged and he stood white-faced. The sight of the lash dark with blood made him feel sick.

'Coal,' said Lloyd Williams tonelessly. 'He used to be a collier.'

The pain consolidated the hate. The hate made the pain tolerable. Blood ran in a glistening crimson stream down the small of the torn back and soaked into an ugly blotch on the white undress trousers. Still the little Welshman snarled, his face a greasy gargoyle.

It was over. After a few staggering steps as he was untied Connelly pushed aside the supporting arms. Snatching the towel from the surgeon's assistant, he mumbled throatily: 'Walk, can't I?'

He made his way, under escort, to the hospital tent and threw himself face down. The bastards. The bloody bastards. Still, it was better than the pit.

Lala Rai, who had brought over the limber, waited until the companies marched away before he reclaimed his vehicle. During the flogging he had kept out of the way. The Gorahlog did not like Indian soldiers watching a white soldier being punished. Some years previously, when the East India Company had abolished the lash for sepoys but kept it for Europeans, he had been seen watching a man in the 13th Foot being flogged. The soldiers had chased him for his life afterwards. Now the sepoys could be flogged again but a wise man did not approach the English regiments on such occasions. He was about to mount the limber when something caught his eye. A button glinted on a jacket lying in the earth; a scarlet tunic with brass buttons and green facings. It belonged to the defaulter. Lala Rai looked around but the sandy square was almost deserted. The nearest figure was a young officer crossing the parade ground. Lala Rai hurried over. The Sahib-log was just a boy and the little Indian threw up a tremendous salute to show that he was an old soldier.

Junior Ensign Pennycuick was non-plussed by the appearance of the solemn little Indian. He knew that the man should not have addressed him without going through an N.C.O. but did not know what to do. This was a situation which he had not been taught to deal with at Sandhurst.

Lala Rai explained importantly that he was in possession of equipment belonging to the defaulter and stood waiting for orders. He expected the officer to call for an N.C.O. or to tell him to double away to the quarterguard.

When young Pennycuick took it from him with a mumbled: 'Er, thank you. Carry on soldier,' he was amazed. Officers did not do things in that way in the Bengal Horse Artillery. With an even more impressive salute he regained his limber and rattled smartly out of sight.

Pennycuick went first to Lloyd Williams's tent but could not find him. He lingered for a moment, then set off for the hospital. Connelly, the only occupant, was lying on his belly, with his face away from him. Swart, hairy arms hung limply on each side of the bed. Little drops of perspiration fell from the misshapen knuckles.

'Are you asleep, Connelly?' he asked hesitantly.

The face turned slowly towards him. Tanned as dark as any native's, it still displayed the blue scars under the skin. A broken nose, deep lines across a beetle brow, blackened and broken teeth. Connelly was not a pretty man at the best of times.

'Sir?' he said sullenly.

'You forgot your jacket.'

It was a stupid thing to say, but Pennycuick couldn't think of anything else.

'Jacket?'

Connelly was bemused.

'Oh! My jacket issit, sir?'

There was no chair, so Pennycuick folded the garment and put it beside the head of the bed. Connelly watched silently.

Embarrassed, the young officer stood for a moment. Then he fumbled in his pocket.

'Here. Take this.'

Connelly looked cautiously at the extended hand. A black, round object reposed there. Little bits of fluff clung to it.

'Please, whatissit?'

A pause and then he added 'sir'.

'It's a humbug.'

Connelly stared at the sweet. The young ensign reddened.

'Go on, take it. It's all right. I've still got some in a tin I brought out from home.'

Slowly the sinewy forearm reached out. A quick movement would ripple the agony in his shoulders.

'Thank you, sir.'

'Well, I must be going.'

The airless tent was oppressive and the empty eyes in the iron visage perplexed him. Pennycuick turned awkwardly on his heel and left without looking back.

Connelly lay still. In his left fist the humbug was warm and sticky. If he squeezed, a gooey fluid was forced between the joints of his fingers. Slowly he raised his hand to his lips. He licked the brown sweetness from his palm before he began to suck the sweet. No one could have guessed it by his expression but he was thinking.

Perry brought him two bottles of Bass Stout that night.

'Where did you get that, boyo?' Connelly demanded. 'I thought it was a crate of Burton's.'

'There's nice now. I bring you beer and you call me a thief.'

'Neffor mind the gab, Ivor. What happened to the Burton?'

Perry's eyes narrowed.

'We got that too, man,' he whispered gleefully. 'Put it in the stream, I did. This lot came from a cart belonging to the dragoons. Cost one rupee twelve annas a bottle, if you pay. Belongs to their adjutant, I hear. Drink up so I can get rid of the bottles.'

Connelly raised the bottle, tilted his head carefully on one side and drank from his prone position. Liquor ran down the side of his neck.

'All officers are bastards!' said Perry.

'All officers are bastards!' replied Connelly.

CHAPTER ELEVEN

The sun was drumming its molten fists on the flat roof of the bungalow. Golden arrows blazed through tiny chinks in the split cane tatties shielding the verandah. Occasionally an almost naked coolie dipped a gourd drowsily into an earthenware jar and splashed the bamboo curtains. Seven tatty wallahs in all squatted in the dust of the Wilmot compound. They were ignored by the other servants flitting by in loose white robes. Inside the darkened house Miss Wilmot did not know just how hot it was. Only that it was very, very hot and that her father's rambling was not helping. He was sprawled in an easy chair with extended wooden arms. Across one he hung a long, lean leg. On the other reposed a glass of something. She could not see what it was.

'Look at it this way, my dear,' he said, allowing his Yorkshire accent to intrude in a homely, persuasive manner. 'I've no objection to Leiston calling here to improve his knowledge of the language. Although why you have taken so much trouble to learn it I shall never know – any native who matters can be made to understand plain English. It is just that, well, Leiston is hardly the right sort of person to be seen visiting our home so regularly. If you wish to indulge your expertise, why not encourage the attentions of an officer? There are some 40,000 English soldiers in India and a reasonable proportion of them are officers. Surely you can find one to suit you. Furthermore, there are many admirable Company officials to whom the association could be congenial.'

The Reverend Barnabas Wilmot paused and savoured his drink for a moment. Really it was too early for claret but Colonel Grant had sent him a case from a shipment which had arrived from Calcutta just that day. It would be rude not to have sampled it before he dined at the mess that evening.

Sarah Wilmot remained indifferently silent. She had a feeling there might be something wrong with the thermantidote but did not feel like spending the energy required to explain her suspicions. The fans of the thermantidote drove air through a damp screen. Worked by two men it was supposed to be able to reduce the temperature by as much as ten degrees. Miss Wilmot doubted whether anything could do that in Amballa in the hot season. And yet her father dressed as if he were back in the draughty vicarage at Leeds.

'The Lod' (Mr. Wilmot always referred to the Deity in this clipped manner as it helped him to cut down the time spent in delivering his rare sermons) 'may have made us all equal. I don't deny it. In His sight, my love, we are no doubt even as a humble sweeper – an Untouchable. However, in His infinite wisdom, He has created stations for us all in this worldly life. It behoves us as true Christians to maintain them, if you see what I mean, Sarry.'

Miss Wilmot tussled with the antimacassar in which a pin from her thick, dark-brown hair had become entangled. It never ceased to amaze her how her father could endure his thick clerical suits. Yet she had to admit he was much more presentable than he had been at home in England. There he had always seemed grubby and dishevelled. Never once did he change his clothes during the day and inevitably filled the house with the smell of horses and hounds and wet earth. Being known as a hunting parson had pleased him and kept him in good repute with the local gentry. Now that he had an army of servants to wait upon him he changed more often. He was shaved in bed. His socks were rolled on for him. His horse was waiting for him as he stepped from the door. Servants undoubtedly suited her father. There were some fifty of them in all – or so she believed – grasscutters, grooms, gardeners, the man who did the washing and his brother who did the ironing, the man who kept the poultry and his daughters who acted as maids. The punkah wallahs, tatty wallahs, and the thermantidote men made up the number with the eight bearers for the palankeen. Mr. Wilmot travelled in this old-fashioned oriental version of the Sedan chair when he knew the drinking was going to be serious. At other times the attendants came in handy for odd jobs in the compound. It covered two acres in all and with the families of servants, was a village in itself.

Mr. Wilmot decided to get to the point he was trying to make.

'You see, m'dear, I think it might be more sensible of you

to discourage the sergeant, nice young man though he is, and try to establish a social relationship which may have prospects. I can't be expected to live for ever, you know, and I should like to see you settle down with someone who can provide for you before I meet my Maker.'

'And may I ask whom you have in mind, Father?' she enquired. 'Are you sure you don't want me to settle down with someone who can look after both of us?'

After years of sponging on anyone who would mount him or entertain him, house him and not bother him unduly, Barnabas Wilmot was immune to such imputations.

'Sarry, that was most unkind. You know I want only for your happiness. I cannot help it if it was the Lod's will that I should be called upon to serve Him in this heathen country. It is my cross and I bear it gladly.'

Gladly indeed, because despite the dust and the ever-present threat of disease (which had disposed of his wife and two younger children six years earlier in Calcutta), India allowed an unambitious, ageing Church of England cleric with sporting inclinations and moderate private means to indulge himself to his heart's content.

Although he received regular donations from well-meaning matrons in England, he had no intention of converting anyone, or of doing more than administer in the most perfunctory fashion to the spiritual requirements of a handful of Europeans. The sight of evangelising Non-conformists filled his orthodox soul with horror.

'India has enough tee-total religions already,' he insisted. 'The country doesn't need any more.'

Where his daughter, his sole surviving child, was concerned, Mr. Wilmot felt obliged to ensure that any friendships she formed did not impinge on his own status. Europeans of all classes were welcome in his house, down to the sons of tradesmen and simple clerks. After all, without exception, they were members of 'the club' in India, whatever might be their social shortcomings at home. But soldiers, ordinary, common soldiers, were 'different', regrettable though it might seem.

'Goodness!' He pulled a large hunter from his waistcoat pocket. 'I must be off. I'm expected at the mess to make arrangements for the next shoot. Don't wait up for me, my love.

Think on what I have said. May the good Lod guide you.'

With that benediction Mr. Wilmot departed noisily, creating such a commotion that the punkah wallahs, thinking they were being abused, pulled energetically on their ropes, the tatty wallahs splashed vigorously and the creaking, ricketty thermantidote hustled the memory of a cool breeze reluctantly through the baking bungalow.

Mr. Wilmot crammed a low-crowned hat with a monstrous brim on his white locks, hoisted his angular frame on to a little Kabuli mare and clattered out of the compound towards the cantonments. From a distance the ensemble looked like an umbrella with four legs.

In the dim living-room, with its rosewood piano with the brass candle-holders, its horse-hair sofa and its black papier-mâché sewing table, Miss Wilmot fanned herself absent-mindedly with the Delhi Gazette and wondered how her father would react if he knew that she found Sergeant Leiston of the 29th Foot extremely attractive.

She had liked him from the day he had escorted her father home from a dinner at headquarters. Most of the men who did the job usually explained away the recumbent figure in the dhooli by saying 'Taken ill with the heat, Ma'am'. Leiston had said: 'I'm afraid the old gentleman is drunk, Miss Wilmot. You ought to tell him to take more blitey-water with it.'

It had been on the tip of her tongue to tell him not to be impertinent and to threaten to report him for his impudence. Instead, on impulse, she had called Nahamdeo to put her father to bed and had asked Leiston if he would like a cup of coffee.

He had laughed and replied that he would much prefer a bottle of cold beer. His genuine surprise and enjoyment at being offered one gave her inexplicable satisfaction. A consignment from the ice-club – which painstakingly stored this precious luxury from man-made dew-ponds in the hills – had arrived the previous day.

Leiston drank it standing. On the verandah, of course. Even in a house full of servants it would have been unwise to invite in a soldier at that time of night. Miss Wilmot noted with approval that her visitor was well over six feet tall. Miss Wilmot was five feet nine inches in her stockinged feet. As she said goodnight she enjoyed the experience of having to look up to the sergeant's face. Wearing his shako he looked even taller and she could not take her eyes off him crunching boldly away down the gravel.

When Jamdanee brushed her mistress's hair for the ritual half-hour that night, Miss Wilmot used her knowledge of Hindustani to find out a little more than was really discreet about the whereabouts of the detachment of the 29th Foot.

It was Julius Begg who first commented on the frequent encounters which his friend Leiston had with the padre's daughter – 'the tall, rangy gel in the grey dress' was how he described her.

'Teachin' yer 'Industani, is she?' he asked scathingly, adding more truthfully than he realised: 'You, wot can talk it as well as the niggers can talk English.'

The two sergeants had been sent to Amballa to wait for a convoy of personal effects for certain officers.

'I'm a raw recruit compared with her,' retorted Leiston. 'Mind you, I'm not saying that there are not one or two things that she can learn from me.'

Julius sat on a camp stool with Buddha-like serenity.

'You 'avin' it off with the baggage then? And her a padre's daughter. Gawd, wot will ye get up to next? You, 'oo 'as condemned poor old Begg for making sure that the 29th don't go short of the hessential pleasures of the flesh.'

He stopped as Leiston looked up from his equipment. A crater appeared in the pink mountain and for a moment Begg was lost for words. Then the jaw clamped shut and he rubbed his bristle pate as he considered the matter. He crashed a meaty fist over his heart and rolled his eyes.

'Nary a word, Robert. Nary a word. Thet gel 'as but to raise 'er little finger and Julius Begg will be at 'er bleedin' service, whether she wants a throat cut or a bolt of Kashmir cloth for 'er granny's shawl.'

He paused to study the shining boot which had just been slipped on his foot by a wizened Hindu 'boy'.

'That old father of 'ers don't 'alf like the likker, Robert. If ye gets the chance to put it to 'im, tip 'im the wink that you 'ave a friend wot can supply a nice line in real brandy – at a favourable price, of course.'

CHAPTER TWELVE

December, 1848, became a month that was to be remembered for its long spell of waiting. Shere Singh, secure on the cliffs at Rasul, set his men to work deepening and extending the trenches concealed in the undergrowth on the banks of the Jhelum. Every day that passed without seeing the banners of his father, Chattar Singh, and the Afghan horse, fretted him. The country was poor around Rasul and he could not feed his men there for ever.

Gough, fourteen miles away in his tented city near Wazirabad, looked to every messenger for news of General Whish at Multan. But Dalhousie's dream of an India revitalised by the steel arteries of the railway was yet to come true. And Whish sat before the fortress waiting in his turn for the arrival of reinforcements from Bombay. Two cavalry regiments, six battalions and three batteries were moving to his support by river, in the steamer *Conqueror*, and by road. They included two hard-bitten European regiments, the wild Irishmen of the 1st Bombay Fusiliers and the green-jacketed 60th Rifles. Until they arrived he had to content himself with minor operations.

Within Multan, the population waited for news of relief. Mulraj daily sent his scouts galloping into the hinterland, the British not having enough men to invest the place. But the news they brought was of little comfort. General Whish, a stolid gunner, was building up huge stocks of shells. Mulraj rode regularly round his thirty towers of mellow, burnt brick and studied the walls which in some places soared seventy feet. They looked strong enough to stand any amount of pounding. But he could not be sure. Treatment of the Sirdar, Khan Singh, who had been thrown into the secure interior of the fort's main arsenal after the murder of Vans Agnew and Lieutenant Anderson, improved. Khan Singh assured his son, who had been imprisoned with him, that there was little need to worry. The English would breach the walls in their own good time and he would be freed to rule the city. It was, he explained, just a matter of waiting.

In Gough's lines near Wazirabad there were cricket matches, shooting parties (providing fowl for the pot) and Leiston found himself taking part in a sack race in which the officers also joined. Julius Begg's young ladies did considerable business not far from the lines of the 29th. And the regimental silver was uncrated and set up on the magnificent mess table of the 24th.

Perched on a forage wagon, Private Hacken and his cronies turned their critical eyes on a display given by a troop of irregular cavalry. With fierce cries the turbaned horsemen spurred across the levelled ground. Lance heads dropped and tent pegs whirled triumphantly in the air. Racing hoofs, a sword flash and brass chamber pots were cut clean in half. Carbines cracked, sending dust flying up before the targets.

'They're not so hot with their guns, but they're good with the lance, Hacky,' said a cadaverous-looking dragoon. 'Yer've got to give 'em that.'

Private Hacken, sitting in his shirt sleeves, nodded condescendingly.

'Yerse, they're good with their lances. And them irregulars are handy with their sabres too. All black cavalry are the same. The tulwar comes natural to them. They're slashers. Don't have to worry where a slash goes, do yer? I mean, you just flay away and 'ope someone gets in the way. Usin' the point . . . now that's somethink different. Calls for skill. I don't know why they gives good swords to the Company's regular regiments. Waste of time, if you ask me. They haven't got the same brains as wot we 'ave and so they makes a hash of things.'

If there was one thing the British generals had given a lot of thought to it was the design of an efficient cavalry sword. During the Peninsular War a well-curved sabre had been a popular weapon with hussars and light dragoons. But a study of casualties had shown that the proportion of killed to wounded was unusually high among the British squadrons. The explanation lay in the long straight swords of the French heavy regiments. A point delivered by a fourteen stone man at galloping speed is not only difficult to avoid but crashes home with devastating results. Whereas a sabre slash, which might have to cut through epaulettes, or a thick coat, a collar or a helmet, may make a spectacular scar but is seldom bone-biting.

'Yeah,' said Private Hacken warming to his theme as the light-blue native horsemen continued to dash excitedly over the drill ground, 'they should ha' left them with their old slashers. They knows how to sharpen them all right. The Sikhs and the Paythans knows what's all right too. Catch 'em with a straight sword! With them the bigger the curve the longer the blade. And sharp. Flick! Off goes yer nose. Chop! Off goes yer ear! Swish! It's goodbye to yer eye-lids.'

Hacken pointed to a menacing crescent of blue steel in the hand of a mahogany-faced irregular who was reining his pony this way and that as he cheered on his comrades.

'Look at the curve and the set of the blade on that skimitar. Talk about sharp. Just one touch of that bastard and yer've got a slash a foot long on yer mug. It's what they're made for. All edge.'

He raised his voice.

'Hi, Mohammed.'

A dazzling smile pierced the black beard. Dark eyes gleamed.

'Show us how sharp yer tulwar is,' shouted Hacken. He licked his thumb and went through the unmistakeable motion of testing a blade, rubbing his finger across an imaginary edge. Jabbing a finger towards the scimitar he suddenly slashed the air. The sowar beamed again and nodded. Slipping the sword into his scabbard for a moment he delved into his sheepskin jerkin and produced a blue silk scarf. He held up a silver coin in his other hand and then suddenly knotted it in one corner of the piece of material. Holding it up for the dragoons to see while he drew his sword again the Pathan paused for a second then threw the silk in the air. For a second it sailed in a graceful parabola. Then a gleaming arc streaked through it and two blue strips fluttered to the ground. One of Hacken's comrades picked them up.

'Look at that, Hackey-boy.' He held up both pieces of silk. 'He's cut clean through the cloth and the coin.'

The sowar beamed and smiled and bowed and walked his pony back and forward. Hacken beamed and nodded back.

'We are a clever black bastard and not 'arf,' he grinned.

Then more seriously he pointed to the blade again.

'Tulwar . . . Damascus? Where it made, Mohammed? Tulwar . . . is it Damascus?'

The sowar seemed to understand. He nodded and jabbered and waved his sword in little circles.

'I reckon 'e says it's made in Khorosan,' said the confident Hacken. 'That's where all the best blacksmiths are in these 'ere parts.'

His hand shot out authoritatively.

'No, don't give 'im back the bits of silk, Weller. 'E won't want them back. We're bleedin' pig eaters and feringhee dogs to 'im even though 'e is on our side.'

That evening some of the dragoons tried to repeat the trick with their own swords. The silk fluttered unharmed through the air.

'Might as well use a carpet beater for all the good ye're doing,' came Hacken's considered opinion. He hefted his own sword comfortably in his hand, three feet from hilt to point with only a slight curve. With a flick of the wrist and a lunge towards a guttering candle at the door of the tent he turned the last foot of the blade into shimmering gold for a second.

'Yer can fergit about the rest of it,' he said grimly fingering the twelve-inch point, the only part of the blade which was sharpened on both sides .'It's this little bit that does the dirty work. Pops 'em like bugs on wallpaper it does. Touch 'em with that at the trot and yer can ferget all yer slashin'. And it won't break neither, not if it's handmade of good old English steel . . . a nice bit o' Sheffield.'

Hacken had every reason to be confident in his weapon. All home-produced cavalry swords were tested on an oak block before issue. A neat piece of mechanism struck home the blade with a force of 125 lbs.; the flat was tested to withstand a blow of sixty pounds. It was a formidable test for a weapon only one and a quarter inches wide; but British swords were formidable things. All the same there was a lot in what Hacken had said about their unsuitability for native regiments. It took long months of training and considerable nerve to thrust home when menaced by a howling, frothing Sikh or Afghan with a bright-edged tulwar raised above one's own body. A man had to be cool and to remember his drill. The sowars in the native regiments felt happier grasping the traditional heavy curved sabre with its single plain knuckle bar, rather than thrust their hands into the half-basket hilt of the lighter, near straight British sword.

Sword drill was, however, only a small part of a cavalryman's service on the Punjaub plain. Dust and monotony were much more familiar acquaintances. Daily the squadrons patrolled towards the enemy. Or guarded the baggage animals. Or escorted infantry working parties. Outlying picquets stared at the empty scrub. Inlying picquets swapped jokes with the foot soldiers trudging back and forth on sentry go. And always there were 'our long-faced friggin' friends' to attend to.

For the 14th Light Dragoons, the spit and polish was more irksome than the duties inflicted on the acclimatised 3rd. Colonel King, who had taken over from Havelock, was a conscientious man and kept his young soldiers busy to please his immediate superior, the ageing Brigadier Pope.

Sun covers were removed from helmets and the substantial Maltese crosses were burnished. The Prussian eagle badge in the centre of the helmet plate was polished till it gleamed.

Then the sun covers were replaced.

The highly decorated shabraques which bore the crown and insignia together with the proud 'XIV L.D.' were brushed and cleaned assiduously. White sheepskin rugs were bleached until they dazzled.

Then the magnificent squadrons trotted out on a sweep and returned covered with white Punjaub dust.

The soldiers grumbled – although there were plenty of kit wallahs to do the cleaning – but secretly they were proud of their colonel's attitude. Their friendship with the 3rd, which had grown up at Amballa, was strengthened; especially as the veterans sympathised with them for the shambles at Ramnagar. A lot more swaggering, swearing and kicking of natives went on in the lines of the 14th than had been the case.

Mallindine became more and more impatient as the days passed.

'What we should do,' he informed Lieutenant the Honourable Murdo Jameson, his cousin and frequent companion, 'is to form all the cavalry in one great column, ford the Jhelum up north, and sweep down behind Rasul while the Feet attack frontally. They can throw in the sepoys first to sop up the fire, then let the H.M. regiments rush the position with their bayonets.'

'Yawse,' said Jameson, who cared not one jot and was quite happy lying on a cool rush mat which his servant had spread on a charpoy. Jameson said 'Yawse' to anything. His father had bought him his commission because he said 'Yawse' by mistake. He thought the old gentleman was referring to a frame in the billiards room with some visiting officers when he was asked if he would like to join the dragoons. It seemed too much trouble to explain so he had allowed himself to be absorbed into the army. It was the same when the regiment was ordered to India. Jameson hadn't meant to go.

He'd been given to understand that a gentleman of means like himself would not be expected to do any real soldiering. The custom was for a person of substance to sell out or transfer or go on half-pay or some such boring thing when a smart regiment was sent abroad. And there was no discredit attached to this very sensible arrangement. Some regiments had two complete sets of officers. Gentlemen for home service and military trades people, so to speak, for foreign parts. When old Havelock had asked him if he would be travelling with his brother officers, he thought they were going to a race meeting. When he said 'Yawse' he had no idea the colonel meant 'Indee-ar'. Given his word though. Too much of a bore to explain. Besides, Lord Cardigan had been out there so it couldn't be in such bad taste. Mallindine was going too so he would be useful. Funny fellow. Always looking for something to do. Actually furious because he'd missed that dreadful brawl at Ram-something-or-other.

Jameson shuddered at the memory of the undignified affair. Such a commotion. And so many absolutely awful people. The Sikhs had actually shot at the British officers. It just didn't seem civilised. Jameson had been very glad when it was all over. He'd managed to lead his troop through the melée without bothering anyone when a Sikh had the temerity to try to pull him from the saddle. Jameson had stunned the man with the pommel of his sword. Then his troop sergeant had appeared and said: 'Don't you think we'd better rally on the reserve squadron, sir?' He'd said 'Yawse' and everyone had trotted after him. Damned if he wanted to go through all that nonsense again. Not surprised that gentlemen preferred to stay at home. For the life of him he couldn't understand why Mallindine wished to chase the Sikhs. Too hot tempered. Caused that unpleasant scene at Amballa.

'I say, Mallindine, that reminds me.'

Mallindine, who had been nibbling a biscuit and drinking brandy and water at a little table, twisted on his camp chair and asked:

'What reminds you? I haven't spoken for ten minutes.'

'Oh! Well, I was . . . er . . . thinking.'

A look of incredulity crossed Mallindine's face.

'Good God, Jameson!'

'Meant to tell you earlier. Mr. Wilmot has ridden in from Amballa. With a draft for the 61st. Dreadful journey. Footpads and stray Sikhs all the way.'

Mallindine sniffed meaningly.

'Ten guineas to a pice headquarters have just had a delivery of claret. Either that or he wants me to divert his daughter from associating with a hottentot this time.'

CHAPTER THIRTEEN

Until the advent of Sergeant Leiston Miss Wilmot had regarded men as an unpleasant and overbearing species. It was a view that had been strengthened by her experiences in India. Apart from the animal behaviour she had observed within the compound on occasions, Indian women were treated with less consideration than the oxen which plodded aimlessly round the well. They were undoubtedly the lowest form of life in the country. Chattels who belonged absolutely to their fathers, then their husbands and finally to the elders of their family, who disposed of them cruelly and brutally.

The role of white women in India was so far removed from this slave status as to be incomparable. But that did not blind Miss Wilmot to the fact that Englishmen were still the lords and masters of their womenfolk. She had read that, fifty years previously, daring women had conducted love affairs with the nabobs of Calcutta almost in public and had exercised great influence. She did not approve of the sexual activities of these ladies, but she heartily commended their impact upon public affairs. Above all, she envied them their freedom to mix with whom they chose.

Calcutta had lost attraction for her after the death of her mother and sisters. Miss Wilmot had been on a visit to a missionary family in the hills when cholera carried off Mrs. Wilmot, Charlotte and Eunice. She'd been glad when her father moved 'up country'. But garrison life had serious drawbacks. A woman was expected to keep out of the sun, let the servants do the work, bear babies for her husband (the poor children seemed to die so easily) and flirt with the officers. To devote any time to work such as the study of native languages was regarded as almost indecent. But she had carried on with it all the same. Now she discovered a fellow enthusiast in Sergeant Leiston and he kept interrupting her thoughts. Roshanara was another who thought frequently of Sergeant Leiston.

Roshanara was one of Julius Begg's young ladies. She was

thirteen, rising fourteen, and old Sarojini, who ran the House of Delights in the bazaar, had great hopes of her. Sarojini had spent many years in the business and liked her arrangement with Begg-Sahib. The girls were available to his comrades and even Gorah-log officers visited them at special times. This meant there was not too much work, and the income was guaranteed. The soldiers were happy. So were the girls. Even Roshanara.

Roshanara had been her mother's first-born and a great sorrow. Without sons a family withered and vanished. So her mother had pledged her to the river gods. And the gods had heard her. Two sons had been born. Then a daughter. And another son. But the gods had to be paid.

The white rulers of Calcutta had forbidden it. But they were not on the banks of the Ganges the night Roshanara's uncles tied her hands behind her back and hustled her to the dark, sacred waters. If the crocodiles had not gorged themselves that day on a boatload of drowned pilgrims she would have been devoured like many other unwanted children.

Sarojini had found her on the steps of the ghat when she went to bathe and worship in the cool of the morning – for Sarojini was a pious woman and had travelled far to pay her devotions. The appearance of the dripping child, still dazed from the blow with which the uncles had intended to stun her, was a sign from the gods that could not be ignored. She felt the child's breasts. They were just beginning to firm. That was good. She took the cold, small hand. It remained limp. So! She would be easy to train. A clap of the hands and an old woman left Sarojini's litter and collected the girl.

Later Sarojini decided to call her Roshanara after a daughter of the Emperor Shah Jehan. Even though he had been a Muslim, his love life had been a thing of splendour after the death of his wife. Besides, the Gorah-log would not know the difference.

The finest fruits of Sarojini's orchard were not wasted on humble musket carriers. Some of the older officers paid well for little girls. She told the major with the purple face that Roshanara was a virgin. The child, whose initiation had been accomplished by Sarajini's two nephews, deceived him without difficulty. The squeals she feigned cost the major twenty rupees, money he considered well spent.

A nightmare and a fever had brought Sergeant Leiston to the bed of Roshanara. The regiment had been on an aimless and inexplicable excursion in the blistering heat of high summer. They got nowhere and did nothing. Three men had collapsed and died on the third day out and been buried by the side of the road. On the return journey Leiston marched with the company at the head of the column. As they approached the cantonments, a pack of pi-dogs fled from the iron hard boots. Behind them in the dust lay a ball they had been playing with. The front rank had kicked it out of the way but a tiny gold speck glinting as the 'ball' rolled enabled Leiston to identify it. It was the head of Tam Duncan who had died of sunstroke on the road.

The sailor's gold ear-ring was unmistakable. The jackals had dug out the body during the night. Leiston who had seen many revolting sights since his arrival in India, could not get the little Scot out of his mind. He was haunted by dreams in which they fought with Julius Begg in the tavern all over again . . . but Tam had no head.

Julius himself had suggested the solution. After failing to get Leiston drunk, he announced: 'What you need is a woman.'

'Maybe. But what I don't need is the pox. Remember Wilson? He finished up without a nose.'

'Pah! He went with sandrats. I'll speak to Sarojini. She'll find a fresh little flower for yer . . . honest.'

On a night when Leiston was half-crazed with heat and suffering from a fever, Julius led him to the House of Delights and the girl child the gods rejected. In the cool arms of little Roshanara the horrors were brushed away.

Roshanara lay on her back and stared at the ceiling as the sergeant slept. Here, indeed, was paradise. The thick walls which kept out the heat also excluded the world. To some, the small room, with its simple bed and rush mattress, its cheap copper bowls and sparse furniture, would have been a cell. The intrusion of strange bodies, the exploring hands, the muscular effort, the mechanical laughter and simulated pleasure would have been degrading. But there were many worse things in the world. Roshanara knew that.

Leiston did not go back often. But he did go back. And Roshanara dreamed of him.

'It's only nateral,' said Julius one day. 'A man 'as to 'ave a woman. It's the way the good Christian God made us. Yer can't go on bottlin' it up for ever. Yer'd blow up.'

Julius was firmly of the opinion that his comrade should marry a white woman.

'Don't be bloody silly. If I ever went back to England they'd put me in jail for bigamy. A man isn't allowed two wives. And I've got one. What d'ye think Miss Howick would say? Or that old bastard, Sir Ephraim? Don't be daft, man.'

Julius was not to be put off.

'You ain't goin' back,' he said confidently. 'Only a bleedin' idiot would go back to an English barracks. Marry one of the women in the rigiment. There's never a shortage o' widows. Why, Mistress Galpin 'as bin married six times to a sojer. An' she made each one of them a better man until they got themselves killed or caught the cholera.'

A woman didn't stay a widow long. Unless she married within six months of her husband's death she would be 'struck off' the ration strength and have to fend for herself. The same thing happened to the daughters of soldiers when they reached the age of fourteen. If they did not find a husband within a prescribed time their parents could not draw rations for them. Julius, who had been born into the army, knew all about that. He'd had two stepfathers before he was six years old.

CHAPTER FOURTEEN

With the cool weather, the leaves withered. In September when Whish had first approached Multan the lofty walls had been almost hidden with dark green foliage. By December the towers and bastions were plainly visible. Much of the jungle had been cleared for firewood. Officers using their glasses could see the Sikhs clearly on the defences, deepening trenches, thickening the outworks.

'Can't have that,' said Whish, staring hard at a walled garden with a summerhouse. 'It'll play the devil with us later on.'

The Sikhs were loopholing the walls and a train of camels stood waiting to be unloaded.

As the mists of dawn cleared, two columns moved on the objective. At the head of one marched a company of the 10th Foot. A company of the 32nd led the other. Making up the rest of the force came the sepoys of the 8th Native Infantry and detachments of sappers carrying scaling ladders and crowbars.

An irregular thudding told listeners that the 32nd had opened fire on the move according to plan. Smoke welled round the ranks, which straggled as the men paused to reload, ram, fix the percussion caps and fire independently.

It had taken the British Army nearly twenty-five years to get round to using the percussion cap, but once they had got it, they made good use of it. Where the old flintlock might misfire every six or seven trigger pulls, the caps had a failure rate below four in a hundred shots. The 32nd banged away merrily.

'Ah, here come our friends,' said Whish from his position of vantage.

Yellow turbanned Sikhs were swarming out of buildings and over walls. In reply to their battle cries the 32nd doubled forward with hoarse cheers. Then the Sikhs saw the second column and scrambled back into their defences. The vicious boom of zamburaks, outsize muskets fired from wooden slings carried on camels, added to the din.

'They've got a scaling ladder up, sir,' said an engineer major.

Through their glasses the watchers saw a red tunic at the top of the rungs. A bright light flashed in their lenses and the figure toppled to the earth.

'Sabred, by George!'

But already the next man was on his way to confront the swordsman. Another ladder was up. And another. The 10th, who had not fired a shot during the approach march, arrived on the scene and thundered a volley which could be heard plainly over the clamour. Scarcely had the smoke begun to clear than another crash announced the contribution of the sepoys of the 8th Native Infantry. A milky haze washed round the disputed buildings. Clambering figures, running men, falling men, motionless men, flashes and heavy detonations testified to the strength of the opposition.

'Holy Mother, look at me musket, me beautiful gun.'

On the roof of the summer house Private Kennedy of the 32nd regarded with dismay the once highly polished stock of his Brown Bess, now in splinters and covered in blood. His bayonet had snapped off clean at the first thrust and frantically he had battered a Sikh to the ground with the butt. Only now did he see the man was wearing a medieval helmet with a tall spike. Throwing down his useless weapon he dragged another musket from under a groaning sepoy.

Two other sepoys were trying to batter a hole in the roof. Kennedy took up a position to cover them as they worked. Below in a crowded room a shower of mud and plaster from the ceiling attracted the attention of a Sikh officer. As the crowbar burst through three muskets blasted the aperture.

Kennedy was drenched in a scarlet stream which spurted from the neck of the nearest sepoy. The other man fell like a log. Mad with excitement, Kennedy thrust his musket through the hole and pulled the trigger.

In a room filled with choking smoke and echoing to the crack of shots being fired from loopholes no one noticed a figure collapse lifeless on a pile of dried grass used for bedding. Or the glowing match of the primitive firelock start a pale brown spot on the white cotton tunic, which quickly became black and burst into flames. Soon the flames were licking greedily at a powder keg.

On the roof Kennedy was welcoming a familiar face as he helped to haul his comrade Makepiece over the parapet.

'Thanks be to God you're here at last. It's a hell of a place,' he said.

Just then the summerhouse erupted, belching smoke and flame from every window. The two soldiers of the 32nd picked themselves from the ground where they had been hurled, and stared stupidly at a sergeant, who danced silently up and down shouting orders they could not hear.

It was some time before their ears recovered, but the summerhouse was no longer a serious obstacle.

CHAPTER FIFTEEN

Leiston knew that he was not visiting Mr. Wilmot's bungalow for the sole purpose of learning Hindustani. Miss Wilmot was well aware that she was not inviting the tall sergeant for the charitable purpose of teaching the under-privileged. And both knew that the other knew. But neither could bring themselves to say as much for fear of destroying what little they had. This impasse might have gone unresolved and unrewarded, had not Mr. Wilmot inadvertently intervened.

'I can't understand gels these days,' he told Mr. Rigby, the Junior Magistrate, a young man who thought conversely that he understood everything.

'In my day they knew their place. Learning foreign languages, asking natives about their customs . . . well, it's not nice. Not healthy.'

Mr. Rigby nodded. Miss Wilmot's tall, slim figure had not escaped his attention.

'Come, Mr. Wilmot, surely it is a good thing to see the gentle sex applying their leisure in improving their minds. Why, Mrs. Rigby maintains an excellent scrap-book in which she pastes all items of interest concerning our community.'

Mr. Wilmot, who had called in connection with a forthcoming social function, and stayed for a chat, rumbled on.

'It's not that so much. I mean, it's knowing your place in society, your duty to your family and friends. Keeping up appearances.'

'Appearances?'

'Yes, appearances. Dammit man, how would you like it if you went home every evening and found your daughter talking gibberish to a hulking soldier?'

'I know ensigns are not always the most relaxing company. My young brother . . .'

'Not an ensign, man. Not an officer at all. A thumping, great, clod-booted sergeant.'

'You mean, an ordinary soldier!'

Mr. Rigby was astonished.

'Yes. A sergeant in the 29th. They're the ones with the yellow cuffs, aren't they?'

A nod conveyed Mr. Rigby's awareness that the 29th had yellow facings.

'I must say it is rather unusual to entertain other ranks,' he mused. 'But I shouldn't think there's much harm in it.'

'Well, I don't like it. Place isn't my own. Be glad to be shot of him.'

And Mr. Wilmot went on his rounds.

Ladies not being a subject for discussion in the mess, Mr. Rigby found time to raise the curious behaviour of the parson's daughter during a shooting expedition to the hills. The officers of the 14th Light Dragoons being in the cantonment and Mallindine being a particular friend, he asked his advice as a soldier and man of the world.

'Do you think it would be a neighbourly act if I had a word with the girl?' he wanted to know. 'I shouldn't think she has the vaguest idea what sort of a situation she's creating. It's obviously quite innocent, but there's talk already, you know. Servants. Can't stop it.'

Mallindine was amused. He'd seen Miss Wilmot trotting about the cantonments in a smart pony cart. Arrogant miss, he'd thought her, considering her father was only a chaplain. Still she had a well-bred look, an imperious nose which went with her high cheekbones. Handsome rather than beautiful.

'I shouldn't get involved if I were you,' Mallindine replied. He blew a puff of smoke towards the Sirmoor heights.

'D'you know, Rigby, I've made a mind to take her in hand myself. Not too obviously. Just drop in for a chat with her Pa.'

He smirked.

'You game, Jammy?'

Jameson thought that he was being invited to play cards and answered 'Yawse.'

Miss Wilmot hardly noticed the increasing frequency with which Mallindine and his amusing friend, Mr. Jameson appeared. As for the tall sergeant – as Julius put it when he fitted himself out in a suit of dazzling whites before setting out for the Wilmot compound: 'She's got yer 'ooked, Robert. 'Ooked.'

Miss Wilmot and Leiston were both indulging in the mutual ritual of pretending to talk and listen without doing so. Both were waiting to see what emotional vibrations proximity might engender.

Leiston ran a finger round his collar as he studied a Hindustani noun. Miss Wilmot sat opposite him in the living-room.

'Do you feel it too?' she asked brightly. 'So it is warmer. It's the thermantidote. It sticks a bit, you know. Just a moment and I'll put it right. All you do is give it a knock.'

Nimbly she sprang onto the seat of her chair and gave the whirring contraption a brisk knock. Then she slipped and gave a little scream as she was caught by Leiston who had risen to help her. His fingers closed over the soft muslin round her waist. Miss Wilmot thought for one wild moment that Leiston might kiss her. When he didn't, she was mortified. Flustered, she put her hand to her hair, straightened her blouse and wondered at her thumping heart.

'You all right, miss?'

'Yes, I think so. Do I look all right?'

Leiston regarded her with a poker face.

'You look a real picture to me, miss.'

She caught her breath.

'Why, Sergeant Leiston, I do believe you are paying me a compliment.'

With mounting excitement, she noticed the hot eyes in the wooden face.

A breath of perfume swept through the room as a tatty wallah splashed the grass blind.

Miss Wilmot sent her bonnet sailing over the windmill.

'Were you thinking of kissing me a moment ago?'

Startled, Leiston remained silent.

'Well?'

Miss Wilmot's voice trembled. If he did not say 'yes' she would be humiliated. If he did . . . She gasped as Leiston stretched out a bronzed fist and touched her cheek.

'Truth is, miss, I could have eaten you up. Leastways, you looked good enough to eat.'

A good-natured grin creased his face.

'But sergeants aren't allowed to eat the padre's daughter,' he added. 'So I think you may stand easy.'

Not sure that she wanted to 'stand easy' Miss Wilmot laughed nervously. To cover her confusion she insisted that despite protocol, the sergeant should take tea with her on the verandah. The couple were sitting there when a group of horsemen rode into the compound.

'Why, it's Papa with Lieutenant Mallindine and Mr. Jameson,' she said nervously.

Leiston started to scramble from his chair.

'I'd better be going. It's time I reported for duty.'

But by this time Mr. Wilmot and his companions were making their way up the steps.

'Oh, it's you, Sergeant,' said Mr. Wilmot shortly. He made no further attempt at conversation. Leiston stood to attention.

'Good afternoon, Mr. Wilmot.'

Impetuously Miss Wilmot decided to make the introductions herself.

'Sergeant Leiston, this is Lieutenant Mallindine and this is Lieutenant Jameson.'

'Good afternoon, gentlemen.'

Leiston had become a robot. Jameson nodded and 'hawed' casually. But Mallindine threw a searching glance.

'Afternoon. Hmm! So you're Miss Wilmot's famous interpreter sergeant, are you? What's it been today, then? Irregular verbs?'

His manner was a little too bright and breezy. Miss Wilmot remembered her manners and offered tea to the visitors. Another table appeared.

'Well, if you will excuse me, Miss Wilmot...'

She looked up gratefully and was about to speak when Mallindine interrupted.

'Oh, you're not going, Sergeant? Don't let us deprive you of your tea.'

The voice contained an edge.

'With your permission, sir.'

Leiston sat down abruptly.

Mallindine looked surprised.

For the next half-hour Leiston spoke only when spoken to. Mr. Wilmot chattered, Jameson dozed and Mallindine tried to bait the sergeant. Success eluded him until his eyes rested on Leiston's blue and crimson medal ribbon.

'So you saw action against the Sikhs, did you?'

'Yes, sir. Ferozeshah and Sobraon.'

'Give them a good hiding, what? Plenty of cold steel and sabre work?'

Leiston paused.

'Yes, sir. You could say that.'

'Well, it's a pity you didn't make a better job of it. It looks as though we shall have to do it again. This time I think they'll get a lesson they won't forget in a hurry.'

Leiston stared stolidly at the elegant dragoon. He'd recognised Mallindine despite his silky moustache. But it was obvious that Mallindine did not recognise him.

'Yes,' Mallindine gestured with a cake knife. 'This time when we get him on the run we'll give the Sikh no quarter. No nonsense.'

Leiston, recollecting the shambles at Ferozeshah, commented drily: 'Pursuing them is one thing, sir. Getting them to run is another.'

Immediately he knew he had said the wrong thing.

'And just what do you mean by that, Sergeant?'

'What I say, sir. The Sikh doesn't run easily.'

'They'll run when the 14th Light Dragoons get after them.'

'I sincerely hope so, sir!'

Mallindine's nostrils twitched.

'By the Lord Harry, Sergeant, you seem to have little confidence in Her Majesty's cavalry.'

Muscles were working in Mallindine's neck now.

'Damned if you haven't insulted them. Confound you if you have not called their courage in doubt . . .'

Clumsily, Mr. Wilmot tried to remedy the situation.

'Come, come, Mallindine, I'm sure the sergeant meant no offence. By praising our enemies we praise ourselves.'

Leiston began to get up.

'I'm sorry if I've caused ill feeling under your roof . . .' he began.

'By God, that isn't good enough,' cried Mallindine, now in a passion. He leaned forward and flicked Leiston's chest.

'Don't think that this scrap of ribbon means you can speak

as you like to your betters, my man. Explain yourself, Mr. Veteran. Stand up at once, sir. That is an order!'

With a crash like an exploding shell, Leiston was on his feet.

Mr. Wilmot jumped violently. The tails of his black frock coat whirled and he put out a hand to steady himself. A flood of hot tea poured into Mallindine's lap as the table went over.

'You unutterable swine,' he gasped, staring wide-eyed at Leiston. 'You did that on purpose. I'll see you flogged.' His face was contorted with rage as he tried to mop his dripping trousers. Miss Wilmot looked round desperately.

'But it was an accident. Tell Mr. Mallindine it was an accident, Papa.'

She looked nervously at Leiston, towering impassively with narrowed eyes, and feverishly to Jameson for assistance.

'It was an accident, wasn't it, Mr. Jameson? Dear Lieutenant Jameson, please say it was an accident. It was, wasn't it?'

Blinking his sandy eyelashes in amazement at the uproar, Jameson stuttered his verdict.

'Yawse!'

And as Miss Wilmot squeezed his hand with unladylike pressure he repeated to his own astonishment:

'Oh, yawse, of course it was.'

With a furious glance at his cousin, Mallindine allowed himself to be led off by the parson, while Miss Wilmot hustled the sergeant away.

'Oh dear,' she said tearfully, as she paused at the foot of the verandah steps, 'who would have thought that such a pleasant day could have ended so horridly? Now even you have turned into a stone statue!'

In the bright sunlight Leiston could have been a white-washed pillar.

'You did mean what you said?' she asked timidly.

Leiston looked blank.

'About . . . eating me?'

A faint smile appeared.

'Of course, miss, but . . .'

'But me no buts, Sergeant Statue . . .'

Her eyes sparkled.

'. . . I will send and tell you when we can meet again. In case Papa has any more visitors.'

Then she ran back into the house.

On the verandah, Jameson ordered a servant to bring another pot of tea.

CHAPTER SIXTEEN

The long-awaited reinforcements arrived at Multan just before Christmas. The day after Boxing Day four columns paraded in front of Whish's camp with orders to clear the suburbs of the city so that batteries could be established within destructive range of the walls. Advancing behind a screen of sepoy riflemen, the green jackets of the 60th and ragged red coats of the 10th and 32nd disappeared into a region of villas and gardens. Native regiments followed at a run and the Sikhs opened a crackling fire.

'I don't think I could raise an ass's gallop at this moment,' said Private Kennedy, throwing himself under cover of a substantial wall.

'Just keep yer head down, Pat,' said Makepiece, rolling expertly onto his back, tearing open a cartridge with his teeth and ramming home the ball so that the rod rang in the barrel. Other soldiers of the 32nd deftly went through similar motions.

A perky lieutenant, using his sword as a walking stick, bent over the hilt and declared enthusiastically that someone should take a look over the wall.

'Just a moment, sir, I'll be wid ye,' said Kennedy rising stiffly. 'I'm just about right for another little stroll.'

The lieutenant laughed and heaved his chest on to the parapet. He yelled and fell back and Kennedy, who had followed him, found himself staring straight into the eyes of a scowling Sikh. On both sides of the wall heads bobbed up, white shakos facing blue turbans.

A frantic clashing, clanging and scraping ensued before the Sikhs fled. The lieutenant was helped to the rear with a livid gash from his temple to his chin and the men rushed among the houses, kicking open doors.

'Lord love yez, it's the soldiers we're after today,' Kennedy muttered to a veiled woman huddled in a corner clutching two children.

He snatched up a gilt fan of peacock feathers and stuffed it in his tunic.

'Pani? Any pani? That's what we're wantin'.'

One of the children tore himself from his mother and hurried to a water jar.

'That's the stuff, son,' said Kennedy drinking noisily from a copper bowl. 'More, now. I've got me a comrade to think of.'

He hurried to the door where Makepiece stood guard.

'Drink that and let's be going,' he said, feeling pleased with himself.

They stumbled over debris and corpses in the shade of narrow streets. A blinding glare brought them to a halt. In front of them, across a broad promenade and beyond a wide, dry moat, lay the walls of Multan bristling with yellow turbans and gun muzzles.

'Back for your lives!'

The cry was repeated again and again.

The attackers scattered into cover but not before a one-inch diameter ball from a zamburak had torn the heel off a Bombay Fusilier and ricocheted into the chest of the adjutant's horse. Moaning, the man was removed. The horse stood patiently as if unhurt.

Until the arrival of reinforcements it had been a standing joke that Whish was running a first-class siege with a second-class artillery train and a third-class army. All was changed now. Before the outskirts of the city were cleared, the sandbag breastworks and emplacements were thrown up. At intervals perspiring sappers hastily rammed in huge baulks of timber to form V-shaped gun ports. Work went on ceaselessly through the night. The shivering infantry without tents or coats, were roused by an ear-splitting dawn chorus of thirteen eight-inch howitzers. During the whole of the next day the bullock teams and elephants dragged up the guns, including two massive twenty-fours and six eighteen-pounders with barrels nine feet long. All of them jerked into bellowing, snarling life. As the heavy artillerymen fell exhausted, horse gunners relieved them. Intermingled with the boom of the siege guns, the sharp crack of Brunswick rifles added a note of spitefulness to the crude bellowing of the cannon.

The Brunswicks hurled a ball moulded with a belt to fit into the two-grooved barrel. Any Sikh hit by one of these man-droppers – almost three-quarters of an inch in diameter – was unlikely to rise again. Pools of blood stained the parapet walk of the ancient walls where the Brunswicks found their victims.

As night fell again, lights glared from the walls and narrow streets were crowded with terrified civilians. In the broad bazaar running through the centre of the town, weeping women, screaming children and surly soldiers pushed their way through a press of nervous baggage animals, steaming in the cold air. Multan with its silks, its spices and its drugs had been sacked before. Alexander's Macedonians had passed that way. Sultan Muhammad, the greatest thief of them all, had paused there with 30,000 horsemen while on his way to rob the great temple at Somnath, which 50,000 Hindus died in vain to protect. Muhammad Ghuri halted also, en route to the rich heart of India from his barren Afghan valley. Multan's walls looked down later on the camp fires of Pir, the grandson of Tamerlane, scourge of all lands. Ranjit, the one-eyed lord of the Khalsa, had taken Multan from the Afghans. Now his children waited for the assault of the latest invaders.

The British were concerned for the moment about more mundane things than the lurid past. Entry in the diary of Lieutenant Henry Daly, 1st Bombay European Fusiliers:

'During the night, owing to the kindly arrangements of the commissariat, each man got his dram and biscuit. We received a few shots, big and little, but no damage was done by us.'

At the same time General Whish was rubbing his hands appreciatively at the report that five large mortars had been added to the siege batteries.

For four days and nights, shells rained on the city, stripping the roofs and filling the streets with rubble and bodies. Two dirty grey pillars rose over the targets of the battering guns. After dark, the debris was piled into barricades and timber was jammed against the crumbling towers by Mulraj's men. Along the parapets the sentries prowled ceaselessly looking for the signs of an escalade. But the ladders never came. Only shot and shells. At night tiny sparks traced the path of the missiles hissing over the brooding outline of the Khooni Burj, the Bloody Bastion. On the morning of December 30 a stupendous explosion sent an awe-inspiring mushroom of brown smoke boiling skywards. Its shadow lay across the city all day. Still the assault did not come. Balls of iron continued to slam the baked brick. The first shots had brought down insignificant showers of dirt. But as the battering continued the spoil heaps grew. Each hit brought masonry cascading to earth, filling the dry moat and sending clods rolling over the smooth outer walk. Sloping piles of rubble grew into two broad ramps. At the top of each lay a breach.

The Bombay Fusiliers stood at the head of the column committed to the Khooni Burj. Called from their camp at noon they had waited two hours with two battalions of sepoys, their ranks swollen by bandaged and sick soldiers from hospital. The prospect of loot had proved strong medicine. A few minutes before 3 p.m. the bombardment subsided. Then a shattering salvo gave the signal. Brigadier-General Stalker roared 'Forward' and a six-foot-four-inch tall Fusilier captain, carrying an outsize antique sabre, led forward the first company. Eighteen men abreast, five more companies followed at intervals of twenty paces. After a larger gap came the rest of the regiment. With drums beating and a breeze ruffling the Union Flag and the saffron silk of the Regimental Colour, the 'Old Toughs' entered the breach.

Towards the crest the lines became ragged. Battered boots scrabbled on a rubbish hill, stinking of sulphur and broken tombs. At the summit the tall captain waved his sword.

'Now for it, boys. Charge.'

Up to their ankles in pulverised brick, crumbled mortar and splintered beams, the Fusiliers plunged after him, an avalanche of white cross belts and shakos. At the bottom of the slope the ground seemed to open up. Scores of yelling Sikhs threw aside matting and planks and leapt from a concealed trench. They blazed away with their matchlocks, hurled them to the ground then belaboured their assailants with their swords. The tall captain's sabre snapped noisily on a steel shield and he grunted in agony as a blade bit into the bone of his left shoulder. A musket ball in the right arm spun him round and he staggered away. More men poured past a colour sergeant, standing at the top of the breach with the Queen's Colour. Splinters flew from the staff and the silk jerked and tore, but the sergeant remained untouched.

'Did ye ever see such an eedjit? He'll never die rich, that's for sure,' said Kennedy as he scrambled past. The 32nd were beside themselves with rage. They had reached the breach at the Delhi Gate but it had not been practical. A further wall lay behind the gap and Captain Smyth had smartly brought them to support the Fusiliers at the bastion.

'Oh, the treacherous bastards,' swore Makepiece. 'Those thievin' Irish swine of yours will lift everything if we don't get in soon. They'd skin a rat for its hide. Up, Pat. Up.'

'Please God they'll leave something,' said the dismayed Kennedy.

Mulraj's men withdrew stubbornly before the fury of the assault. Panic-stricken crowds mingled with them as they retreated on the citadel. The leading Bombay Fusiliers burst into a temple amid screams from the civilians sheltering there. Their leader seized two men and forced them at gunpoint to act as guides.

They led the British into the mouth of one of their own guns and were shot for their pains. By nightfall, the city had been taken and Mulraj's garrison had taken refuge in the citadel. Quartermaster sergeants, leading files of coolies with great-coats and arrack for the troops, hunted their regiments in the bedlam. A deafening blast about 1 a.m. showered tiles and bricks over the whole scene and after a moment's silence the shouts and screams began with redoubled intensity. Multan was enduring yet another pillaging. Bayonets, ruddy in the glare of burning buildings, pistols cocked in gloomy alleys, alien faces, foul-breathed and menacing, haunted the streets.

Makepiece had found some native liquor and gulped it down savagely. His left eye was almost closed where a Sikh had clubbed him with a musket butt. He lurched into an almost undamaged house followed by Kennedy.

'Listen. What's that?'

Kennedy had stayed sober. His ferrety eyes were sharp for plunder.

A muffled sob came from a curtained recess. Makepiece drew back his musket and bayonet but Kennedy held up an arm. Creeping up he pulled the curtain aside. Two shrouded figures cowered on the floor. Kennedy grabbed one by the wrist and pulled a stout, sari-clad woman to her feet. A slimmer figure lay on the floor gazing up, eyes shining with terror.

Makepiece wiped his lips.

'Just what I need. Come on luvvy. Make your old Uncle Tom's eye better.'

The older woman struggled and tried to shout. Kennedy's hand clamped over her mouth. The woman frantically pointed to the girl on the floor and shook her head. She pointed to herself, stabbing her breast repeatedly with her finger.

'Looks like you've got her daughter, Makepiece. The old lady wants yer to do her instead.'

Makepiece did not answer. The girl screamed momentarily as he pulled her to her feet. A curse and an unmistakable gesture reduced her to silence. She was dragged sobbing into another room. Kennedy heard the clatter of a musket on the floor, then a desperate scrabbling and moaning.

'Aw, to Hell with it,' he said and, laying down his own gun, pulled the mother to the floor.

'Wot's the matter wid yer?' he snarled as she struggled violently. Tearing the silk trousers from her limbs, he raised his fist threateningly and repeated the question. As she sagged in acquiescence he muttered between grunts: 'Ten minutes ago you were begging for it. Now ye're getting it.'

The stormers were marched out the next day to make way for fresh troops. Dishevelled, unwashed and red-eyed, they tramped past the smouldering ruin of what had once been an imposing gate. Arms and legs protruded and a distorted face returned their gaze with sightless eyes.

'Bengal sappers,' said Kennedy. 'Sure, that must 'av been the bit of a bang we heard last night.'

'Took a torch into the powder magazine, they reckon,' retorted his right-hand man.

'Well, that's one way of opening a bloody door,' added Kennedy.

CHAPTER SEVENTEEN

The message that sent Amballa into a ferment was brought by a travel-stained camel rider who padded into the cantonments in mid-morning. By three in the afternoon the 3rd Light Dragoons had packed their barrack boxes into store, kissed their wives and families goodbye, given three cheers and set off at a brisk trot.

'Keep 'em moving at a decent pace,' the Colonel growled as the cheers died away. 'We don't want any womenfolk hanging round the tents tonight.'

Miss Wilmot watched the sunburned wasp-waisted men of the 3rd jog cheerfully out of camp, a handful of wives and children bobbing in their wake. The 14th were not long in following them. As they passed the compound an orderly detached himself from the ranks, saluted and handed her a letter.

Curiously Miss Wilmot tore it open. As she read a flush came to her high cheek bones. She pursed her lips and her knuckles paled as her grip tightened. She tossed her head angrily so that the little hat she was wearing jerked on its frothing veil like a boat hit by a sudden swell.

'Dear Miss Wilmot,' she read. 'Since the unfortunate incident which marred the visit of Mr. Jameson and myself to your father's house on an unhappy occasion recently, I have caused certain inquiries to be made. As my regiment is now ordered on active service, I feel it is my duty to impart to you information of a delicate nature that I am sure you would want to know. To whit, that Sergeant Leiston, to whom you and Mr. Wilmot have shown unusual Christian charity and kindness, is indeed a blackguard, as his conduct might have implied.

'By coincidence it seems that he is the son of a tenant of my uncle and, it has come to my knowledge, deserted his wife and child and abandoned a secure position in order to evade his responsibilities.

'I tell you this because I feel you will no longer condescend to allow Leiston to indulge in the familiarity he has assumed in the past. I will be glad to make it my duty to see he is properly rebuked.

'I have written to your father in similar vein, but I thought that you would like to be informed at first hand by someone who has your best interests sensibly in mind. I remain yours to command, respectfully, Eldred Mallindine, Lieutenant, XIV L.D.'

Miss Wilmot stared at the crumpled paper in her hand, her tight-buttoned bodice heaving with agitation. As disjointed thoughts raced through her mind, a growing noise compelled her attention. Behind mounted officers, solid red-coated ranks tramped past. With fifes shrilling and drums clattering, the 24th Foot were stepping out jauntily to 'The Girl I Left Behind Me'. She wondered bitterly what tune Leiston and the 29th were marching to, wherever they might be.

After the tempestuous tea-party on the verandah she had seen Leiston only briefly, when he had called unexpectedly to say that he and his detachment had been recalled to the regiment. Although there had been no obvious show of affection, they had shaken hands most warmly. She had gone so far as to let her fingers linger longer than was seemly. And she had blurted out: 'You will come back to see me . . . come back to see us . . . won't you?' She hadn't imagined that Leiston had responded to the pressure on his hand, surely. Certainly he had made it quite plain that he would return to Amballa if he could.

Contrarily, when her father raised the subject, on receiving Mallindine's note the next day, she refused to hear a word against the tall sergeant.

'I'm sure that Lieutenant Mallindine is making wicked imputations because of his own disgraceful behaviour,' she declared hotly. 'I shall not believe a word until I hear the truth from the sergeant's own lips.'

Mr. Wilmot, who feared his headstrong daughter might discover that he had encouraged Mallindine's visits deliberately, discreetly remained silent. With little chance of Leiston reappearing, it seemed the wisest course to take. Only when his daughter announced her intention of accompanying her father to join the army, where he intended to pursue his ministry, was he vociferous.

'It is not only foolish, it is preposterous,' he declaimed. 'I am sure it is not the Lod's will that I should allow my only daughter to embark on such a perilous journey. I will not permit it, Sarah. I forbid it.'

'Then I shall make my own arrangements when you are gone,' she replied firmly, her own Yorkshire accent becoming decidedly pronounced. 'With the Lod's will or without it.'

'Be sensible, Sarry.' Mr. Wilmot adopted a conciliatory tone. 'What on earth does a woman want with a conflict of this nature? There is no practical application in your intent.'

'Pa, you speak but three words of Hindustani. Not only do I speak the language, but I read it as well. I shall act as your interpreter. As for ladies not going to the war – Sir Harry Smith took his wife with him throughout the last Sikh campaign. At Ferozeshah when she must have been fifty, she watched the fighting from the back of an elephant, I believe.'

'Sarah. We do not possess an elephant.'

'Then I shall travel by pony cart and on horseback. The camels can carry our tents and my trunks.'

Although the 29th did not set out to 'The Girl I Left Behind Me' it is unlikely that Miss Wilmot would have found any consolation from the tune that did play them out of camp. 'Hearts of Oak' might have seemed only too appropriate to a young lady who could hardly be expected to appreciate its significance to a regiment proud of its service with the fleet on The Glorious First of June. With the mustering of the 29th for action, Sarojini too found herself faced with trouble. Roshanara refused to remain behind at the house of pleasure when Sarojini prepared to follow her clients into the field.

'This is not work for you, Rose Petal,' the old whore-mistress told her. 'Campaigning is only for the strongest girls. The Amritzar girls and the half-caste have broad backs that will not bruise with a pebble under them. They are well used saddles and can bear the roughest riders. You must stay behind, with my other jewels, until the war is over. It does not matter who wins, there will be work for us afterwards. They cannot kill a fat elephant like Begg-Sahib. If the Sikhs beat the Gorah-log he can take service with them. But he says they will be beaten even though the Jang-i-Lat-Sahib is a mad old man who worships the bayonets on the soldiers' muskets.'

Smooth though her tongue, and strong though her arm, Sarojini was unable to convince Roshanara. When her dhoolis set forth on the trail of the army one of them bore the little girl the river gods had spared.

'I will let her wait on me,' Sarojini told her old uncle who supervised the bearers. 'There is much she can learn.'

On the outskirts of Wazirabad not far from the tent metropolis of Lord Gough, the man who worshipped bayonets, the house of pleasure surreptitiously opened for business.

Julius Begg was relieving Leiston on picquet duty on the banks of a little tributary that ran back into the Chenab when a light winked briefly under the river bank.

'That's hinterestin', Robert,' he said, wrinkling his pudgy nose. 'Most hinterestin'. 'Ere, Freeman, get yer long, useless body into the water and see what it is over there. Never mind yer boots, lad. They'll dry. Just give me yer musket and git in.'

Freeman splashed across the shallows, bent down and whistled.

'It's beer,' he shouted. 'Two bleedin' cases of it.'

'Orl right, lad. Not so loud. Now then, let's get it on the bank.'

Within minutes the hoard that had cost Connelly of the 24th the skin off his back, and which his comrade Perry had carefully hidden, was dragged clinking to the bank.

'Well, I'll be damned. If that ain't what some thievin' hounds scrounged from the hofficers' mess when we first got 'ere. Leastwise, that's where the Burton came from. Don't know about the Bass, though. Don't know about that at all.'

The picquets looked hopeful. The Burton could go back to the mess. You didn't rob your own regiment. But the Bass . . .

'Tell you what, Robert. Take 'em both back to the lines and 'ave a word with the adjutant. Me name's not Julius Aloysius Begg if 'e don't turn a blind eye to the Bass. That way, we do it all legal-like.'

Sergeant Begg casually slipped a bottle into his pocket as he spoke.

'Better take a couple for yerself before yer 'ands them over. Orl right, lads, look lively. Leiston will guard the ale and we'll make sure Shere Singh don't spring no surprises.'

The picquet trudged on and Leiston's party set off with the crates.

They had not gone a hundred yards when a line of dragoons trotted by in twos, shouting good-naturedly at the sight of the beer crates. Unexpectedly a moustachioed sergeant-major swung his horse towards the straggling foot soldiers.

' 'Ere, that's our officers' soddin' Bass,' he said. 'Where did you bastards lay your hands on it?'

Leiston halted his men.

'Just pulled it out of the stream,' he said warily. 'Found some of our own stuff, too.'

'Ho, yes. A likely story! Well, yer'd better 'and it over. I'll give yer a receipt for it.'

The big soldier smiled blandly.

'You needn't bother, Sergeant-major. I'm under orders to deposit any valuables with my own main guard. Ye'll find it there if you want it.'

An imperious voice cut the air.

'What's going on here, Sergeant-major?'

A dragoon officer and two N.C.O.s who had been coming up fast in the rear of the cavalry patrol, cantered over.

Leiston and the sergeant-major began to speak at once when the officer interrupted.

'So it's you, Sergeant Insolence, is it?'

Leiston, who had not recognised Mallindine at first, jerked his head.

'Sergeant Leiston and picquet, 29th Foot, returning to camp from duty, sir.'

'More like a brewer's outing, by the look of things,' Mallindine sneered. 'Well, Sergeant-major, what's it all about. We can't waste all day talking to these louts.'

The sergeant-major explained.

'Found our ale, have they? Well, you can just put it down there, Leiston. My men will see to that.'

Leiston shrugged and signalled to his men.

'And Leiston . . .'

'Sir?'

Mallindine walked his horse over so that he could look down on the sergeant, and said in a lower voice:

'I think you might like to know that I've put paid to your little game. Didn't remember your name at first, but it came to me later, when I'd made one or two inquiries. If you've designs on the padre's daughter at Amballa, you can forget them. She knows you're a married man.'

Leiston's ruddy weatherbeaten countenance took on a darker hue, but he said nothing. Mallindine, not content with his victory, went on:

'You may rest assured I shall pay the little baggage the best of attention in your absence. It's about time she was broken in . . .'

Leiston's left hand shot out and clamped numbingly on Mallindine's sword arm.

'Say no more, Master Eldred.' The words came out fast and harsh. 'You've said enough . . .'

'For God's sake, Sergeant . . .'

An elderly corporal seized Leiston's hand and tried to drag it away. Leiston, breathing heavily through his flared nostrils, let his hand remain for a moment, then dropped it. His eyes never left Mallindine's.

It took the young dragoon officer a few seconds to find his voice. His throat muscles were almost paralysed with rage. When the words did come they were almost incoherent.

'See that? See him . . . assault me? By God! Striking an officer . . . threatening behaviour . . . You swine! You clod-hopping swine!'

When the abuse ceased Mallindine caught his breath and regained some sort of control.

'Sergeant, you're under arrest,' he spluttered. 'Hand over your arms to the corporal. Corporal! You will march the prisoner to the Main Guard of the 29th with this note. My troop-sergeant will go with you to deliver it to the officer of the day.'

He scribbled furiously in a pocket book, tore out a page and handed it to the dragoon N.C.O.

'We'll see the colour of your backbone for this, Leiston,' he hissed. 'If the court-martial doesn't decide to hang you.'

Quietly Leiston handed his musket to a private of the 29th

and told the corporal: 'It's all right, Baggott. Do what the officer says.'

'You'd better, Corporal,' said Mallindine, wheeling away. 'I'll be back later.'

In a passion he spurred his horse after the distant patrol followed by his escort. They disappeared in a flurry of sand and dust.

'Well, ye've done it now, Robert,' said Julius as he sat in the guard tent excavating the nails of a filthy bare foot with his large horn pocket knife. 'Struth! Strikin' a hofficer! Thought you 'ad more sense. And on active service. In the presence of the henemy. Ooh, it don't bear thinkin' about.'

He leaned forward confidentially.

'Shall I leave me sticker? Yer can cut the canvas and be off tonight. Make fer the river and I'll contact yer . . .'

'Thanks, Julius, old son, but I think I'll take my chance.'

'Wot'll ye tell 'em?'

'Nothing.'

'*Nothin'?* Look, lad, yer in trouble. Yer'll 'ave ter say somethin'. Shall I . . .?'

'Shall you say nothing? Yes!'

'But what about 'er? The gel in the grey dress.'

'What about her?'

'Well, she's in Wazirabad wiv 'er boozy old pa. So I 'ears. Can't she put in a good word for ye? Or the old feller?'

'Look, forget it, Julius. She wouldn't want to know. Not now. And anyway, you can't bring a lady like her into a dirty business like this. What can she say? She wasn't there. Mallindine's got a couple of hairy dragoons who saw me grab him.'

Oh, Mallindine was going to triumph all right. Any military court was unlikely to look with favour on a soldier who tried to defend himself by bringing in a woman's name – and a lady at that.

'Well, suit yerself, old son. Floggin's mighty 'ard on the back, but it don't kill strong men.'

Leiston smiled ruefully.

'And you did say it wouldn't be 'orl glory, didn't you, Julius?'

CHAPTER EIGHTEEN

Keen eyes stared from the cover of a clump of thorn bushes. A group of horsemen sat silently watching bulky shadows shift restlessly in a night filled with belches, rumbles, groans and the sullen stirrings of a herd of camels at rest. Truly this was a wonderful war, thought one-eared Mirza Khan. A man could grow rich in the Punjaub without much effort. On the Khyber where his estates could be covered by the soles of his boots the sum total of Mirza Khan's possessions consisted of a sword, an inflatable bullock skin and a rope. With these a man could kidnap a victim, float him across the river and wait for the ransom. But it was a risky business even for a Eusafzai bred to the life like himself. Here, in the service of the Sikhs, it was child's play to steal from the feringhees. They had brought thousands of baggage camels with them into the Doab and as these had to be grazed, it was an opportunity too good to be missed. Mirza Khan raised his hand.

'Now . . .'

His wild horsemen surged behind him yelling.

Mallindine, whose dragoons had formed part of the outer patrol line, heard the commotion and, cursing, spurred to a hillock to get a better view. As he did so a swarm of startled beasts burst through the bushes. His horse reared, kicking and neighing, a stampeding camel crashed into it, and Mallindine rolled on the hard ground. As he staggered to his feet a blinding light flashed before his eyes.

The following day Leiston was released under open arrest.

'Cor, yer a lucky cove, there's no two ways about it,' said Begg, shaking his head. 'An officer puts you in clink and within a few hours the Sikhs put paid to 'im for yer. They ain't found 'is body yet, although they brought in a couple o' dead dragoons, wot got stamped by the camels. Narsty . . .'

Leiston stared moodily from the door of the tent.

'Can't say it makes much difference,' he replied.

The Reverend Barnabas Wilmot's long nose had appeared

in the lines some time earlier and he had requested that Leiston visit his quarters.

'I believe you have something to say that my daughter would like to hear from your own lips, young man,' he declared with a frown. 'I hope you will be good enough to deliver yourself of the truth.'

'Well, yer'd better get it over with,' Julius advised. 'She can't eat yer. Tell 'er about it like yer told me. Woman's only 'uman, ain't she?'

Miss Wilmot felt far from human. The journey had been much worse than she cared to admit. Although she had had a dak ghari all to herself, instead of sharing with another traveller, the progress had been an ordeal. Every four miles when the horse was changed it took a swearing coachman, whip in hand, and half a dozen coolies to reduce the reluctant beast to subservience and back it between the shafts. Her trunks had fallen off the roof regularly despite the attempts of the kit wallah to save them. And once a perverse horse had run away downhill with the conveyance. She had finished the journey on a saddle horse, congratulating herself on having had the foresight to bring a habit with her. When Leiston arrived at the door of her tent she was still aching and bruised.

A servant showed in the sergeant, who stood awkwardly fingering his shako. Miss Wilmot winced, shifted on her canvas camp chair and said sharply: 'I believe you know why I require to speak to you.'

'Yes, miss, I saw your father.'

'Is it true that you are married?'

'In a manner of speaking, miss.'

Miss Wilmot's eyes flashed.

'Come, come, man, are you or are you not? Did you or did you not leave your wife and child to fend for themselves?'

Leiston's jaw jutted.

'Like I said, miss,' he continued stubbornly, 'I'm married in a manner of speaking . . .'

She stared at him uncertainly. She did not know what she had expected. Hardly this brazen confession.

'But you deliberately gave me an entirely different impression.' A red patch glowed on her neck. 'You allowed me to become . . . to look on you with . . . affection.'

Suddenly the scarlet patch spread over her face.

'Sergeant Leiston,' the hard Northern tones were unmistakable, 'you trifled with my feelings for you. Deliberately.'

He gazed at her bull-necked, tight-lipped and wordless. What was the point of trying to explain to this parson's daughter about Miss Howick and Mallindine? What did she know about jumping when a squire said 'jump'. She had guts though. Travelling for days in a bone-breaking ghari just to . . .

Leiston realised with disturbing certainty that this lean spinster with the Yorkshire accent had come out solely to ask the question she had just put to him. He began clumsily to try to say something. Anything.

But Miss Wilmot had regained her composure.

'There is nothing more I have to say to you, Sergeant.'

Her lips were compressed and her eyes were blazing but hurt.

'Well, you see . . .'

'I see, Sergeant. I see I was deceived into thinking you were a different person. Good day, Sergeant Leiston.'

'Miss Wilmot . . .'

'Good day.'

The pitch of her voice rose unsteadily.

Leiston left.

Miss Wilmot did not let her father see the depth of her injury. She kept her tears for the privacy of the curtained dak ghari at the beginning of the long journey home. After the first change of horse she returned to her saddle horse and felt much better. On her way she was able to avail herself of the protection of Lord Dalhousie's entourage, which was heading relentlessly into the seat of war.

It was very easy to dislike young Lord Dalhousie – for young he appeared to many of the more venerable members of the East India Company's establishment. He was full of ideas which upset the order of things and he busied himself when he might have taken his ease.

Dalhousie himself had been rather surprised at the power he possessed, although that did not spoil his taste for it. Quickly he was learning that what the Governor-General said one minute was either common gossip or rigid law the next. There had been the affair of the Cucherry Hussars, the nickname given to the civil servants who inhabited that place. Why, Dalhousie had declared, did they wear moustaches like so many Frenchmen when they were Englishmen to a man? Although the remark had been intended only as a joke, moustaches had fallen 'like leaves in October'.

Then there had been his speech after the ball at Barrackpore. He had said merely what he had said before – and what, in any case, he believed. That the Sikhs had forced him into war. So he had not only drawn the sword but thrown away the scabbard. Within days he had been assailed in the press. Accused almost of conducting a ruthless, merciless campaign in a quite ungentlemanly manner. Vengeance was un-English.

Just as well he had kept to himself the sentiments he had expressed in a letter to a friend:

'If the Sikhs, after this war is over, rise again, they shall entrench themselves behind a dunghill and fight with their fingernails, for if I live 12 months they shall have nothing else to fight with.'

Such critics as there were, however, made little impression on the assured little Scot. Have things his way he would, and did. Even the best was not good enough for the Marquis of Dalhousie. Her Majesty had bestowed the Order of the Thistle on him soon after his arrival in Calcutta. And whereas he was sensible of the honour done to him, he was far from satisfied with the quality of the decoration. No 'tin and wedgewood' star for him. No abomination looking 'like a piece of cut beetroot at a ball as it usually does'.

A discreet emissary had been despatched to Abuds in Conduit Street with instructions to order and have sent out to Calcutta a star 'not a diamond one . . . but a plain, handsome star, not very large or very small,' to take the place of the official one. Alas, when it arrived in October, although an improvement, in Dalhousie's view 'the enamel might have been likened to a Thistle'.

Other honours were in Dalhousie's mind, however, as the brave new year of 1849 was ushered in. Intelligence came from Whish that the city of Multan had fallen and that Mulraj was besieged in the citadel. Whish, whom he had berated in private when he had pulled back from Multan in September. Amends would have to be made. Maybe these old generals had something to commend them after all. It would not be long now, perhaps, before he could quit the discomfort of the tented camp and retire to the comparative luxury of the *Soona Mookee*, the Governor-General's splendid yacht, all green and gilt with its punkahs, sofas and civilised bedrooms. Towed by a steamer, the *Soona Mookee* needed no crew and provided a haven of privacy. Dalhousie saw himself floating back to Calcutta to dispense nineteenth-century wisdom for the benefit of an almost medieval community. He chuckled at the picture he conjured up of his wife bowling along in her phaeton with an escort of dragoons. Yes, the end of the conflict was undoubtedly in sight. He must write to Gough immediately.

Not all the news was good. Amir Dost Mohammed, the Afghan, had joined old Chattar Singh in the west and this combined force had compelled the surrender of the little fortress of Attock. They were now marching to join Shere Singh at Rasul. From urging caution and instructing Gough to wait for the arrival of the reinforcements that would become available after the fall of Multan, Dalhousie tried a more optimistic note. Writing to the Commander-in-Chief of Whish's victory, he declared he would rejoice to hear of a similar blow struck at the Sikhs entrenched on the Jhelum.

'Ah, that's better.'

Gough tapped the letter meaningly as a smile flitted across his russet features.

'He wants us to be at them, Mackeson. 'Bout time, too. The longer we sit on our honkers here the more confident thim Saikhs become.'

'And stronger, sir. We shall have to fight twice their number when Chattar Singh and the Afghans arrive. The sooner we can crush Shere Singh the better for our prospects in general. They won't be so keen to take on the combined army after the Multan troops join us.'

'Quite so, Mackeson. Quite so. We shall be at 'em before long and Dalzie will be content to leave us to our business, I hope.'

Lord Gough, who had spent much of the past weeks prowling impatiently through the countryside, scanning the Sikh positions with his mighty telescope, felt decidedly more cheerful. Earlier he had written to Dalhousie to say that he felt perfectly competent and strong enough to beat Shere Singh with his existing force – some 12,000 men and sixty-six guns excluding the camp guard. Now he wrote confidently:

'With God's blessing I propose to attack the enemy. It is my intention to penetrate the centre of their line, cutting off the regular from the irregular portion of their army. The only fear is that the former, when routed, will throw themselves into the jungle close to which they are stationed. But I hope they will fight for their salt, and if so, and if I can get close to them, it will be hard if I cannot take their guns, twenty-two in number.'

CHAPTER NINETEEN

Jawahir Singh hummed contentedly as his grey Arab mare trotted through the moonless night, carefully avoiding the clutching scrub. Soon the English would come. And because their eyes were dim from drink and their necks were stiff in leather collars, they would not see the trap. They would die, mangled and torn, like his cousins who had been caught on the bridge at Sobraon. Jawahir Singh was lucky. If his pulton had not been in reserve he too might have died that day instead of looking on helplessly as the desperate throng retreated across the single chain of bobbing pontoons. The English horse artillery had appeared out of the smoke and opened fire with case-shot. When the bridge broke and the Sutlej was choked with men, camels and horses trying to save themselves, the English foot soldiers and their Bengali lick-spittles had lined the banks and fired volleys. Ten thousand Sikhs had died. The Sutlej was swollen with a sudden icy spate from the Himalayas and the wounded drowned.

The little mare pricked her ears at the authoritative click of a musket being cocked.

'What, would you shoot your own captain?'

A half-moon beard wagged silver in the dusk.

'You told us yourself nothing coming from the south could be allowed to live, Rissaldar. To hear is to obey.'

'You will have slaughter soon enough, old man.'

Jawahir Singh waved vaguely in the direction from which he had ridden.

'I have been as far as their outposts. They will not come tonight. The feringhee captain will have to wait. Have you made him comfortable?'

The soldier, a dafadar, laughed.

'See for yourself,' he said.

Jawahir Singh threw his reins to a sentry and walked across a clearing to a mound topped with sandbags. His escort snatched a brand from a heap of embers and held it over his head. A brass twelve-pounder gleamed dully in the glare.

Jawahir Singh bent down and peered under the cannon at two eyes as dark as any Indian's.

Mallindine was filled with an overwhelming desire to kill. He wanted to smash, grind to pulp and obliterate his captors.

The Sikh looked at him curiously. The English were strange people. This officer ought to be grateful to be alive. The Pathans might as easily have cut his throat as taken him prisoner. But not satisfied with having his life spared, he had gone on to insult Ameer Singh, who had offered him a commission in the cavalry of the Khalsa. Why not? Other Europeans had served it well in the past. They might not have taken the field – Commedan Canora, the American, had actually tried to prevent his Sikh gunners from joining their comrades at Haripur and been cut down for his pains – but the Europeans had helped to make the Khalsa the power it was. This dragoon had sneered and called the other foreigners mercenaries. But did not the English officers get paid for fighting? Albeit not as much as if they had served the Khalsa. They took loot as well. Combermere Sahib had been given prize money worth 60,000 gold sovereigns after the fall of Bhurtpore, it was said. Bah! The English were just like the Afghans, interested in money, women, horses and drink. Their pride was hypocrisy.

'Well, Feringhee, would it not be better to become one of the Khalsalji than lie here?'

Mallindine, who did not understand a word, tried to spit, but his cracked lips refused to function and his swollen tongue jammed in his throat. The dafadar, sensing the defiance, thrust out the torch letting a spark fall on Mallindine's crotch. The hair crackled momentarily. Mallindine drew his breath sharply but did not cry out. Darkness flooded into the gun pit as the Sikhs walked away. With it came the recurring vision of the day's events.

After he had spurned the offer of a post in the Sikh army he had been handed over to two black-bearded sowars.

They threw him face down on the ground and pinned him there. As he squirmed frantically, fingernails dug into the small of his back. A roar of laughter arose as his tight-fitting overalls were ripped from his body exposing his backside to the jeering crowd. A boot pressed his face into a steaming pile of camel dung. As he slobbered and choked, his tunic was ripped from top to bottom. His guards, heaving on the sleeves, rolled on the ground as the material gave way. Shrieks and hoots followed them as they dragged him off, naked, dung-smeared, dazed. Lashed by the wrists under a gun, Mallindine found refuge from the mob and the sides of the emplacement gave some shade. But insects crawled over his legs and explored his body. Flies settled in droves on his face. He was unable to get to the bucket hanging under the gun, but once a Sikh had thrust the cannon sponge to his mouth. The sheepskin dripped bitter water which he had sucked at eagerly. Later as the night fell he shivered uncontrollably and suffered agonies of belly cramp. Unable to control his bowels, he squatted in his own filth on bleeding haunches chafed raw by the sandy soil. The torchlight visit of the Sikh had been almost a relief, distracting him momentarily from his wretched state. At intervals through the night he fell asleep, only to be nagged awake by a variety of pains. The first flies returned with the rosy dawn of January 13.

Private Hacken was not feeling well disposed towards life as the skirmishers of the 3rd Light Dragoons trotted forward in the morning light. They had moved out at 5 a.m. and he had time only to gulp down a cup of rum before mounting. His stomach was protesting angrily.

'Any 'opes of getting a bite later, do you think?' he asked Sergeant Wood morosely.

'Not much chance at the moment, Billy,' replied his comrade. 'It looks as though the Old Man is going to do something big, but what it is Gawd knows.'

The whole army was on the move, twelve thousand men. Five dense scarlet columns, each of three battalions, kicked up the dust as the infantry brigades moved forward. Elephants, towing the ponderous 24-pounders, loomed among them like ships in a fog. On each flank the tall plumes of the Red Men marked the passage of the Bengal Horse Artillery, covered by the cavalry moving in columns of regiments.

Lala Rai, clinging to a jolting six-pounder in No. 3 troop, looked at the bobbing pennons of the 9th Lancers and felt comfortably secure. The 14th Light Dragoons and two regiments of Indian light cavalry completed the formidable mounted contingent on Gough's right. Only two native regiments supported the 3rd Light Dragoons on the left.

To Junior Ensign Pennycuick the lumbering phalanx seemed invincible. Alexander the Great had defeated a great Indian army on these plains. The ensign looked at the hazy silhouettes of the elephants and tried to imagine they bore the war castles of King Porus. Colonel Mackeson, whom he had met in the company of his father, had laughed at the theory that the Jhelum was the river of the ancient battle and said it had changed its course a score of times since then. But young Pennycuick just knew. The shades of the Macedonian host were watching.

Private Connelly trudged on effortlessly, wondering when he would get a drink. The days when each man carried his own waterbottle had yet to arrive. The bhistis humping their waterskins and the occasional well were a soldier's only hope. Perry reckoned there was a town ahead called Rasool or some such heathen name, and that they were going to storm it. Connelly's eyes brightened in anticipation of loot.

Miss Wilmot filled Leiston's thoughts. He could not get over the fact that she had travelled so far simply to find out whether or not he was married. If she liked him that much . . . For the thousandth time he tried to find the opening phrases he would use if ever he got the chance to talk to her.

'Can't see that gel hidin' her long legs be'ind a curtain at the end of a barrack room, even if you was in a position to marry 'er,' Julius had commented. 'A parson's daughter and a common sodger? No, if I was you, I'd marry inter the rigiment, Robert.'

'Keep in step there,' Leiston barked savagely.

''Ello, 'ello,' muttered Julius, his short, powerful legs keeping up well with much longer ones, 'somethin's upset our Robert, 'as it? Must be that bit o' skirt.'

Julius Begg ran an expert eye over the marching columns, took in the sky, sniffed, spat the fine sand from his mouth and decided the omens were not good.

'Don't like the feel of it, Freeman,' he announced to a lanky, young soldier. 'Don't like the look of it one little bit.'

'Garn', Sergeant. It's a bleedin' parade. We'll be tucked up in our tents like good boys tonight, you'll see. Old Paddy knows what e's up to.'

'I 'opes so,' replied Julius, 'but don't blame me if it's not orl glory terday.'

Lord Gough, trotting along in his fighting coat, was as uneasy as Sergeant Begg. He wondered whether Shere Singh was going to stick to his hit and run manoeuvres – 'dhai pat' tactics, the Sikhs called them. To the left the jungle was thicker than it had seemed and towards the right, near Rasul, ravines and brushwood provided ugly obstacles. Water seemed to be non-existent.

About mid-morning the Commander-in-Chief called a halt. Reports came in confirming the presence of good wells at a village about two miles away where Sikh outposts held a small hill. The elephants lugged their heavy loads to the front and the 24-pounders opened fire briefly. The troops waited expectantly for the order to form a line of battle, but it did not come; only silence. Trumpets, bugles and drums set the columns in motion, the left-hand units marking time as the right flank swung round. Then the army halted again.

Cantering over fresh furrows made by the 24-pounders, the Commander-in-Chief dismounted and climbed to the flat top of a mud-brick house. The country between the village and the Jhelum was unrevealing in the sunlight. Small parties of Sikhs could be seen, but thick bushes and occasional tall trees hid any other movements. Lord Gough descended and decided to pitch his tents for the night before exploring this miniature jungle.

'What'd I tell yer, Sergeant?' said Private Freeman. They could see the Royal Engineer officers riding over the proposed camping ground. Small groups of Indian sappers followed, hammering in bright marker flags.

'Hmm. We'll see 'ow long they stay that way,' said Sergeant Begg as the order came to pile arms. He delved into his knapsack and produced a piece of cold goat's meat. Leiston watched from a distance as the familiar figure waddled towards him.

'What's bothering you, Julius?'

'Take this, Robert, lad,' he replied, handing over a piece of the meat. 'Dunno as 'ow we shall get much else today. Somethin' wrong somewhere. Weather's changin' for a start.'

Leiston looked up. Despite the sun there was a sultry feeling in the air.

'Somethin' in me bones tells me there's trouble. I smells it. Them Sikhs aren't going to let us put our tents up under their black noses without a protest. No, Robert, they're up to somethin', mark my words.'

He screwed his fat face into a scowl and bit off a chunk of meat. Leiston glanced towards the silent undergrowth and remarked:

'Bit close to the jungle, I give you that.' He tore at the meat with his teeth.

'By God, you must have jaws of iron, Julius.'

Industriously the engineers continued flagging out the ground. The 24-pounders were parked and a troop of cavalry unsaddled its horses. A quarrel developed between two quartermasters about the right to a patch of ground.

The 24th had broken ranks and Connelly and Perry were squatting with their backs to a tree when a sergeant ordered them to unload a cart containing officers' stores.

'Why does that bastard always pick on us, Ivor? That's what I want to know, boy.'

'Tell you why – because he wants to prove what a bloody pig he is so he can stick a Union Jack on his arm.'

'Shut up and get on with your work, Connelly. Another word and I'll crime you,' rapped out a voice.

Connelly's face became a blank.

'Colour sergeants!' he muttered once round the far side of the cart. 'Bloody show-offs!'

Junior Ensign Pennycuick stood disconsolately in front of his company.

'Now I suppose we'll sit here for weeks,' he called sulkily to Lieutenant Lloyd Williams.

'Patience, fire-eater,' the Welshman replied. 'We'll see action soon enough.'

Pennycuick stretched, yawned and tried to spot his father among the bustling staff officers. Another yawn. From a tall tree nearby a startled shout roused him.

'Sikhs. Thousands of them. I can see their turbans in the jungle.'

As if to confirm this unsuspected presence a cannon shot

crashed out. And another. A young lieutenant half-climbed, half-fell out of the tree and dashed past Pennycuick yelling. His voice was drowned by the urgent bugles of the 24th. Connelly let an officer's dressing case fall with a thump and ran for his Brown Bess. Stacks of muskets vanished into grasping hands.

Away to the left flank Billy Hacken was spurring his horse for his life. He had walked it into the jungle looking for water. He had found it all right – the place seemed to be dotted with mossy, dank holes. But as he threw his leg over the saddle he saw long ranks of Sikh infantry forming in the bushes. Without bothering to re-mount properly he sent his horse racing for the regiment.

'An officer. For Christ's sake get an officer. Half the soddin' Sikh army are after me bollocks. The jungle is stuffed with them.'

On all sides alarms sounded, but Lord Gough had already received a personal warning from the Sikhs. Two six-pound cannon balls had just bounced past him.

CHAPTER TWENTY

Mackeson had seen the general angry before, but seldom in such a passion. Gough's eyes flashed as they followed the bumping missiles.

'If it's shot they want they shall have it, and with interest,' he growled. 'Send up the 24s.'

The elephants came lumbering back.

The first British shells had hardly struck when an even louder salvo roared out in reply. Clouds of white smoke rose for a considerable distance inside the near edge of the jungle. The Sikhs had pushed forward a line of guns which successfully commanded the site chosen for the British camp.

Champing at his moustache, Gough studied his options. He could not stay where he was. The Sikhs would blast him from the safety of their concealed positions. He could not pull back. The village contained the only wells in the area. There was nothing to stop him falling back on the camp he had left that morning. But that would be construed as a retreat. Some important native chiefs were still undecided which way to jump. If they heard that the British had been driven back from the Jhelum, Shere Singh would double his strength.

'We shall have to be at them, gentlemen,' he told his assembled staff flatly. 'I see nothing else for it.'

'If I may be permitted, your Excellency . . .'

'Yes, Mackeson.'

'It is nearly two o'clock, sir. The day is well on. Might we not be involved in a battle at dusk?'

'If so, it can't be helped. With God's help we may be able to settle this thing before sunset.'

Gough turned to issue instructions to an aide-de-camp.

'With respect, sir, the afternoon will be gone . . .'

The white-coated figure whirled in the saddle, mouth trembling in a crimson face.

'I am Commander-in-Chief of this army, sir, and I desire you to be silent.'

Mackeson felt the eyes of the staff upon him.

'Very good, sir.'

Gough's ruffled features relaxed slightly. He continued to give orders concerning the line of battle evolving on the plain. He'd never met anyone who could not do better than the Commander-in-Chief.

At Ferozeshah he'd had Hardinge telling him one minute that as Governor-General he would leave military affairs to Gough – and then interfering when decisions had to be made. Young Dalhousie was beseeching him to be cautious with one breath and urging him to seize Shere Singh by the scruff of the neck the next. Now this young politico, Mackeson, was trying to tell him how to run things. Yet the responsibility was his alone. Well, he'd decided. The Sikhs wanted a fight. By all that was holy they would have it. They'd left themselves with a river behind them again and once he had got his infantry through the trees they would be trapped.

'Make sure you cover my right now, Pope,' he called to the pot-bellied old brigadier who commanded the cavalry on that wing.

'Ye can count on it, sir,' he replied hoarsely.

Alexander Pope was almost as old as Gough and felt his age much more. The motion of the horse jarred every bone in his ancient body. There had been a time when he could have outridden the lot of them, British and Indians. He returned the salute of Colonel King of the 14th Light Dragoons. Nice boy, King. Kept his men smart. Two of them had helped him into the saddle earlier on when the Commander-in-Chief had sent for him. If only his knees were not so stiff these days. Now what was it Gough had said? There seemed to be an inordinate number of squadrons.

Pope had never commanded more than a regiment in serious action before. Now he had four under him. But his right to command was unchallengeable. Gough, remembering him from the old days, had expressed no doubts as to his fitness for command and was hardly likely to on the grounds of age.

Of Gough's senior officers the youngest was the goatee-bearded Colin Campbell, commanding the infantry division on the left wing. The cautious Glaswegian had spent his youth fighting the French in the Peninsula and had led the 98th Foot under Gough in China in 1842. At fifty-seven he was still a regimental officer at heart. Now he had three brigades to lead.

At the head of the right division was Sir Walter Raleigh Gilbert, seven years older than Campbell and a veteran of the First Sikh War. Thackwell, commanding the army's cavalry, was even older, at sixty-eight. The one-armed Waterloo hero stationed himself with the left brigade under another of Wellington's men, Brigadier White. Pope he left to his own devices.

The line was formed hastily. In the centre Gough massed his scanty heavy artillery with one infantry division to the right, the other to the left of it. The horse artillery he divided in support of the cavalry on the flanks. Having drawn up his army, Gough then found it lay at an angle to, instead of parallel to, the Sikhs. With more trumpeting and bugling the huge line pivoted through forty-five degrees.

Pope had additional problems. A large body of Sikh cavalry had moved from the ravines and jungle near Rasul. He detached two squadrons of his lancers and four of native cavalry with horse artillery to confront the white-robed regiments moving forward under brilliant silk banners. Fussily he began to rearrange his remaining troops. Squadrons wheeled this way and that until everyone, including Pope, was bewildered. While Gough's guns continued to send shredded jungle greenery flying, Pope formed nine squadrons in one long line.

With even Gough's telescope unable to pierce the thick foliage, the battle was beginning to take charge of itself.

'Can't see a damn' thing,' he muttered, staring into the smoke. A procession of mounted orderlies brought reports which only confused matters. The only certain thing seemed to be a slackening in the Sikh artillery fire. The flashes and smoke clouds in the jungle were diminishing. A fleeting thought occurred that perhaps Shere Singh was going to slip away as he had done at Ramnagar and Saddulapore.

'Divil take me, but he won't get away with it this time,' growled the old warrior. 'Like as not he's pulling out his guns at this very moment. We shall have to be quick if we're to have them. Orderly. *Orderly.*'

His voice betrayed surging excitement.

'Deliver this message into the hand of General Campbell,' he said scribbling furiously. 'Into the hands of himself, d' ye hear!'

Earth and sand flew as the dragoon saluted, wheeled his horse and jagged it savagely into a gallop. As other riders raced to different parts of the line, Mackeson fished out his pocket watch. It was just three o'clock. To use one of the Commander-in-Chief's favourite expressions, if the Sikhs were going to fight for their salt it was going to be a bloody business before sundown.

Gough blew his nose heartily on a large blue handkerchief and turned amiably to his political adviser. He bore no ill will for the earlier contretemps.

'That's what'll do the work for us, Mackeson.'

Mackeson followed a wave of the handkerchief. Over the shakos of one of the infantry regiments a line of bayonets had appeared, flashing in the sun. He regarded the spectacle with a dispassionate eye. The Cult of Cold Steel had been enshrined in the Army ever since Waterloo and Paddy Gough was its arch-priest. It was no good telling him that he regarded the bayonet as little improvement on Cromwell's pikemen. As the years passed the veterans who had served under Wellington seemed to forget more and more the other events of that June day; the long ordeal of the infantry squares and the slaughter caused by the British horse artillery. All they could see in their mind's eye was the magnificent spectacle of the general advance of the whole line at the end of the battle, when the bayonets had swept the French before them.

'They make a gallant sight, Your Excellency,' was all that Mackeson said.

'That they do, my boy,' said Gough proudly. 'That they do. I only wish I was going in at the head of one of the regiments myself.'

Gough blew his nose again, loud and long.

'Yes, I'd give a lot to show them the way,' he added in a softer tone. And Mackeson was surprised to see a tear glistening on the old man's cheek.

CHAPTER TWENTY-ONE

The furrows cut deeper into Colin Campbell's brow. He glanced at the jungle uneasily.

'Ye'll have to take them in yersel', Pennycuick,' he told the waiting brigadier. 'I'll no be able to look after three brigades at once in this. Penny' (the similarity of the names of two of his brigadiers irritated him) 'will be in reserve. I'll be marching with Hoggan and the 61st. It'll be warm work in there . . .' he nodded towards the undergrowth, '. . . so ye'll have to get to them quickly.'

As he rode away he turned to shout: 'Remember now, dinna load. This work is to be done by the bayonet.'

Junior Ensign Pennycuick watched excitedly as his father took his place at the head of the 24th. The regiment formed the centre of the brigade and the 25th and 45th Bengal Native Infantry the wings. Each contained about 1,000 men. When the bugles sounded advance they carried nearly three tons of burnished steel with them on the ends of their muskets.

'Sod this friggin' "bayonet only" rubbish!'

Private Connelly's company had loaded with ball ammunition earlier and their officers had wisely decided to leave matters as they were.

'Any bastard Sikh who gets in my way is getting the bloody lot,' he stated grimly as they moved off.

In the ranks of the supporting horse artillery the speed of the brigade's advance caused a hubbub of shouting.

'They're crossing our field of fire,' said their commander. 'They're going to get to the Sikhs before we've given them a round. God help them is all I can say.'

Brigadier Pennycuick was a fiery, middle-aged officer. Having set his young soldiers in motion he urged them on impatiently. Restricted to the use of the bayonet, it seemed to him that survival could best be assured by closing the gap as quickly as possible.

Responding eagerly to his leadership, the 24th Foot plunged on. They had entered the brushwood in line with the sepoy regiments on each flank. But within ten yards the line was bent. In twenty-five it was in shreds. Companies and even sections began to force their way through. The pace became hectic. The shouts louder. Those in the van saw twigs and greenery rushing towards them, brushing their faces. Those behind saw the jerky movement of white shakos and pipe-clayed belts and packs. Bayonet scabbards and cartridge boxes clattered as the thorns clutched them. Random yellow flashes betrayed Sikh sharpshooters ahead.

A tearing sound like the splintering of a thousand bamboo canes began in the distance and rushed terrifyingly towards Junior Ensign Pennycuick. It seemed to swallow him and then rush past and disappeared. Before it had lost itself in the general bedlam another crackling, snapping terror was speeding towards him.

'Round shot,' panted a hatless corporal. 'Don't worry sir. Too high.'

The noise came a third time and the top half of the corporal disappeared. His legs crumpled in a heap on the ground.

A blue turban rose unexpectedly from behind a log and a Sikh with a bloodstained face aimed at Lieutenant MacPherson. Connelly fired hopefully, slipping on the cap as he ran. To his surprise the turban jerked viciously and the firelock toppled from the dead man's hands.

'Take that man's name, Sergeant,' shouted MacPherson. 'We must stick to the bayonet.'

But the sergeant had other things to do.

Towards the edge of the jungle, cool, green patches of light beckoned invitingly. The 24th Foot burst suddenly onto a sloping green sward dotted with pools.

'What a place for a picnic,' was the first thought that came into Junior Ensign Pennycuick's head.

The bearded men in the yellow turbans had been firing slowly since noon – mainly round shot with an odd shell or two. But at the sound of the bugles and the approach of the British battle line they bent to waiting stacks of sinister iron tubes. Slipping a metal rod through two small handles, they lifted them to the muzzles for loading. According to the size of the cannon, the tubes contained anything from forty to a hundred balls of lead. Some of the missiles weighed up to two ounces each. Propelled by a hefty charge of gunpowder the tube, or canister, disintegrated at the muzzle, freeing the shot in arbitrary deadly flight. It was like using a cannon as a shot gun and was effective up to 300 yards.

The waiting Sikhs got the first glimpses of red coats through gaps in the trees – vague darting figures. Bushes waved and a solitary soldier burst into the sunlight looking about him anxiously and shading his eyes. More men followed including a mounted officer waving a sword. Two standards emerged tossing defiantly and the British line thickened about them.

Glowing matches hissed in the vents and the cannon vomited their loads and leaped back. Red coats slumped, screamed, started in agony, threw up their hands and collapsed. A howl of rage rolled across the clearing. As the Sikh gunners frantically pricked out smouldering fragments, sponged their barrels, loaded and rammed, the maddened British were racing towards them. Here and there gouts of flame stabbed the smoke and brought down more of the running figures, but the 24th were already on the batteries. An avalanche of butts and bayonets battered the Sikh defenders to the earth. As the mêlée subsided officers hurried to spike the captured guns. Ramrods were hammered into touch-holes and snapped off at the vent. But the regiment was disorganised. Some men tended wounded comrades. Others sought their company commanders and N.C.O.s. Some simply tried to regain their breath. Only the brigadier saw the oncoming line of Sikhs halt and level their muskets and he fell at the first volley.

Ensign Pennycuick felt bewildered and alone despite the milling confusion. The sight of a wild-eyed Sikh raining blows on his father's spreadeagled body was like a terrible dream.

'Stop it! Stop it, I say!' he shouted as he rushed at the man. With an oath, the Sikh whirled the heavy tulwar towards him, shattering the flimsy infantry pattern sword. In impotent rage, Ensign Pennycuick battered his assailant with the hilt.

Connelly was loading when he saw the slight figure struggling with the Sikh. Whipping a percussion cap onto the nipple of his musket, he scrambled over the corpse-littered ground.

'Hang on, sir. For God's sake hang on. I'm coming!'

His voice had reached screaming pitch when the Sikh drove

home the blade and stepped back to give Connelly an easy target. Even as he fired Connelly knew he was too late. Junior Ensign Pennycuick staggered with the shock and looked down at his stomach in amazement. The broken sword slid from his fingers, with which he clutched at the unbearable pain growing in his belly. A heavy hand pushed him slowly to the ground. He fell across his father's chest and crumpled to one side. There was something terribly wrong somewhere. He felt his shoulders being tugged and turned a puzzled gaze on a beetle-browed little soldier with a broken nose. Why was the soldier crying? He clutched the weeping man's tunic and tried to speak.

'It's all right, Connelly,' he whispered. 'I'll know what to do next time.'

In his death agony he tore away a brass button, which remained clutched in his hand.

Sikhs were now swarming all around. Connelly seized the little ensign's sword hilt and sent it whirling into their midst.

'Share that among you, you bastards,' he howled. Then turned and stamped blindly back to the knot of soldiers clustered around the Regimental colour. To his amazement he saw it was held in the grimy hands of Private Perry.

'What's happened to the officers, Ivor?'

'Most of the poor sods are dead as far as I know. You're standing on Lieutenant Phillips, look you.'

'Where's the other Colour?'

'In bits, boy. Somewhere down there too.'

Connelly bent and with some difficulty picked out the Union Flag from among the tangled uniforms. Hardly six inches of the pike staff remained in one piece.

'No bloody good like that, man.'

He tore the silk free, slipped it hastily under his cross belts and knotted it round his waist.

As the 24th retreated he fell back with them, pausing only to unship a bayonet from a dead man's Brown Bess. His own was bent and useless. The appropriated blade shone with a clinical brightness. Any Sikh wanting to lay hands on the Queen's Colour of the 24th Foot would have to get past that first.

It was a matter of conjecture whether any of the troops

falling back would escape. Despite determined attempts to keep pace with the 24th, the sepoys had been swept by case shot and over-run by a fierce onslaught in which infantry and cavalry took part The sight of a stream of wounded coming back from the 24th's shattered line was too much for them and they retired as best they could with the Sikhs seeping around them.

Colin Campbell, unaware of the disaster which had befallen Pennycuick's brigade, led the 61st on at the head of Hoggan's. When the accompanying sepoys showed signs of faltering he rallied them and now his whole force was attacking the enemy flank. Unseen by Campbell, a cloud of Sikh cavalry loomed threateningly. Sir Joseph Thackwell nudged his empty left sleeve in their direction and ordered a squadron of the 3rd Light Dragoons, supported by the 5th Bengal Native Light Cavalry, to charge.

'What? Do we 'ave to take on all of them?' Private Hacken stuttered in alarm as the dragoons trotted forward. 'It's not even our bloomin' squadron, Joe. We've got the wrong colour 'orses.'

Hacken and Sergeant Wood had been attached to the grey squadron and their bays stood out.

'I'll tell Lord Gough about it later,' said Wood abruptly.

The dark blue dragoons on the grey horses turned into line. A bugle sounded. Watchers held their breath as the trot became a canter, the canter a gallop and the gallop a full-blooded charge. Behind the racing squadron trotted a longer supporting line of Bengal light cavalry in pale tunics, scarlet cummerbunds and white jodhpurs.

The speeding blue wave disappeared into a gentle swell of white foam which suddenly boiled violently and evaporated. The Sikh cavalry had scattered and the wave raced on. In its path lay a dark breakwater of infantry. They greeted the oncoming cavalry with a disciplined volley. As the charge sounded again the Sikh bugles answered and the well-drilled regiments swung into a dense wedge. With its apex towards the enemy the triangle presented the smallest target to frontal attack and at the same time allowed the men on both sides to bring the maximum fire to bear on their attackers.

Hacken saw the ominous movement, swallowed and looked discreetly behind.

'Jesus Christ, Joe,' he yelled. 'The niggers are not coming on.' The 5th Light Cavalry had halted. Their bugle was sounding but nothing was happening. The dragoons were charging on their own.

With an enormous, explosive grunt the wedge swallowed the careering horsemen. The impetus carried them far into the packed ranks. White shakos bobbed over a sea of turbans.

With wrists bent until they hurt, the dragoons stabbed furiously at the fierce upturned faces. Jammed shoulder to shoulder, the infantry struggled to thrust with their bayonets until old soldiers began to shoot neighing grey horses and riders vanished into the swaying mass. The rest forced their way through and rallied some distance beyond in the scrub. Led by a pale captain, whose bloody shirt flapped through a tunic ripped by a lance, tight little knots hewed their way back. This time the shaken Sikh infantry opened their ranks and contented themselves with abusing the battle-crazed British as they passed through. Troops of gorchurras coming up to cut off the dragoons took their cue from the foot soldiers and backed off.

Hacken, head low and sword high, fixed his eyes on a familiar bay horse in front.

'Keep goin', Joe,' he yelled. 'They've 'ad enough. We're nearly there.'

To his amazement a troop of Bengal cavalry scattered wildly at their approach. It was only when the pace slowed and he rode alongside Wood that he saw the sergeant no longer had a head.

CHAPTER TWENTY-TWO

Lord Gough reined his grey charger first one way and then another. Every few minutes he stared through his telescope at the tossing jungle with its flying twigs, billowing smoke and bright flashes. It remained inscrutable. Two of Campbell's brigades had disappeared from sight and the third was moving forward in support. Wounded were straggling back and it was obvious from the noise that heavy fighting was taking place. Before him the heavy artillery stood silent, unable to fire because of the possible movement of British troops across his front. On the right Gilbert's six battalions had moved forward in fine style but he wished he'd had a third to back them up, as on the left. He hoped that the extra weight of cavalry would make up for the shortage of infantry.

Having led a division which sustained heavy casualties storming the trenches at Ferozeshah and which saw hard fighting at Sobraon, Sir Walter Gilbert had considerable respect for the Khalsa. His men advanced at a controlled pace, firing volleys and supported by a horse artillery battery. The Sikhs replied in kind. From the packed ranks on both sides a blizzard of lead lashed the diminishing space between the lines as Gilbert's men advanced.

'Easy, boys, take it steady! Close up now. *Close up!*'

Officers and N.C.O.s shouted reassuringly.

'No need to rush, there. Wait for the order.'

Hands in cartridge boxes, teeth tearing paper, spit, ram. 'Present . . . fire!'

'Never mind him. The dhooli bearers will pick him up later. It's only a scratch.'

A malicious hiss and a thump followed by shouts staggered the line for a moment. A round shot had killed two men and half a dozen others had been knocked to the ground by the impact of the mangled bodies.

'Close your ranks. Close up. Those fellers have nothing to worry about now. Look to your front.'

Another volley flamed and crackled.

'There, now look what yer done, lad. That's what comes o' bein' in too much of a hurry.'

Julius Begg shook his head vigorously as a ramrod sailed into the distance and vanished.

''Ere. Use this until yer gets a decent one.' Begg fished a ramrod from a discarded musket of ancient design and handed it to the dismayed soldier. 'It's a wood 'un so be careful with it.'

The man took it gratefully.

'Yer'll be able to pick up one o' ours soon enough,' the fat sergeant added grimly.

'What yer tryin' to do, son? Choke yerself?' Begg stretched out a pudgy hand and tugged at a stout youngster's collar.

'Ain't I allus told yer that the first rule in haction is to loosen yer toonic and stow that bleedin' neckpiece?'

A black leather stock looked smart on parade, but it stifled a man strung with cross belts, a pack and musket.

'Dress by the left. Keep up there. By the left.'

Leiston waded through a little pool, aiming a kick at a soldier who halted to scoop a handful of water. He strained his eyes into the drifting smoke. The Sikhs were standing their ground. It was going to be close work again, just like Ferozeshah. The muscles in his neck tensed.

At thirty yards range the Sikhs delivered a final volley as the British sounded the charge.

The 29th Foot struck the Sikh line where a pulton of irregulars stood alongside solid ranks of red-coated Khalsa veterans. Bearded warriors threw down their long matchlocks, drew their swords and hurled themselves forward dashing their shields in the faces of the British. The 29th responded with a hoarse cheer.

Leiston wielded the thirteen and a half pounds of musket and bayonet swiftly and with a calculated economy of effort. He was unaware that his teeth were clenched and that his face was set in a mask of ferocity. A wild-eyed figure dressed in blue rushed foaming at the mouth towards him. Leiston coolly directed his stained blade to where he judged the man's breast bone to end. Throwing his arms wide, the Sikh threw himself onto the point. The weight of the body almost jerked the weapon from Leiston's hand. For a few brief seconds the Sikh lashed out in a frenzy with his tulwar, slashing the raised white 'wing' from the sergeant's shoulder. Then Leiston heaved him to one side like a farmer moving a sheaf of corn with a pitchfork. He turned panting and threw up his point to protect a young soldier who was sobbing as he tried to extricate his bayonet from the rib cage of a writhing, cursing Sikh.

'Not so hard, son,' he shouted. 'Six inches is enough for any man.'

A warning yell made him turn. The Sikh in the blue robes had lurched to his feet and was fumbling with his turban. As his eyes glazed in death he hurled a razor edged steel quoit. The shining metal ring, a traditional weapon often worn ceremonially round the head-dress of religious extremists, carved through the top of Leiston's shako, leaving the truncated peak still on his head.

As the British gradually pressed back their opponents, Leiston twice saw Sikhs seize bayonets and slash soldiers about the head before other red coats dispatched them.

'Hasn't anyone told these black bastards they're supposed to run at the sight of cold steel?' gasped a breathless corporal.

The killing went on until the smoke thinned and the 29th stood beyond the Sikh batteries. Officers and N.C.O.s began reforming the disorganised ranks.

'Come on, get fell in there.'

Leiston started to push and shove men into line. Some were white-faced. Others dripped sweat. Most were shaking with excitement. To the right and to the rear a mounting din made the men glance over their shoulders nervously.

'Look to your front, damn you,' shouted a young officer bleeding from a cut across the head.

The men muttered and scowled, but obeyed. Shoulder to shoulder they emanated a controlled savagery.

Jawahir Singh studied the thin line of British cavalry cautiously. They had made such a hesitant start that he suspected a trap.

'Bring the feringhee captain here.'

A sowar trotted forward tugging a rope and a naked filthy figure staggered and fell against Jawahir Singh's horse. He seized the captive by the hair and forced him to look in the direction of the British.

'Well? There are your soldiers. What are they doing? Is it a trap? Or are they as stupid as they look?'

A croak greeted his question.

'What's that? Speak up, Captain. We can't hear you.'

Another croak.

'Ha!' Jawahir Singh was amused. 'You tell me to go to Shaitan. To go hang myself.'

He called out loudly to his men, translating liberally. A rumbling laugh greeted his words. Only the sowar who held the rope did not join in.

'Shall I kill the feringhee now?'

'No. Leave him where he can see his comrades slaughtered.'

The Sikh trotted to a tree, lashed the rope round it and as a farewell kicked Mallindine hard in the stomach. He collapsed on his knees, groaning. Jawahir Singh led his men forward, waiting for his chance to descend on the approaching enemy.

An orderly galloped up to Brigadier Pope. The old man studied the message petulantly.

'Orders, orders, orders. Now this. It's too much.'

The horse artillery accompanying Pope's brigade had already reported that the squadrons were obscuring their line of fire. Now the infantry brigade were complaining that the cavalry had drifted in front of the right battalions, who could not use their muskets because of them. Pope's head was beginning to ache as much as his back. It had been the devil of a job getting his nine squadrons in line, and now somehow they had moved too far to the left. They would have to be moved to the flank again.

Colonel King, at the head of the 14th Light Dragoons, watched the brigadier conferring and hoped he would not dither again. Since two o'clock his men had faced in half-a-dozen directions and he could sense that their confidence was draining away. Uneasily he glanced behind the long trotting line. As far as he could see, Pope had left nothing in support for them to rally on if necessary. A handful of guns dotted the otherwise empty plain.

'Oh, my God, this is ridiculous!'

Jameson, in front of his troop, slowed to a walk in response to the bugle calls now sounding along the regiments.

In the native cavalry regiments sowars were beginning to look over their shoulders.

Pope made up his mind. The whole brigade came to a halt. He held a short consultation with his staff. They would turn the line into column facing right and move clear of the infantry they were masking. At that moment an ominous movement began in the wheeling mass of opposing Sikh cavalry.

'Threes right!'

The thin piping voice of the old man was incoherent.

In the distance the 6th Bengal Light Cavalry could see a regiment of Sikhs begin the unmistakable preliminaries of a charge.

'Threes about!'

That was what the brigadier had obviously shouted.

Smartly, as if on parade, they wheeled and began to trot to the rear. The British squadrons followed suit. A derisive yell broke from the throats of Jawahir Singh's oncoming warriors. 'Feringhee baghatjen!' The rearward motion became noticeably quicker. A sowar touched his horse with his spurs too sharply. It snorted, tossed its head and bounded forward. Before he could rein back, the soldiers on either side had kicked their horses into a canter to keep up with him. The pace became faster and faster. Tight-knit ranks were opening. The neat rows of pennants of the 9th Lancers broke up into ragged clumps.

Colonel King rode desperately across the front of the regiment waving his sword. He cut at one galloping dragoon but the man dodged the blow, swerved, and raced on.

'*Halt!* Halt, damn you,' roared Jameson. But his own horse was pounding along as hard as the rest. Panic seemed to have communicated itself to the animals as well as the men.

Lala Rai was straining at an upturned limber when he heard the drumming of approaching horsemen. He and Mahdo Dinnath carried on with feigned unconcern. They had been posted to a new troop and wished to impress. But the thunder became compelling. They straightened and gazed with disbelief at the line bearing down on them. They were being charged by their own cavalry! It was incredible, but they were running away. Terrified sowars of the Bengal Light Cavalry were galloping through the battery. The gun lascars threw themselves to the ground as a lancer, eyes staring, cleared the limber with a bound. Horses cannoned off the wagon with violent thuds as the torrent swept over the gun positions. When the uproar diminished Lala Rai and Mahdo Dinnath cautiously peered round the side of the wrecked vehicle. The Red Men were struggling to limber up but the Sikhs were among them, stabbing horses and gunners as the teams came up. Two of the British had given up the hopeless attempt to flee and were desperately loading. The first fell with a Sikh lance in his back. He left the rammer protruding from the gun muzzle. The other was cut down over the handspike. As the Sikhs galloped on triumphantly the little Hindus raced for the six-pounder. Lala Rai wrenched out the rammer and threw himself flat as Mahdo applied the match. A furnace door opened and Lala Rai cringed. In the distance a knot of gorchurras collapsed in a heap of flailing hoofs and waving arms. Lying under the wheels of the gun Lala Rai thrust his rammer between the legs of a Sikh's horse and Mahdo leaped on the fallen rider, clutching a sword taken from a fallen Red Man. Each crouched low with a foot in a stirrup and let the dead man's mount carry them after the runaways.

The doctor did not believe in chloroform. He held that it interfered with the 'natural benefits' conferred by shock and pain. The Reverend Barnabas Wilmot did not believe in prayer when he could be doing something practical. So he had no objection to holding down the pale warriors who were beginning to arrive by dhooli. Amputation took, on average, three minutes. The knife and the saw were always sharp at the beginning of an action and the surgeon's muscles were not yet weary. A seventh leg had just been added to the pile under the awning when the first of the fugitives rode through the hospital. A guy rope parted with a twang and a tent collapsed. A soldier of the 61st, with a bullet as big as a pigeon's egg bulging blue under the skin of his bare chest, put his head in the operating tent and shouted:

'Come out quick as you can. The cavalry are running away.'

The surgeon, being as stubborn about his medical obligations as he was dogmatic about chloroform, ignored the plea. Not so Mr. Wilmot.

'Here, you,' he growled to the soldier, 'hold this fellow for a moment. I have other things to do.'

Horsemen who had been fleeing blindly from one nameless terror now found themselves facing another. A patriarchal figure in a black suit and huge mushroom hat assailed their mounts and bodies with a hammer-headed riding crop.

In a voice of thunder he was declaiming: 'Back, before I brain you. Back in the name of the Lod. Halt or I'll break every bone in your body.'

A bony hand shot out and snatched the weapon from the hand of a passing lancer. The riding crop hooked a dragoon from his horse. Mr. Wilmot swung nimbly into the saddle and proceeded to use the shaft of his lance to belabour Pope's absconding brigade, now entangled with blaspheming artillerymen rescuing their guns and limbers.

Gough himself saw the confused mass rolling past in the distance.

'By God, Pope's made a hash of it,' he roared. 'Get over there and stop those fools. Or I'll do it myself.'

He turned as if to carry out his words and his staff galloped determinedly towards the threatened flank. The welcome crack of six-pounders told them that the reserve horse artillery were engaging the Sikh pursuers.

The slaughter of Pennycuick's brigade on the left and the flight of Pope's cavalry on the right, placed Gilbert's division in a critical position. Although they had taken the enemy's gun line, they were in danger of being attacked from both flanks. The 2nd Bengal Europeans, with the supporting sepoy regiments, found themselves completely hemmed in by Sikh cavalry and infantry.

Brigadier Godby, who had distinguished himself at the vicious battle of Aliwal in 1846, coolly ordered the whole brigade to retrace its steps.

'Right about face!'

The order was repeated and the three battalions began a steady march back through the jungle over their fallen comrades. Volleys drove back the enemy. As they approached their original positions Godby ordered his horse artillery to 'put a shower of grape in there' and behind a hail of canister the whole brigade crashed through the Sikh cordon and re-formed in safety.

Gilbert's other brigade, meanwhile, was heading in another direction, in an attempt to capture the guns which had taken such a toll of the 24th. A wave of cavalry galloped ominously down on the 29th Foot who halted in line.

Ramrods rang in musket barrels. At less than two hundred yards a hail of heavy Brown Bess bullets brought down scores of horses and men and the Sikh banners ebbed away.

The 29th resumed their steady advance upon the enemy cannon where the gunners were hastily limbering up.

CHAPTER TWENTY-THREE

Mallindine leaned against the tree watching Jawahir Singh's regiment advance. In the distance he saw the long British cavalry line drop its already moderate pace to a walk and then halt. He tried to shout a warning, but the words would not come. And even if they had, no one would have heard them. Helplessly he looked on as Pope's brigade broke the golden rule of keeping on the move when in the presence of an enemy likely to charge. If that was unnerving, the sight of the British squadrons' undignified retreat was anathema. As they broke into disorderly flight he tugged madly at his bonds and shouted 'No! Oh, no!'

The sound of his voice attracted attention. Mallindine pressed himself into the tree and waited tensely. A muttering soldier appeared, saw him and glared. The Sikh wore a red tunic with green facings. Seeing that Mallindine was bound by the wrists he uttered a shout of surprise. Then with a wolfish snarl he levelled his musket and bayonet, screamed his war cry and rushed headlong at the bound man.

Mallindine's frantic jerk was a reflex action. The bayonet scraped his flesh and thudded into the tree with a force that jarred the musket from the holder's hands. As the Sikh shook his wrists in pain and rage, Mallindine threw himself forward and looped the rope around the bearded throat. Both crashed to the ground. Frantically the man clawed at Mallindine's face and tried to free the rope from his neck. With the tree securing one end of the rope and the naked Briton the other, the pressure was unendurable. Tongue and eyes protruding, the Sikh died, unable even to groan. Mallindine rolled him over and fumbled with the knife in his belt. When he had freed his hands he pulled the musket and bayonet clear. Dark red sap trickled from the torn bark. Even the trees were shedding blood.

Julius Begg extracted a short clay pipe from his pocket and lit it with the slow match of a cannon. He puffed the strong black tobacco solemnly on his perch on the gun trail. With a perfunctory kick at a sprawling white-robed body he jerked the yellow turban loose and wound it slowly round his torn trouser leg just above the left knee. After regarding his handiwork contentedly for a moment he looked round carefully.

'Hmm!'

He puffed and spat. The Sikhs didn't go much on baccy officially. Said it destroyed whole nations. They couldn't know what they were missing.

The cannon, a six-pounder with decorative brass let into the wheels, had been hit earlier in the day when the British heavy artillery opened fire. Its snout had been snapped off clean by a 24-pound shot which had also wrenched it from its housing. An undamaged companion piece stood in the same sandbagged emplacement. Its crew lay where they had fallen under the bayonets of Begg and Private Freeman. The squat sergeant and the scrawny soldier had been knocked unconscious by the same shell as the 29th advanced through the Sikh line. It was unforunate for the gunners that they were gazing the other way when the two red coats, having recovered their senses, crept up behind them.

'Don't look at me like that,' Begg muttered reprovingly. He tore a strip off a dead gunner's uniform and threw it over Freeman's face, concealing the fixed, glazed stare. 'I did tell yer it wasn't orl glory. And it ain't. That's for sure, son. Ask the angels if yer don't believe me.'

Begg rose gingerly and limped over to where a long matchlock lay. He inspected it and propped it against the sandbags alongside two other muskets, his own and Freeman's.

'Now,' he addressed himself aloud, 'the question is, 'ow do I find the rigiment?'

He sat down and puffed and spat again as he considered the problem.

To Mallindine, the sound of an English voice was better than a tot of arrack. He slithered cautiously towards the sandbag redoubt. The bayonets of two soldiers were just visible. A rapid booming followed by rippling volleys near at hand forced him to hug the ground, but the noise subsided and he crawled closer. Supposing he had imagined the voice?

He had been light headed for some time now. An unmistakable curse reassured him.

'Soldiers! You in the gun pit,' he called softly. 'Soldiers!'

At the sound of Mallindine's voice the tip of one of the bayonets had vanished.

'Don't shoot. I'm a British officer. When I count three I'll make a dash over the sandbags, so don't shoot.'

A moment's silence, then a low voice challenged:

''Oo are yer? What's yer name?'

'Lieutenant Mallindine, the 14th Light Dragoons.'

''Oo?'

The voice sounded suspicious.

'Mallindine . . . 14th Light . . .'

'Orl right, sir. Advance an' be recognised.'

The voice was mildly mocking.

Mallindine scrambled over the side of the emplacement and looked round. An ugly, perspiring barrel of a man stared at him through piggy eyes down the barrel of a musket.

'Cor!' The musket was lowered. 'An' where the 'ell 'ave you bin, sir? Sellin' yer clothes fer beer money? Yer looks more like one of them there saddhus than a hofficer!'

Mallindine ignored him and walked shakily to the pail hanging under the damaged gun. He scooped water up with his hands and drank carefully. Then he held out the bucket to Begg, but the sergeant merely wetted his lips.

Begg gazed at the naked scarecrow, covered in sand and filth and bleeding from a score of scratches.

'Better get some togs on sir. Try 'is, 'e won't be needin' 'em.'

Mallindine pulled off Freeman's boots and trousers.

'Lucky it was 'im and not me what copped it, ain't it, sir?' Begg continued cheerfully. 'Yer'd 'ave looked a right duck in my toonic and pants.'

'Where are the rest of your men, Sergeant?' Mallindine asked anxiously while trying on the sandals of the dead Sikhs, Freeman's boots being too small for him.

'There ain't any more. Me an' Freeman got knocked out by a shell and got in 'ere by accident. The rigiment was doin' fine at the time . . .'

'What's the matter?'

Begg had turned a pale shade of green.

'Nothin', sir. Jest a scratch.'

'Here, have some water.'

'Nooo . . . noo water fer the minute.'

A little pool of blood was spreading from Begg's boot.

'Can you walk?'

'Not fer the moment. I shall 'ave to sit, sir. Best thing yer can do is make yer own way back. Try 'eadin' down to the big tree there. Should find somebody. 'Ello – trouble.'

Begg seized his musket as the noise of battle rolled closer through the jungle. Mallindine grabbed the matchlock. Bullets whistled overhead and a fusillade of shots banged deafeningly near. There was a sound of racing feet and two panting turbaned figures jumped into the emplacement and made for the stacked case shot. The Englishmen's muskets boomed and Begg seized the spare gun.

'You load this one,' he said, thrusting his own smoking weapon at Mallindine. 'Go on, get 'is cartridge box, son.'

Mallindine bent over Freeman and heard another shot.

'Some beggar 'ad a peek first. 'Ope 'is mates don't come lookin' fer 'im.'

Angry voices filled the air. Mallindine peered over the sandbags and saw a group of Sikhs gesticulating toward the emplacement.

'It looks hopeless this time, Sergeant. There are dozens of them.'

'Pop up an' give 'em a shot, sir. It'll puzzle 'em a bit longer. They obviously wants to get 'old of that there gun and the case shot, 'cos the boys are comin'. Cop this!'

He threw over the matchlock. Mallindine caught it, moved to another position, rose and fired. His shot was greeted by a howl of rage. Begg threw him another musket and Mallindine repeated his performance. With a spontaneous roar the Sikhs charged. Mallindine placed his back against the sandbags, held his musket in front of him and wondered why the bayonet wasn't shaking.

CHAPTER TWENTY-FOUR

A six-horse team galloped along a rough track with the gun bounding over the ruts scything down overhanging bushes. It was followed by another and another. The Sikhs were clearing out hastily from the path of the 29th. Leiston counted six guns in all heading for Rasul. A team was brought up for a seventh but by then they were within easy range.

'Present . . . fire.'

The volley brought down most of the horses in a tangle of harness and lashing hoofs. A solitary animal bolted through the jungle with a dead Sikh bouncing behind it, one foot caught in a stirrup. The remaining gunners darted expertly around the stranded cannon. One of them seized the handspike and the muzzle swung round slowly towards the oncoming line.

'Canister,' Leiston noted as the shot was rammed home. 'Now we're for it.'

Dazzling orange flames blinded him for a moment. Coughing and spluttering he emerged from the rolling smoke and saw that the Colour party was no longer in the centre of the line. The young lieutenant who had been carrying the Regimental Colour was kneeling in an attitude of prayer but his body was propped up only by the staff of the fallen flag. Leiston stumbled towards him over groaning bodies and clutching hands but before he reached the spot a young ensign wrenched the pike from the dead fingers and was rushing forward with it. Daylight showed clearly through a ragged hole in the centre of the silk. The Queen's Colour had been picked up too and was waving its tatters in cocky defiance. The gunners were overwhelmed but not before the man with the handspike had battered two of his opponents to the ground.

Disorderly bodies of Sikhs were falling back in all directions before the advance of Mountain's brigade. One crowd of irregulars was making for a supporting redoubt where the snout of another gun could be seen. Something, or rather someone, was making them hesitate. Leiston saw a red coat appear, fire and then vanish. The Sikhs had halted in bewildered rage. Behind them were the 29th. In front an entrenchment which had been seized by the feringhees. A second shot doubled up a man in agony. With a howl the Sikhs swarmed towards the obstacle brandishing their weapons. Fast as they were moving the 29th were unlikely to reach it before them.

'Waaaaa!'

Leiston heard the roar of alarm and saw the mob split and swerve round the sides of the redoubt.

A massive figure was silhouetted against the sky. The arms jerked and poised the barrel of a six-pounder momentarily over its head. Then another heave sent the heavy brass missile smashing into the milling Sikhs. Screaming in terror the lucky ones fled. The figure toppled out of sight.

Begg sat down on the sandbags with a thud. He slid slowly backwards until his back rested on the shattered trail of the gun. His hands were shaking uncontrollably.

'Wet me mouth.'

Mallindine, mesmerised by the monstrous figure, cupped his dirty hands in front of the pudgy, powder-stained lips.

'That's better. Now 'and me me 'at. That one. Without the sun cover.'

Feebly Begg rubbed the helmet plate with a grimy sleeve.

'That's better.'

He planted it firmly on his bullet head.

'Is it on straight? I 'ates 'ats wot lean. Gotter set an example. Ther boys'll be 'ere any minute.'

The English cheers drew nearer. Two red-coated figures leaped over the walls of the redoubt.

'Cor, was that you, Sarn't Begg? What the hell have ye been drinking?'

'Gerron wi' ye, lads. Ek dum! If ye don't want my boot.'

'You hurt bad, Sergeant?'

It was the young lad who had fired his ramrod by mistake.

'Wot me? No. It's only a scratch.'

Leiston scrambled over the parapet.

' 'Ello, Robert.'

Begg was grinning through his pallor.

'Did yer see me?'

Leiston nodded.

'I saw you, Julius.'

A fractional shaking of the massive shako beckoned Leiston closer.

'Let yer inter a secret. I couldn't ha' done it if it 'ad bin loaded. Another six pun' would ha' bin the death o' me.'

A stifled wheeze shook the bulky frame. Pink pubbles oozed from the mouth.

'He's . . . he's laughing.'

Mallindine was still propping Begg's shoulders.

'He's dead,' said Leiston.

'It must have been his heart when he lifted that . . .'

'Nothing wrong with Julius's ticker.'

Leiston was almost scathing.

'His leg – it's just a scratch.'

A blackened hole with a musket ball still bulging in it came to light as the yellow wrapping was removed.

'It's not that.'

Leiston busied himself at Begg's tunic and stood back with dripping hands.

'There must be the best part of a load of canister in his guts. His belly is almost solid lead. It's a wonder he ever got here.'

Mallindine fastened the top button of the private's tunic and stood up red-eyed, filthy and unshaven.

'They tore off my clothes when they took me prisoner,' he explained almost casually.

A bugle sounded urgently.

'You'd better join with us, sir. I don't know where your regiment is.'

Picking up a musket Mallindine nodded towards Begg.

'What about him?'

Under the prodigious black shako the little piggy eyes were closed and the pudgy cheeks pulled down in a scowl.

'Just leave him where he is, sir. For the moment.'

As they ran to join the British line Leiston added:

'Don't you worry about our Julius. He can still look after himself.'

The 29th began to advance towards the growing racket which indicated that Campbell's brigade was making a last assault under the darkening sky.

Leading Hoggan's brigade in person Campbell renewed his attack on the Sikh flank, pressing down the gun line. Even before the brigade could form, and as the 46th Bengal Native Infantry were moving to their place on the left of the 61st Foot, a horde of gorchurras charged. The sepoys halted and delivered volleys by companies, so that a constant ripple of fire played on the enemy. Through riderless horses the sepoys marched on. More cavalry swept round behind the brigade. Campbell faced the rear ranks about and unleashed a withering hail of musketry. Twice more this happened before the Sikhs retreated.

As Campbell attacked, the Regimental Colour of the 24th once more came tossing forward through the smoke, although the men clustered round it were pathetically few. Private Connelly plunged savagely through bushes with bayonet fixed. He saw a Sikh horseman stop and slash at a wounded officer lying on the sward where the Pennycuicks had died. He shouted and ran towards him. The officer had raised his arm defensively and Connelly clearly saw the fingers fly as the Sikh sword fell. He paused and fired. The Sikh tumbled forward over his horse's neck.

Another gorchurra, seeing his comrade fall, pulled his horse on to its haunches and jabbed his lance furiously at the helpless figure on the ground. Connelly hurled his musket with its fixed bayonet from ten yards into the small of the rider's back. With a shriek the lancer galloped blindly away, the weapon protruding over his horse's hindquarters.

Connelly did not notice another Sikh taking aim. A blow in the chest brought him to his knees. He lurched to his feet like a prizefighter and tried to stand erect. Despite all efforts to make them move forward his legs obstinately staggered back down the slope. He was down on his knees and clutching the grass as he slithered gently into a muddy pool. For a moment his hands clung to the bank. Then he was gone. Mud and blood soaked into the flag around his body. The colliery was a dark, unrelenting place.

CHAPTER TWENTY-FIVE

A cool breeze rustled the shattered acacia trees, thinning the powder fumes. Sporadic bursts of firing replaced the non-stop clamour of the afternoon. Light drizzle turned to chill rain. The parched red coats and sepoys held up their faces and tried to let the drops run into their mouths.

'What d'ye reckon we'll do now, Sergeant?'

The 29th were formed up beyond the Sikh gun line with their muskets tucked under their arms to protect the locks from the weather. Behind them, in the broken bushes and churned up ground, search parties were gathering the wounded.

'Wait for orders. How the hell do I know?'

To Leiston it was like the night of Ferozeshah all over again. No one knew where anyone was or whether the Sikhs were likely to come back at them.

'It's bleedin' cold.'

'Think yourself lucky. It's colder if you've snuffed it.'

'Water . . . water . . .'

Groans and hoarse cries drifted in from the darkness. The wounded always called for water. Half a cup would kill those with belly wounds, but they wanted it all the same. Julius must have known he hadn't much of a chance, but he hadn't risked a drink. Not according to Mallindine. Just dabbed his lips.

'Water . . . water . . .'

'Can't we get something from those ponds, Sergeant?'

'What? And poison the lads. Those ponds are full of dead horses and men and all sorts of muck. I wouldn't even give it to you lot.'

'Water. In the name of heaven, water.'

Weeping could be heard among the whimpering.

Lord Gough too was parched. He glared round the faces in his candlelit tent and turned his attention to the table. Rasul, Chilianwala, the river, the jungle, the roads were as neatly marked as they had been when he studied the map that morning. Nothing was changed on paper. The still lines of red coats, the piles of Sikhs and the mangled horses did not show. Some day someone would add nice red and green squares with a few arrows to indicate the positions.

The staff chatted in low voices.

'What was that?'

Thackwell gazed at a paper in his hand.

'Another request for permission to draw water, sir.'

'Hmmmp!'

Gough turned away without saying anything and Thackwell dismissed the messenger. Others with similar requests had been dismissed earlier.

'Who was it from this time?'

'Penny. He says the 15th Sepoys are having great difficulty moving their wounded and are short of officers. Can we send someone.'

'See to it, Gilbert.'

A dripping dragoon clanked in with another message, asking where water details should be sent.

'They'll have to wait.'

Shadows danced across the map as the candles flickered. Muffled voices outside and a champing of bits announced another visitor.

'Well, Campbell? Did ye find out any more?'

'It's nae better, y'r Excellency.' Campbell was a stickler for protocol. 'The right of my division is still where it was and has closed up on Gilbert's. But the brigadiers dinna know where their colonels are and the colonels are no certain of their men's positions. Hoggan's well enough but Penny is worse hit than I thought. What is left of Pennycuick's brigade is gathering on the edge of the jungle.'

'Gilbert! De ye think ye can bring off the guns?'

'Well, we've spiked them, but they'll have to wait until the morning when we can bring up fresh horses . . .'

Sir Colin Campbell, who had just sunk wearily on to a camp chair, cocked his little beard.

'The morning! We'll no have any men, never mind horses, if we stay where we are. The sepoys are jumping at every shadow as it is.'

Silence fell on the company.

'You've no need to worry for your flank, Campbell. The cavalry are covering your left.'

Thackwell waved his stump as he spoke. He meant to be reassuring.

'Och, man, there is no enough water for the men, never mind the beasts.'

Campbell turned his mournful eyes on the Commander-in-Chief.

'The men are desperate for water, sir. With your Excellency's permission . . . I would like to pull back my division.'

Gough remained poring over the table. But he was not seeing anything on the map. Only a vision of helpless men lying in the dark. He'd been wounded himself, more than once, in the Peninsula. He'd not forgotten the agonies of thirst.

A clenched fist crashed on the table.

'No, Campbell, no!'

'Y'r Excellency!'

'I will not pull back and leave the wounded to be slaughtered. You know what will happen out there. I saw them today with my own eyes. Those gorchurras take a delight in cuttin' up a man when he's on the ground. No. I won't hear of it. D'ye hear!'

'Out there' the Sikh guns were waiting, glistening in the rain. They were already spiked. British soldiers were standing to arms alongside or near them. To pull back now would be to concede . . . the only proof of victory that was acceptable. And he'd told Dalzie he would have them.

An aide-de-camp offered him a glass.

'Hmmm?'

'Brandy and water, sir.'

'No . . . no. Not at the moment.' With all the requests for water coming in it would choke him to drink.

'General Godby's compliments, sir.'

A staff officer accepted another demand for water. Gough merely shook his head. Where were all the men who knew best now? Mackeson had not been so quick to offer advice. Although no doubt he'd be penning a letter to his political friends that night. Dalzie would be in his bed before long at Ferozepore with all the water in the world to drink.

'I'm not moving until all my wounded are safe, gentlemen.'

Campbell remained sitting.

'Is that clear?'

From a little rise beyond the tent it was possible to see lanterns glowing dimly in the jungle, leading pale dhoolis with their burdens. Gough stood bare headed and wondered how long he could wait. An ammunition cart drawn by oxen and filled with wounded trundled slowly past.

He went back to his headquarters and waited, but nothing had changed. No solution appeared miraculously on the map. No officer arrived with tidings of a Sikh capitulation. The clock had moved remorselessly away from the time when his men were whole and unspent. What had been done had been done.

It was a bitter decision but it had to be made. As the casualty reports flowed back and the orderlies brought messages clamouring for tents, medical supplies, ammunition, relief and water, always water, Gough steeled himself. He asked, of course, as a matter of form; and the generals told him as a matter of form that all the wounded who could be found had been removed to safety. But Gough knew, and they knew, that it was an impossible task. Just as impossible as leaving the battered army on the battle field.

'What's that, Sergeant? What is it?'

Leiston jerked himself awake at the voice of his company commander.

'It's the recall, sir.'

'But we haven't got in all the wounded yet. We can't have. Are you sure?'

'The people on our right are falling back already, sir.'

Crashing and shouting confirmed his statement.

'Bugler . . .'

Plaintive notes rang out and the weary regiments stumbled back onto the plain.

Within an hour the creaking of wheels and snorting of horses could be heard as the Sikhs returned to drag away their abandoned guns. Occasionally a shot or a scream rang out as search parties discovered wounded British and Indian soldiers overlooked in the undergrowth. Sometimes it was the cry of 'Water, water . . .' which betrayed them.

In the tent of the Commander-in-Chief the reports were still coming in.

'If we go on like this we shall have lost two thousand and more by the morning,' commented a harassed staff officer.

'Be grateful that we haven't lost India. We might well have done if we had not given battle today.'

Pausing, Gough added fiercely:

'Although I doubt if anyone will see it that way in England.'

CHAPTER TWENTY-SIX

A slight, stooped figure gazed from an elegant upstairs window at the yellow London fog hanging over the greasy cobbles of the courtyard. It reminded him of gun smoke. Creases deepened by the side of the aquiline nose. The lip curled. With no one else to rebuke him the Duke of Wellington was reproaching himself. Perhaps, after all, he should have gone. Dalhousie had been quite specific in his letter.

'In public, I make, of course, the best of things. I treat it as a great victory. But writing confidentially to you, I do not hesitate to say that I consider my position grave.'

The pale, almost translucent, hands fidgeted with the paper. Three years earlier the Duke had agreed to a victory medal being struck after Gough had beaten the Sikhs at Sobraon. It had seemed such a conclusive action that he had permitted the ribbons to be just like the Waterloo medal only with the colours reversed. Now there was the Devil to pay at this Chilianwala. Out of 12,000 men Gough had lost nearly three thousand. And half a dozen guns. Two of the sepoy regiments had come back without their Colours. But the battle flags and guns were not the problem. The casualties were the real worry. The 24th Foot had been slaughtered and the 29th had suffered severely. Good, sound regiments both. A spark flickered in the pale, blue eyes. For a moment he saw the 29th storming the hill in the dusk at Talavera. The eyes hardened as the vision passed. Someone had bungled the cavalry. Pope would get the blame no doubt as he had conveniently died of his wounds. Still, most troops ran away at some time. It didn't matter an awful lot if they were well supported. His lips pursed. From what he could gather the brigade had been left without anything to fall back on at all. Damn' fool thing for anyone to do. To judge from some reports the Bengal cavalry had not been rounded up until dark. He hoped that someone sensible would get them in hand next time. They'd get over it if they were properly handled. But he still had his doubts. It was all right sending Napier out to take over from Gough. He might be unscrupulous but he knew his stuff. After all, who had taught him? No matter. Just supposing . . . just supposing the troops knew that Wellington himself were on the way. He was only nine years older than Gough. Just one last battle . . .

'Bah!' The man renowned throughout the world for his common sense told himself sharply that he had been dreaming and returned to his desk.

From Calcutta to London the reaction was similar to that of the Duke. Letters in the Indian press, rumours and official despatches indicated that a calamity had befallen the army on the banks of the Jhelum.

As the politicians had given Dalhousie a free hand they couldn't blame him. The public had been brought up to believe that the British soldier was invincible so they couldn't blame him.

And as no one in India wished to have trouble with the sepoys, Gough got the blame.

'The fact that the Sikhs might have had anything to do with it quite escapes everyone,' Sir Charles Napier confided to a close friend. 'So I must be off.'

With him went a letter making the gravity of the situation abundantly clear. Written in the Duke's unmistakable hand was the uncompromising sentence: 'If you do not go, then I must.'

Reluctantly Sir Charles packed his bags and went. Even though the Duke was within four months of his 80th birthday one did not question a message like that.

At least, thought Napier, he would escape from the foul English winter. But what would Paddy Gough say?

On the morning after Chilianwala the General rode among his men in the drenching rain. Cheers followed him throughout the camp. The soldiers cheered because he looked a kindly soul, because by some fluke they were still alive and because most of them had got hold of an issue of rum. Search parties brought in the dead and some wounded men who had survived the night.

Private Perry dug silently and expertly in the sodden earth. Two mass graves were to be used for the dead of the 24th. The N.C.O.s had told him that he was excused duty. One of the officers said he was a hero for saving the Regimental

Colour. But he said he'd dig all the same. It took his mind off Connelly. No one had seen the little bastard since the last charge.

Perry had checked the dead lined up for burial, furtively kicking certain N.C.O.s and examining with morbid curiosity the badly disfigured. He'd even looked at the officers laid out on the big polished table in the mess tent. His spade bit into the ground. Stupid bastards. Couldn't forget their bleedin' privileges even when they were bleedin' well dead. Well, sod 'em. Down here . . . the spade bit deeper . . . the ruddy colonel, the major, the captains and all would be the same height as the privates. It was almost worth getting killed to be planted alongside the nobs. Almost. Still. He wished Connelly would turn up.

Of the 24th's fighting strength of 1,100, thirteen officers and more than 200 men had been killed and 276 wounded. The 29th Foot had more than 200 wounded but less than forty fatal casualties.

'Reckon old Shere Singh didn't do so well, either,' Leiston told Corporal Baggott as they led a train of camels squelching through the mud to the scene of the attack the previous day. He nodded towards Rasul where a thick black pall climbed slowly to the lowering clouds.

'A mighty lot of dead are going up in smoke, if that is anything to go by.'

After the heavy rain it was hard to recognise the scene of the previous day's struggle. Everything looked different.

'Are you sure old Begg is dead?' asked Corporal Baggott suspiciously after a while. 'It isn't like Julius to go and get himself killed.'

But Julius was sitting where they had left him.

During the night the Sikhs had stripped most of the dead. Begg they had left severely alone. He sat, forbidding and mysterious, with the rain trickling off the peak of his mighty shako. After the perspiring burial party had finally got his body roped to the camel they had to lash two corpses on the other side to balance the animal. Leiston carried back the shako to wedge it on the fat man's head when he was buried. As he explained, Julius had always wanted to be buried in his 'regimentals'.

For the 14th Light Dragoons the task of burying the dead was not a problem. Only three men had been killed during the disastrous 'retirement'. One officer had died too. Lieutenant Cureton had survived his father by only two months.

CHAPTER TWENTY-SEVEN

Muffled in their cloaks against the driving rain, a detachment of dragoons splashed wearily down the Lahore road. The horses had hardly a jog left in them. Mallindine would have trotted past the ghari without stopping but his sergeant heard the insistent voice and turned aside to investigate.

'It's an English lady, sir. She says she wants to speak to the officer.'

'Goddamit! What's she doing in this hell hole?'

Mallindine walked his horse alongside the vehicle and bent down.

'What can I do for you, ma'am?' he shouted.

The reply was indistinguishable above the wind so he dismounted and squelched closer. The woman behind the rattling, half-lifted blind sounded surprised and relieved.

'Oh it's you, Captain Mallindine!'

He stared.

'Miss Wilmot! You shouldn't be here. You never can tell what you'll meet on the road. There are Sikhs and budmashes all over the place.'

'I'm trying to get news of my father. I hear there has been a great battle.'

'So there has, but Mr. Wilmot is all right. I have not seen him but I'm told he greatly distinguished himself at the hospital.'

The wind almost jerked the slats of the blind from Miss Wilmot's hand.

'You can't go on in this. You must turn back. I have despatches for Lahore. I'll be happy to escort you.'

Miss Wilmot shook her head helplessly and pointed towards the horse. A glance told Mallindine that it was unfit for further hard work that day. Miss Wilmot's servants were huddled in the lee of the ghari which was parked in the shelter of a clump of trees where some other travellers were sheltering from the storm.

'Could you ride? We have spare mounts.'

'Will you wait while I change?'

Mallindine nodded and went off to speak to the dragoons who had dismounted in the shelter of the trees with their horses' rumps to the wind. An elderly Indian clutching an unruly umbrella was talking to them.

'He's asking about the battle, sir. Says his mistress is a rich lady and has friends in the 29th.'

'Has she, by Jove? I've friends in the regiment myself. Take my horse.'

The old Indian led him through the puddles to a roomy if aged carriage parked at the head of two smaller ones. A veiled head appeared at the window in answer to the assault of the umbrella handle.

'Can I help you? I understand that you are seeking news of the 29th Foot.'

Dark eyes studied him. The woman was obviously getting on. Her dark hair was tinged with grey – where it showed.

'There has been a battle on the Jhelum?'

'That's right. At a place near Rasul.'

'The 29th were in it.'

'Yes. I happened to be with them for a time.'

'Were many killed?'

Another umbrella man had appeared making it easier to hold a conversation.

'Not really. None of the officers.'

'But what about the men? Do you know what happened to the fat sergeant? To Sergeant Begg? He is my friend for many years. He has helped me in business.'

Astonishment must have shown immediately because the woman put a much-ringed plump hand on the sill and demanded:

'Please – you know him?'

'I'm sorry to have to tell you, ma'am, that I was with Sergeant Begg when he died. It would not be too much to say that he saved my life.'

The woman did not hear the second sentence. At the first she burst into a wail and collapsed sobbing and crying inside the coach. Another woman comforted her and a different veiled face appeared.

'You know where Sergeant Begg is buried? Please?'

'I'm sorry but . . .'

The girl burst into a torrent of Hindustani. Some of it Mallindine made sense of, the rest was lost to him. Under other circumstances he would have shrugged his shoulders and left but the mention of Begg intrigued him. He hurried back to Miss Wilmot's ghari and knocked. The blinds were raised quickly.

'I'm ready.'

'Before we set off do you think you could use your knowledge of the language to speak to some Indian ladies who are sheltering here? It's amazing, but they're inquiring after a man who saved my life only a few days ago. Do you remember that stout sergeant who came with the detachment of the 29th to Amballa . . . ?'

He struggled to hold open the door as Miss Wilmot emerged. She nodded and hurried over to the coach. After a brief conversation she was allowed to climb inside.

Sarojini continued to weep as Roshanara asked the English lady in the riding clothes questions which she translated and passed to Mallindine standing at the window.

'In truth, I think you're too hard on Sergeant Leiston, ma'am.'

Miss Wilmot had called in the cantonment in Lahore as Mallindine was about to return to Helan.

'But I've already explained to you what sort of women they were in that coach. They follow the regiment. They have already been at Wazirabad for a time and were returning there.'

'That means little. There is no indication that Sergeant Leiston had anything to do with their . . . activities.'

Miss Wilmot was pale and haughty.

'You did not speak to the young one, Lieutenant Mallindine. I did. She was overjoyed when she heard that he was uninjured.'

'Well. Aren't you pleased?'

A buttoned boot stamped imperiously.

'I dislike to hear of any British soldier coming to grief, but . . .'

'Yes?'

'He deceived me.'

Sitting upright with a sniff she added: 'It may surprise you to know, Mr. Mallindine, that I actually contemplated . . . marriage . . . with that brute. Had he been free.'

Mallindine nearly dropped the belt he was buckling on.

'My God. But the man's just a common soldier. Your father . . . er . . . you're a lady.'

'I would have made him something else. Have no fear of that.'

Looking at the determined jaw, Mallindine did not doubt it.

Heading back into the Doab that afternoon Mallindine reflected that he had been tempted to tell Miss Wilmot the truth about Leiston's marriage and was glad that he had not. Miss Wilmot was a fine looking woman who had ridden through the storm like a seasoned dragoon. There was no nonsense about her. The sort of woman who would make a general a good wife. And Mallindine intended to be a general himself some day.

On the road into Wazirabad the dragoons encountered a messenger moving fast on a camel. The shootar sowar brought the news that the citadel in Multan had fallen at last.

Mulraj sat in a guardroom underneath a solidly built medieval gate listening to the howitzer shells landing. Every explosion brought down little showers of dust from the ceiling. Screams and whimpers echoed in the corridor where he had installed the ladies of his zenana. For two days and nights he had been sitting clothed from head to foot in chain mail pondering on the practicability of a break out. The guns had never ceased. All his overtures for a truce or an armistice had been refused. So had his request to negotiate a surrender. General Whish, it appeared, was not empowered to discuss terms. Only to smash the ancient citadel to powder. Or accept the unconditional surrender of its garrison. Including Mulraj. Unless the Sikh chieftain surrendered by midday, Whish had announced his intention of storming the citadel, just as he had stormed the walls of the town. Despite the earlier resistance of his troops Mulraj was no longer confident. His magazines had been destroyed. He fingered the iron bangle on his wrist uneasily. What, he wondered, would the British do to him?

'They ought to 'ang the bastard. That's what.'

Private Makepiece was disgusted. For nearly a fortnight the howitzers had been pounding Mulraj's stronghold to dust. Unceasingly the sappers had dug and burrowed nearer and nearer the walls. Barrels of powder had been brought up to charge the mine which had been driven under the counterscarp. The stormers had been marched out and were poised, waiting for the big blast which would give them access to Mulraj's treasury, when the word had flown round the ranks. He was going to surrender after all. Then the clouds opened and the rain came down.

'Isn't hanging too good for him, the heathen bastard?' demanded Kennedy vociferously.

Makepiece waggled his toes in a leaky boot and swore softly under his breath.

'If he leaves us out here much longer, Pat, we'll have to surrender or swim for it.'

If Mulraj had kept the British waiting, it was only so that he could surrender with dignity. He rode out of the gates of the citadel clad in scarlet from head to foot with his horse draped in silk of a similar colour. To General Whish he extended a jewelled scimitar in a green velvet scabbard. The old man weighed it in his hands and calculated ruefully that it had cost him 12,000 explosive shells and 13,000 heavy round shot. Plus more than 1,200 killed and wounded.

Before the besiegers reorganised for the march to join Gough they performed one last task. Men of the 1st Bombay Fusiliers retrieved the bodies of Mr. Vans Agnew and Lieutenant Anderson from the shallow grave where they had been buried. Wrapped in Kashmir shawls, the remains were carried solemnly up through the breach which the regiment had stormed and buried on the summit of the citadel. For Khan Singh, the man who was to have replaced Mulraj as Sirdar, the British could do nothing. He and his son had been blown to pieces by the explosion of the main magazine after it was pierced by a British shell.

CHAPTER TWENTY-EIGHT

Crowds filled the narrow streets of Wazirabad. Pathan horsemen in the service of the British clattered through the bazaar laughing and shouting. Peasants pushed carts full of produce. Cows wandered at will. Leiston kicked a scratching beggar from the steps of the House of Pleasure and called loudly. One of Sarojini's relatives, an uncle or a cousin, appeared and started to beat his breast at the sight of him.

'All right. All right. Go and get Sarojini for me. We haven't got much time.'

Corporal Baggott, who had accompanied Leiston on a mission to collect some returning wounded from the nearby hospital, threw himself in a cane chair and heaved a sigh of relief.

'Don't hurry. Nice to be able to get yer bottom down for a few minutes.'

'Well? Are ye going to get Sarojini or not?'

The old man disappeared mumbling, and a slight figure in a green and gold sari appeared through a bead curtain.

'Have you come to see me, Leiston Sahib?'

Leiston smiled uncertainly.

'I'm always pleased to see Roshanara. But it's Sarojini I must talk to. We have little time.'

'Sarojini is dead.'

'Dead?'

'Yes. She is dead.'

'What happened? Cholera? A fever?'

'She is dead because Begg Sahib is dead. She said Begg Sahib was her husband and so she did what she had to do.'

Roshanara placed her hand delicately but firmly against the door post in an unmistakable gesture.

Leiston knew what she meant. He had seen houses before carrying a small vermilion handprint by the front door. Although the authorities had firmly condemned the practice of suttee, some Hindus still forced widows to follow their husbands to the funeral pyre. They seldom went willingly.

But few neglected to dip their hands in a pot of paint and leave a mute symbol of farewell as they left their homes for the last time.

'But we buried Begg Sahib in the big trench.'

Roshanara nodded in a matter-of-fact way.

'Sarojini did not have to do anything. She just sat and waited for death near the babul trees. There was no pain. When she was dead we burned her near the place where Begg Sahib is buried. Some soldiers came but they did not hurt us. They said we were mad and let us go.'

But Leiston wasn't listening. He was fiddling with a piece of tarpaulin. When he had unbent the stiff folds he pulled out a grimy white strip of cloth covered with dark stains. Pulling out a large horn pocket knife he proceeded to slit the stitches. A small pile of gold coins rolled onto the table.

' 'Ere. That's old Julius's money belt.' Baggott's remark was ignored.

'I brought it for Sarojini. Who will run the house now?'

'Sarojini told me that I was to be the new mistress,' Roshanara replied. 'She said I had to find a protector and that I was to take her place.'

'What about the uncle and his sons?'

'They will do as I say. They have not got the knowledge.'

Leiston pushed the coins towards her.

'You'd better have these.'

The girl let them lie.

'Tell me . . . can a man leave the army of the British when he wants to?'

'Not young men – unless they are sick. Or pay a sum of money. What we call buying themselves out. Old men can go free after serving many years. But not the young ones.'

'Would that money buy *you* out?'

Her voice was soft. Tempting.

'Many times over.'

'Then I will buy you.'

Her eyes shone at the thought.

Leiston laughed. It was a pleasant enough prospect. Kept man in a house full of whores. No more marching. No more fighting. A distant bugle call roused him.

'Put it somewhere safe, Roshanara,' he said, pushing the

coins nearer. 'Put it somewhere where those old rogues can't lay their hands on it. Go on. Begg Sahib wouldn't mind. Don't waste it on buying soldiers out of the army.'

'Wot about me?'

'Especially Corporal Baggott.'

The eyes behind the veil darkened.

'Will you come back?'

'Of course, I will. Some day.'

He made his way out into the alley followed by the grumbling figure of Baggott.

'You must be barmy,' said the corporal. 'She'd set you up for life.'

Leiston was swinging through the bazaar with a jaunty step.

'What? Me start counting the takings and acting as chucker-out for a bunch of whores? Not on your life. There was only one Julius. That's enough for me.'

Corporal Baggott was still determined to have the last word.

'Can't see there's much difference, anyway. A whore gets paid so ye can do what ye like with her, and the army pays us so they can do what they like with us.'

'Mind you,' he added thoughtfully. 'I suppose both of them can get to like it in the end.'

CHAPTER TWENTY-NINE

Scratch, scratch, scratch. Lord Dalhousie's pen moved busily over the paper. Whatever happened, his private correspondence went on remorselessly. The previous day by a freak sound effect cannon fire had been heard in the distance. It had not inspired him.

'In former days the mere sound of guns would have enabled one to feel sure that it was a battle fought and won; nowadays one cannot be so sure of it . . .' he wrote.

With Lord Gough, he had become completely disenchanted. In his view the Commander-in-Chief's handling of the troops at Chilianwala had been below contempt. Each night he prayed for the arrival of reinforcements from Multan. In this respect General Whish was doing his best to please him. The irregular cavalry were heading up the 250-mile road from Multan to Wazirabad and the Chenab fords as fast as they could trot. Horse gunners supporting them were pressing on at a gruelling pace which enabled one battery to cover forty miles in a single period of 24 hours. To the nagging beat of the drum the infantry were making marches of eighteen miles a day. Behind them in the stormed city flocks of vultures and dense clouds of flies blackened the ruins. In the great camp near Chilianwala conditions were not much better. Packs of jackals and scavengers had glutted themselves but the stench still drifted over the area. No one bothered to bury the dead horses and rotting camels. Steady rain made conditions even more loathsome. Reconnaissance became difficult for both sides.

Massive pyramids of mud sprouted along the perimeter of the camp so that sentinels could look out over the countryside. An informal competition developed to out-build one's neighbours. On the tallest of all, Lord Gough surveyed the landscape on the rare fine days. His men spent much of their off-duty time on the sides of the primitive watch towers. Otherwise they manned the defences and patrolled the scrub.

'Lucky we didn't all get hanged this morning,' said Private

Hacken gloomily pricking out the nipple on his carbine. 'Mr. Westley Richards here almost had the General for breakfast. Came straight out of the jungle, old Thackwell did, where we'd been looking for Sikhs. Wanted to know what we were doing so far forward. Silly old sod! With his one wing he'd be a fat lot of good in a barney. Just laughed when the sergeant said we were scouts and told us to be careful.'

He lay back and sighed.

'Don't know what I'm going to say to my feet when I see 'em. Won't recognise 'em, it's so long since I 'ad my socks off. Won't bother with boots in future. Just have the soles of my feet cobbled.'

Footwear was a pressing problem throughout the army. In another tent Leiston sat with other N.C.O.s carefully picking through a black leather heap.

'I don't know who thought of taking the boots off the stiffs before we planted them, but I wish he was here now,' said a disgusted voice. 'This boot's got a bit of bleedin' foot in it.'

Leiston pulled on a pair of Sikh sandals.

'Ah well. Time to take my mud bath. I'll keep the water nice and warm for you.'

Outside a little group of men draped in various garments to keep off the rain slopped after him towards the trenches. It was turning out to be a long time between battles.

Shere Singh had decided to evacuate Rasul. The arrival of his father's troops and the Afghans had made it impossible to remain on the Jhelum. The country was too barren. Furthermore he had to move somewhere and it could not be back the way he had come. He led his troops gradually towards Gujrat from which he could threaten the crossings at Wazirabad. A strong garrison with a few guns kept the British occupied in their camp near Chilianwala. But even this force was withdrawn in the second week in February.

Two options lay open to the Sikh commander. He could try to provoke Gough into another headlong assault on his superior forces before the arrival of the Multan army. Or he could strike across the Chenab for Lahore seventy miles to the south. From Lahore, Dost Mahommed's wild tribesmen could terrorise the hinterland while the Khalsa marched on Delhi.

Such a bold thrust might bring results but Shere Singh was still unhappy at the thought of leaving Gough's army in his rear. In the end his strategy fell between two stools. Edging nearer the crossings he tried to invite attack. But Gough would not be drawn. Brief outpost clashes flared, but that was all. Hodson's irregulars screened the approaches to Wazirabad and, as Whish drew nearer, guns and infantry were ordered forward by forced marches to reinforce him. Shere Singh sought to inspire his troops by a great parade at Gujrat in which he displayed the captured Colours of the 25th and 45th Bengal Infantry, and the horse artillery guns taken at Chilianwala.

He had English prisoners brought forward as he reviewed his army, marching past to the beating of tom-toms and belligerent blasts on cow horns.

'See the Khalsalji!'

His arm waved in the direction of the infantry columns moving past in unending procession.

'Look at these men well. For they will stamp on the red necks of the soldiers of the Engrese Sirkar and it will be as if it had never been.'

'Then the Khalsa will have to learn to kick high,' retorted a dignified civilian, 'for English necks are devilish stiff things and don't bent easily. And if our necks are red . . . you must put some of your men in our collars, Sirdar, and see how they fare.'

Shere Singh was amused.

'Oh, we shall, Colonel. We shall take them from the English dead.'

'Well, you won't get them any other way.'

With another wave of his arm Shere Singh dismissed the captives. His confidence was not altogether genuine. The Khalsa had shown great resilience in reforming to counter-attack after the British onslaught at Chilianwala. But the red coats had come on time and time again as if they were mad with drink. The Colours of the English regiments had fallen . . . only to be picked up.

A line of earthworks started to rise a few miles from Gujrat. Like Multan it was an ancient city and had been important enough to incur the wrath of the Mongol invaders who had levelled it to the ground. But it had risen again around a fort built by the Emperor Akbar which was turned into a formidable stronghold by the redoubtable Gujar Singh. Unlike Multan it lacked strong outer defences but its approaches were covered by two river beds, one wet and one dry in the spring of 1849. The distance between these watercourses was some three miles and it was there that Shere Singh took his stand and raised his entrenchments. By doing so he forced Gough either to attack him on a narrow front where he could concentrate his artillery, or to cross the river beds. Until such time as the British attacked, the renowned smiths of Gujrat were obliged to ply their tools on the refurbishing of the Khalsa's weapons and equipment.

On February 15 Gough broke camp in front of Chilianwala and marched in battle formation towards Gujrat. Each night he pitched his tents at a different spot as he neared the army of Shere Singh. On February 18 cheering swept through the tents. Whish had arrived. The next day the lean, weather-beaten men of the 60th Rifles swung into camp followed by the 1st Bombay Fusiliers. Behind them, cutting deep furrows in the road, came the heavy cannon.

On the night of the 20th the opposing armies were in sight of each other. Sikh cavalry sentries could hear singing coming from the British tents and the sky was ruddy with the glare of hundreds of camp fires.

'Here y'are, son. Take a drop of this.'

Private Makepiece proffered his bottle and looked blearily round the circle of soldiers clustered before the blazing logs. Green jackets, red coats, blue tunics swam before his eyes.

'Poor bastard,' he said, throwing his arms around a shabby dragoon. 'Yer didn't get no loot, did yer? Yer didn't get nothing in that old jungle fight but bleedin' 'ot lead. An' yer lost yer best mate! 'Ere, stick this where the Company's prize agents won't sniff it out.'

He thrust a handful of rupees into Billy Hacken's calloused hands. A regal wave of the arm dismissed all protests.

'Plenty more where that came from, ain't there, Pat?'

Private Kennedy took a pull from a bottle and threw a crackling thorn bush on the fire so that the sparks flew.

'They searched the rigimint through and through a dozen times. They took the milk and left us with the cream,' he said, smacking his lips.

A concertina began to wheeze out a doleful ditty.

'Aw, for Gawd's sake give us something cheerful,' grumbled Makepiece, swaying.

'Yes, give us a lively 'un,' shouted a young private of the 10th. 'Give us "The British Bayonet" . . .'

A roar of abuse greeted him and a big sergeant of the 29th stepped forward and spoke to the concertina player. A mutter of protest rose again as the squeeze box uttered the first notes of 'The British Bayonet' but it died as the voice began loud and clear:

'They gave me a red coat, they gave me a gun,
They gave me a shillin' and the sergeant told me "Son,
When they give you your medal, to stick upon your chest,
Hoooo! Remember that of all your friends,
The mutton bayonet's best."'

The last line was roared out deafeningly by the crowd around the fire and silence fell again as the rich baritone voice went on:

'A nigger boy told us, "soldier follow me,
My sister costs a rupee, the jig-a-jig is free,"
But the girl cried out "let *me* pay" as I stood in me vest,
Hoooo! Remember that of all your friends,
The mutton bayonet's best!'

The noise came faintly through the glass windows of the Commander-in-Chief's tent.

'Listen to that, gentlemen,' he told his assembled brigadiers. 'The rogues will have their revenge tomorrow. What's that they're singing? "British Bayonets" isn't it?'

Major Mackeson who stood near the window cocked his ear. The words were plain.

'The ladies were weeping, the men had gone to war,
Except Widow Murphy, who jumped up with a roar,
"My dears the sentry's willing, to be put to the test,
Hooooooo!
Of all the friends . . ."'

Mackeson turned and replied stonily:

'Yes, sir. "The British Bayonet" is what they are singing.'

Gough beamed.

'Good. They'll get their chance to use it tomorrow.'

'You got a good voice, Sergeant,' Corporal Baggott called as he rolled up in his blanket. 'Old Julius couldn't have done better himself.'

CHAPTER THIRTY

It was going to be hot. Leiston loosened his stock and wiped his greasy chin on his sleeve. Like the rest of the skirmishers, dark patches of sweat discoloured the back and armpits of his faded red coat. Ahead, across a patchwork of greens and yellows, marking the young crops of the Jat farmers, lay thick brown parapets topped by turbans. They had been clearly visible since the army had mustered at five that morning.

'No dust. They must have been there a while,' he remarked to his neighbour. 'Waiting for us.'

'Thank Christ there's no jungle this time. Those thorns nearly tore me trousers off. Quiet, though, aren't they?'

'Waiting for us to get into range. Shouldn't be long now.'

Behind the lines of skirmishers, a solid mass of men was moving forward, Colours flaunting under the cloudless sky.

'Hello. There it goes.'

A single puff of smoke appeared ahead, followed a split second later by a crack. Bright lights danced down the Sikh trenches which disappeared under a wall of boiling smoke as the rest of the guns chimed in. Whistling, hissing and roaring shells flung up their geysers of rich earth. A smouldering clod rolled at Leiston's feet.

'Steady as you go, boys,' called a voice. 'They're firing short.' But bugles had already called the skirmishers back to leave the way clear for the guns.

'Forward!' Lala Rai was nearly jerked from his perch as the gun jolted through a cactus hedge. He could see gaps all along the battle line as the artillery detached itself. Trumpeting elephants advanced with a stately tread, two to each 'heavy'. Medium pieces were being dragged forward by oxen, whose patient plodding was in marked contrast to the galloping teams pulling the six-pounders. Lala Rai's position with his back to the enemy gave him an excellent Sikh's eye view of the army.

'The fools have opened fire too soon,' he shouted to Mahdo Dinnath. 'They have unmasked their batteries for nothing.'

'Action rear.'

The gun skidded to a halt, the lascars raced for the charges and the teams galloped back.

Lala Rai was right. Fifty years later, at Omdurman, the British colour sergeants carefully marked ranges by hammering stakes into the ground to be traversed by the Dervish horde. The Sikhs at Gujrat neglected this simple precaution. In the clear light the solid British line had appeared, impossible to miss. But it was well beyond range. The Khalsaji watched hypnotised as the stationary British mass heaved and disgorged scores of draught animals towing guns which rumbled, squeaked and jingled over the ground. It was a discordant tuning up before a brutal symphony.

Lord Gough was enjoying the unrestricted view. There were no acacia or tall dhak trees to obscure the enemy; no thorns to slow down the infantry as at Chilianwala. At 9 a.m. Brigadier Tennant, commanding the entire compliment of artillery, got the signal. Deft hands had already seized the clamp handles and twisted the worm so that the muzzles of the big guns had an elevation of five degrees. At just under 1,000 yards they should be out of harm's way and able to inflict the maximum damage. Two degrees were all that the six-pounders needed, having been pushed forward to within five hundred yards of their target.

At Tennant's order a devastating bombardment was unleashed on the Sikh entrenchments and battery positions. Dust, flames and soil formed a thick curtain which jerked and glowed. At the base of the inferno lurid flashes denoted the explosion of missiles from the eight-inch howitzers. Eight of these monsters plus ten long barrelled 18-pounders gave Gough an explosive hammer of unparalleled violence. In the centre of the hurricane, amid collapsing trenches and blasted barricades, the Khalsa's dazed infantry waited. Black pillars shot skywards as limbers and ammunition dumps blew up, but the minutes ticked by and the deluge continued without a sign of slackening.

Gough had ninety-six guns to call upon. Shere Singh had fifty-nine. All added their brazen clamour to the uproar at once. While the artillery battle raged, fragments broke away from the snowclouds on the Sikh wings. The cavalry advanced under blue, red and gold banners to attempt to relieve the pressure on the infantry.

Billy Hacken, with the 3rd Light Dragoons on the British left, neck-reined his horse as the bay squadron turned and trotted back to take up position behind the waiting greys. The whole regiment was retiring by squadrons as the enemy flank attack developed.

'Come on, you bastards. Come on and get it.'

His hands tightened on the sharkskin grip of his sword. A horse-drawn battery was advancing with the Sikhs. He saw it unlimber and the gunners lift the heavy balls to the muzzles.

'Going to make a hole in us and let their sowars charge through it,' he informed his left hand man. 'Well, they've got another think coming to them.'

As the gunners put a match to the first touch-hole a field of young corn sprouted a new crop of black shakos and green jackets. The heavy Brunswick rifles of the 60th roared out and the ambushed gunners crashed to the ground as the belted bullets tore into them. Plunging horses scattered with toppling riders and falling lances as the 60th switched its fire to the cavalry. The 3rd Light Dragoons trotted forward and spiked the guns. Out of the smoke staggered a wounded Sikh officer clutching his arm.

'Sorry, matey, but you might shoot someone's napper off if I let you get better,' said Private Hacken running his sword through him.

On the other wing, the Afghan horse were finding it difficult to come to grips with the enemy. The British cavalry advanced, threatened, charged and retired like robots.

'Are these, then, the jackals who ran at Chilianwala?' asked Akram Khan, son of Dost Mahommed, riding at the head of 1,500 horsemen. 'They are not fleeing today. Even when we strike at their rear they come back at us. Now they threaten ours.'

Mallindine, at the head of his troop, was hoarse from shouting orders. They had hardly crossed swords with the enemy but had spent most of their time manoeuvring and feinting. He and Jameson had spent the previous night superintending the wrapping of yards of muslin around their shakos so that the material hung down their backs. Jameson and other officers had assured him it was an excellent way of guarding against the 'caput' or chop delivered by the gorchurras at the back of the head when opposing horsemen crossed. Someone had revealed that even Paddy Gough had a stout leather protector sewn under the sun flap of his fighting cap for that very reason. All the same, Mallindine felt rather foolish.

From the roof of a house behind the trenches, Shere Singh saw his defences pulverised. One by one his cannon had been dismounted and the carriages smashed into splinters by spinning, fizzing howitzer shells and screaming solid shot. Partly deafened by the bedlam, it took him some time to realise that the British fire was slackening.

'Look! Here they come.'

Shere Singh stared through his glass at a brick red wall lurching ominously through the smoke. A bayonet glinted where the sun struck through the murk.

'There must be six miles of them,' growled an old chieftain. 'It is well that we have two surprises still in store.'

The soil was soft and reeking of burnt powder. Cannon balls littered the fields and the advancing skirmishers had to avoid their own gunners limbering up after their labours. Leiston saw two silent villages looming dark through the drifting smoke on his right. His own men were mingling with the Rajputs from the 31st Bengal Infantry. The villages were more their concern than his and he headed for the battery positions straight ahead, pausing frequently to fire. A staff officer galloped behind him and advanced with the Rajputs, cheering them on. They swerved and, shouting 'Raj . . . Raj . . .' started to run towards Bara Kalra, the nearest village. Like a combustible material that has been smouldering for some time it burst into flame, stabbing fire from scores of loopholes in the walls. The advancing Rajputs staggered under the onslaught then went on, leaving the ground strewn with moaning wounded and sprawled dead. With a roar the twin village of Chota Kalra became wreathed in smoke and the 10th Foot, veterans of Multan, absorbed another volley. An officer halted Leiston's section and ordered them to concentrate on Sikh sharpshooters in the villages who were picking off the gunners of a nine-pounder troop one after the other. Obediently the men of the 29th opened fire but as Leiston put it 'we may as well be armed with broomsticks at this range.' Dead horses now littered the gun position. More were brought up at a gallop along with fresh gunners.

General Gilbert rode scowling up to the colonel of the 2nd Bengal Europeans.

'Officers to the front!' went the cry. 'Lead your men!'

The Europeans doubled forward cheering, carrying the Rajputs with them, and burst into the village streets. The 10th Foot secured a hold in Chota Kalra and a vicious battle ensued in which the Sikhs, the cream of the Khalsa, barricaded the doors of the mud huts. A splintering of wood and crackling of musketry told listeners the villages were being cleared.

From Bara Kalra the Sikhs retreated sullenly but in good order. Then they saw what a toll they had taken of the attackers and returned to the fight. A killing match of volleys began in which the Bengal Fusiliers and Rajputs benefitted from the Sikh tendency to fire high. Rounds of canister from the nine-pounder battery put an end to the contest. As the Sikhs streamed back from the village their own horse gunners opened fire on both sides indiscriminately. But the spine of the Khalsa was cracked. In an effort to cover the retreat, the cavalry launched one last attack on the British left.

Lala Rai and Mahdo Dinnath worked like demons preparing the charges for their six-pounder. The Red Men fired half a dozen rapid rounds at the Sikh horse and then the gun fell silent. Lala Rai looked round and gasped with relief.

The red and white pennons of the 9th Lancers and the Sind Horse were coming fluttering down to the charge. He could hear the shrill cries and whoops as they surged across the fields. With a splintering crash they were among the leading enemy and the rest did not wait. Individuals were already drifting away. Groups came hurrying after them. The lancers rallied and watched the Sikhs split up and disperse. The infantry too had begun to dissolve. Disintegration followed. The approaches to Gujrat became a seething mass of fugitives throwing down their arms and equipment so they could run faster. Blue turbans, yellow turbans, red tunics, white robes, all swirled helplessly in front of a four-mile line of cavalrymen now in pursuing order, three yards apart. Here and there a white bearded Sikh chief flung up his shield, wheeled his horse and rushed upon his enemies yelling his war cry. Lances dipped, sabres flashed and the wave of snorting horses, creaking harness and cold-eyed men closed over the debris.

The path of the 29th led them over demolished earthworks, shattered wheels and abandoned guns around which lay the corpses of men and horses. Beyond were the Sikh tents and baggage. And still the cursing officers urged their men on.

'Keep them on the run, my boys. You don't want to do it again, do you?'

Many Sikhs had taken refuge in the trees. Leiston brought one tumbling down with a shot and a cry of: 'Out of it, you silly sod.'

Finishing off the man with the bayonet he muttered: 'You should have run for it. We're not bothering with prisoners today.'

Lord Gough rode behind his victorious troops beaming, waving his hat to cheer them on. His leg was bleeding from a graze caused by a spent shell fragment, but he felt overjoyed.

'Make sure you don't let them get their breath,' he told his staff. 'Run them off their legs. Gallop until the cavalry drop. And gallop some more.'

For mile after mile the fugitives looked back only to see the dread horsemen, lance pennons now stiff with blood, coming after them.

For many infantrymen events had been less exciting.

'Divil me bones, but it's a poor sort of a battle when you finish up the day as badly off as ye started,' groused Private Kennedy as the 32nd, having suffered only half a dozen casualties, pitched camp under the strict supervision of their officers.

'Never mind, Pat,' retorted Makepiece soothingly. He looked wistfully at the inviting dome of the shrine of the revered saint Shah Daula and added: 'There'll be other places.'

In Gough's headquarters the brandy and wine flowed freely. This was no wake as at Chilianwala. Of the 24,000 men he had put into the field only 96 had been killed – 29 of them gunners – and less than 1,000 had been wounded. And he had scattered an army of 50,000 taking all their artillery.

Limping about the camp with his silver hair shining, the old man made a joke of the fact that the provost marshal was among the wounded. Jokes apart, he could not wait to get off his despatch. It would reveal that three British regiments, one of them the 24th Foot, had not lost a single man amongst them.

Gough did not commit his troops to Gujrat that night but pitched his camp outside the town where the cavalry returned exhausted during the evening, some having ridden fifteen and more miles after the enemy before drawing rein. As Mallindine rode in he was told that the pursuit was to be resumed the following morning. The 14th Light Dragoons would be in the van. He ordered his second charger to be saddled in readiness and told his orderly to bring him something to drink. Gingerly he put his hand to his neck and felt the tender spot where an Afghan sword had trimmed the muslin neatly but failed to cut through the quilted neck flap. He would buy Jameson a dozen of champagne when they returned to cantonments again.

CHAPTER THIRTY-ONE

The familiar hills drew nearer and Mirza Khan, the one-eared Eusafzai, felt the air to be cleaner. Trotting down a stony track towards the Khyber, he took a deep breath and began to laugh. He laughed until the tears rolled down his cheeks into his red beard. The idea of the mighty Khalsa and the braggart horsemen of Dost Mahommed being chased out of the Punjaub and into the hills by the red-faced, stiff-legged, pot-bellied British generals with their wooden, swine-eating soldiers, struck him as being a joke of immense proportions. Only seven years previously he had helped to harry the red coats up and down the passes and seen the men with 44 on their helmets die at Gandamak. True the British had returned to Kabul and blown up the Bala Hissar, but they had lost face on the frontier. No self-respecting tribesmen took them really seriously. And now here they were like wolves at the heels of a herd of sheep. He, Mirza Khan, had been lucky to escape with a sword wound in his buttock at Gujrat, although the feringhee officer's neck must bear his mark. Truly this was rich. The Sikhs had always boasted they had legs of iron and yet the Engrese soldiers had marched for three days after the battle and hardly stopped for breath. He shook with mirth. These English were strange people. One had to make fools of them before they could be stirred into life and then . . . the memory of the plain covered with fleeing Sikh soldiers proved too much for him and he threw back his head and let his laughter have full rein. He would come back and take service with these English when things settled down and the hounds had been called off.

At the head of the pursuit rode Sir Walter Gilbert, much to the disgust of General Thackwell. Thackwell was the senior officer and during his career had been General of Cavalry of the Armies of the Indus, of Gwalior and of the Sutlej. But Gough had not forgotten his hesitation after Maharajpore or Saddulapore. Instead Gilbert, famed steeplechaser and flat-race rider in his earlier years, was given the job of harrying the fugitives. And Thackwell, the 'Old Sabreur' could sulk as much as he liked. The Sikhs had to be given no rest.

Sikh infantry travelled light. Their tents went on pack horses along with their cooking pots. Relying on sturdy legs and powerful physique the remnants of the Khalsa tramped speedily along the road to Peshawar, stronghold of Chattar Singh, governor of the city and surrounding province. Behind them came Gilbert's seemingly tireless cavalry and the dogged red coats.

In the ranks of the 29th, Corporal Baggott swung along easily, his spare frame having lost even the memory of any rare surplus fat. He held his musket by the muzzle with the butt comfortably over his shoulder.

'I suppose we'll start coming down some day,' he complained gloomily. 'Or else we'll get lost in the mountains and freeze. Not that what I couldn't do with some of that there snow.'

Distant peaks gleamed frostily on the parched columns.

'How're your boots doing, Jasper?'

Leiston had begun to have an obsession with boots. The corporal decided to humour him nevertheless.

'They're wonders, absolute wonders, Sergeant. I'll always have them cobbled with paper in future. It helps you to get the feel of the pebbles on the road better.'

'Wouldn't make no difference if you had no boots at all,' grunted a voice. 'This old bastard is going to wear our legs down to the ankle before he lets up.'

'Never mind,' said Leiston. 'Think of all the batta the Company will dish up. Ye can get drunk for a week.'

'I'd rather have a drink of Adam's Ale right now than all the bleedin' batta in the world. I hope to Christ there are some decent wells ahead. That last one . . .'

They'd had to hold their breath while, lungs bursting, they hauled up battered buckets full of stinking black fluid.

'I reckon there was dead Sikhs down that 'ole.'

'Maybe.'

'Did yer see them wounded sowars.'

'Yeah. And they was half mad with bhang, when I found 'em.'

''Ow'd yer know?'

'Their eyes was staring and the black bits in the middle was like tiny points. Poor bastards had both been run through by lancers. That bhang stops 'em feelin' the pain. They was stuffin' it in their mouths like good 'uns.'

'Wot d'yer do?'

The soldier made a rasping noise and drew his finger questioningly across his throat.

'Nah. I got out that pesh-kabz I picked up at Chilian, but I thought, what the 'ell? The Sikhs are sendin' our prisoners back now. So I stuck it back in me belt. I think I'll chuck it away. It's bleedin' 'eavy.'

Corporal Baggott pulled out a large knife with a bone handle.

'If you don't want it, I'll have that, Jasper. Sort of keepsake of the campaign.'

Baggott handed Leiston the knife.

'Reckon I'll put my corns and blisters under a glass case like wax fruit to remind me of the Punjaub,' he added. 'That ways I can warn my grandchildren against joining the infantry. An 'oss soldier I'd be, if I 'ad my time again.'

But the cavalry had blisters too. In other places.

'I shall never ride anywhere ever again except in The Row when we return to England,' said Jameson. 'My backside is like leather and I've callouses like walnuts on the inside of me knees. Just how long, pray, does Sir Walter think a gentleman can go without a change of linen? Unless the camels come up tonight I shall begin to smell like the men.'

'Could be worse,' remarked Mallindine. 'You could smell like the camels.'

'Damn. What is it now?'

Bugles brought the column to a halt. Horsemen could be seen on a nearby hill-top. Presently a squadron of irregular cavalry raised a cloud of dust as they disappeared towards the mouth of a ravine. Within an hour word went round that Shere Singh had come to surrender, bringing British hostages with him.

As dusk fell thunder roared through the inhospitable peaks of Hazara and Kashmir. Leiston huddled in a rain-battered tent checking equipment by fitful candles and the baleful blue glare of lightning.

'What's it all in aid of, anyway, Sergeant?'

'Old Shere Singh's bringing in his men to surrender to-morrow.'

'Balls to Shere Singh. And his daddy.'

'Tell that to the colonel. He says he wants the 29th to look like soldiers, not chimney sweeps. Right. Let's see those packs.'

A glistening shako pushed through the tent flap.

'Sergeant Leiston to report to the main guard.'

Leiston threw a tarpaulin across his shoulders and squeezed out into the storm. He found Mallindine waiting for him.

'Evening, Sergeant.'

'Good evening, sir.'

Mallindine looked a deal better since he had last seen him. Harder altogether.

'I tried to get in touch with you before Gujrat, but it wasn't possible. I saw the 29th were near, so I took the opportunity to call in and say that I have had news from home which concerns you.'

'Very good of you, sir.'

'Well, I'm afraid it's bad news, really.'

Leiston wondered what Mallindine considered bad news. He couldn't think of anything that might cause him to lose a wink of sleep.

'I had a letter from home a month ago telling me that there has been an outbreak of fever at Cleadon. I'm afraid your wife and eldest sister have died.'

Mallindine paused for a few seconds.

'General Mallindine died too.'

He added as an afterthought: 'And some of the Portuguese.'

'It sounds a very sad affair, sir.'

'Yes . . . I'm sorry about Miss . . . er . . . your wife, and your sister.'

'And I must offer my sympathy on the death of the general, sir. Must have been getting on.'

The big sergeant stood looking thoughtfully at the dragoon.

'Funny, isn't it, sir? We come out here and go traipsing all over India, where folk are dying all the time of sunstroke, plague and cholera and the like. Others never stray from their own county and die of fever. The women at Home Farm, I mean.'

A brilliant flash lit the tent and thunder boomed overhead.

'I suppose the funeral and all that was taken care of?'

'Yes, your father saw to that.'

'I suppose he's *your* bailiff now, sir.'

'Yes. He is indeed.'

Mallindine came out awkwardly with what had been on his mind.

'If you can arrange to return home, there'll be a job for you too.'

The words sounded a bit lame.

'I mean . . . your father must be a fair age.'

Leiston looked honestly taken aback.

'Oh, I don't rightly know that, sir. About going back.'

'You have other plans? Well, let me know if there is anything.'

'Thank you, sir. I've one or two things to sort out. But, with your permission, I'd better get back to the men.'

'Carry on, Sergeant.'

'Good night, sir.'

Back in the tent, Leiston threw his tarpaulin in one corner and resumed his kit check.

'Let's hope we have some fair weather for the surrender tomorrow,' he said to no one in particular.

The march the following day took the 29th through a pleasant valley of cornfields and orchards. Peach and apple blossom flecked the lower slopes of the hills which were carpeted with dandelions and purple, aromatic heather. At the top of a steep pass a row of guns had been drawn up as the first token of formal surrender. Polished brass 18-pounders shone like gold. Inviting storm-washed roofs appeared and a troop of dragoons went clattering past the infantry towards them. Word came down the column that the town was Rawal Pindi. On the plain in front of it a mass of cavalry was assembled. The Khalsa was gathering to capitulate.

There were twenty thousand of them and they walked their horses before the assembled British in twos and threes, proud men, descendants of the tough old Sikhs who had taken to the hills rather than give way to the Moguls. Many of them had lived through the great days of Runjit, when the Khalsa held the lands from Kashmir to Peshawar and down to the gates of Delhi itself. Now, before the assembled British, each warrior laid down his arms, metal shields which had been in the same family for generations, long matchlocks, spears and muskets. As the procession continued the pile grew.

'They look half-starved to me,' said Jameson. 'It's just as well they can keep their horses. They'd never walk back to their homes.'

A white-bearded chief on a fine mare dismounted, unbuckled his sword, kissed it and laid it reverently on the ground. There were tears in his eyes. Then he rode away erectly, ignoring the rupee which each Sikh was given as he handed over his arms.

'Now, there,' said Jameson, 'goes a gentleman.'

'Aj Ranjit Singh mar gaya!' the old man said clearly as he trotted past. 'Aj Ranjit Singh mar gaya!'

'What was that, Daly?' asked Jameson, turning to a bearded infantry adjutant.

'He says that Ranjit Singh died today.'

'But he died ten years ago.'

'Not really,' replied Daly.

'Oh. I see what you mean,' replied Jameson, although he was not altogether certain.

By dusk the pile of surrendered weapons was more than ten feet high and covered many square yards.

The formal surrender later at Wazirabad, when Shere Singh and his father placed themselves in the hands of Lord Gough, was a more ceremonial affair. The two chiefs appeared on horseback followed by elephants with magnificent howdahs. Chattar Singh wore fine gold spectacles for the occasion. But even though the scowling escort were required to hand over their weapons to a dafadar, it was agreed by officers present that it was nothing compared with Rawal Pindi.

And so peace returned to the Land of the Five Rivers. Lord Dalhousie, unable to get any instructions from England on what to do with the leaderless nation, annexed it. He also added the famous Koh-i-noor Diamond to the possessions of the East India Company, an act which did not seem like looting at all – it had been stolen by Persians and Afghans before he got his hands on it.

This new acquisition attained complete respectability when it was presented to Queen Victoria to shine on in the Crown Jewels long after the Indian Empire had vanished. But in 1849 The Raj was merely beginning. Political agents, engineers and surveyors were returning once again to the Punjaub to sweat out their lives in a mixture of spartan discomfort and torrid luxury, preparing the way for the railroads and the canals.

The Governor-General found the arrival of Sir Charles Napier in India somewhat embarrassing, as the general had been instructed to take over from the Commander-in-Chief immediately upon his arrival. Diplomatically Napier procrastinated until the Victor of Gujrat could resign with dignity. Dalhousie compounded this discretion by laying down that Lord Gough should be accorded the honours due to a commander-in-chief until he departed for home.

In England more honours came Gough's way. Parliament voted him a pension and he was made a viscount. But he regarded as an even greater honour the tribute paid to him at a dinner in the United Services Club in Pall Mall. There the Duke of Wellington, no less, made a speech in which he described Gough as 'affording the brightest example of the highest qualities of the British soldier'.

The other ranks themselves spent the ill-gotten gains of Multan and the lesser pickings of Gujrat on riotous living, drink cutting them down as savagely as case shot. They noted sardonically that within two months of Gujrat the ex-soldiers of the Khalsa were being put into British uniform in great numbers.

CHAPTER THIRTY-TWO

The iron-shod wheels crunched on the macadam, blending soothingly with the steady clack of the horse's hoofs. The carrier tried hard to make out the expression of his passenger, but as he was slumped and the soldier sat bolt upright, all he got was a close up of stripes and embroidery.

'What's the flag fer, Sergeant?' he asked after they had proceeded in silence down the curving lane past Cleadon Grange.

'Bein' a bastard . . .' said a voice from behind.

'Watch your language, Witham. They're not used to barrack-room talk here.'

The voice was hard but there was no venom in it. A grunt answered from a second soldier perched uncomfortably on the tail of the cart.

'Colour Sergeant! I look after a half-company,' the hard voice continued by way of explanation.

'Ho! You're sort of in charge, are you?'

'Not sort of. I am in charge.'

The trio proceeded in silence past a park wall. Slate roofs came into view beyond oaks and elms, drab in the damp autumn afternoon.

'Who lives there nowadays?'

'The Grange? Oh, that's old General Mallindine's place. Least, it was. His niece lives there now with one or two of the family. Rightly it belongs to Colonel Mallindine, I believe, though he's away soldiering most of the time. Hoss soldier, I hear tell.'

'Stop just beyond the bend, if you please. I'll walk from here. Witham! See our kit into the Limeburner's Arms and tell 'em we're used to good rations. I'll inspect the quarters when I get there.'

Hobnailed boots stamped out a truculent challenge to the quiet hedges as Leiston shook the creases from his thick serge trousers. He squared his shoulders, hitched his pipe-clayed belt and strode up the drive to Home Farm. There were weeds in the gravel and the ditches were partly overgrown. Fences had a patched appearance. But if the farm had become unkempt the house had been transformed. It stood spick and span in marked contrast to its surroundings. Instinctively Leiston headed for the back door but deliberately switched his track to the front entrance. He had banged hard on the knocker before he noticed a polished brass bell pull.

'Yes?'

A rosy-cheeked parlour maid stood looking at him in amazement. It was obvious she was not used to seeing soldiers standing on the step.

'I wonder if I might trouble Mrs. Leiston to spare me a moment?'

He was beginning to wonder if it was such a good idea, after all, to arrive unannounced.

'Well, I don't know . . .'

The maid was flustered.

'Come along. Jump to it, my girl.'

His doubts put an edge into his voice and the girl vanished mumbling, returning a few moments later to show him into a room which he could not remember. A piano, fine carpets, a blue velvet tablecloth . . . things had changed. He picked up a photograph from the mantelpiece, framed in heavy silver filigree.

'Who is it, Ethel? Who? Oh, you silly girl, come out of the way.'

A stout woman, with a questioning frown on her flushed face appeared at the door. As he caught sight of her in the mirror, Leiston's eyes narrowed and he froze. When he did move it was to brush his thick moustache defensively. The woman too was transfixed. Disbelief was written all over her face.

'It . . . it . . .'

He swung around, erect and cool again.

'I didn't expect to see you either,' he said simply. 'They told me you were dead . . . of the fever that killed the general.'

As the woman swayed he caught her arm and pulled out a chair for her. As she sat down he noted that although her thick hair was streaked with grey, Miss Howick was still quite a comely woman.

'What do you want?'

'I don't know now. We were drumming up recruits in the county and I thought I'd come over and see my mother.'

A limp hand gestured.

'She died during the epidemic. When the servants at The Grange became ill, she went to nurse the general. He wouldn't have anyone else near him in the end. She died about a week after him.'

The woman shut her eyes. But when she opened them whatever she hoped to banish was still there.

'What about Father?'

'He lives with your sister over at Hetherington.'

Leiston looked round the room and out of the window.

'Who looks after all this, then?'

'I do.' The voice was aggressive. 'It's mine now. General Mallindine left it on trust to me. When I pass over it goes to Ralph.'

'Ralph?'

'My son . . .'

'Oh!' Leiston picked up the photograph.

'Soldier?'

'Sandhurst. It was the general's doing. He took to him when he was very small. He said that Ralph was the only child in the family who looked like a Mallindine. The general had him at The Grange a lot.'

'What did you tell the boy about his father?'

'I said he had been killed in India. We heard that you went there some time after you left home.'

Leiston chuckled wryly.

'Aye, I was out there all right. But I was only half killed.'

The gap between them filled with silence. Only the high colour of the woman and the slight quiver of the lips betrayed her anxiety. The mahogany complexion of the man gave away nothing.

'Who else lives here?'

'The maids. The bailiff has one cottage and the hind has the other.'

Leiston waited.

'Then, of course, Ralph stays here sometimes when he is on leave, although he spends a lot of time at The Grange.'

The woman's hands fluttered at the jet beads around her throat. Black bombazine suited her, thought Leiston.

'So you've plenty of room?'

'Yes . . . I mean no. We have visitors . . .'

Leiston indulged in a little mild cruelty.

'So you could put me up for a few days.'

A stifled shriek greeted his sally.

'I thought as much,' he said. 'A fine homecoming for a husband, to be sure.'

'You can't stay here,' she replied defiantly, clasping her hands firmly in her lap and sitting up straight without looking at him. 'I'm a respectable widow.'

'Hmm. You'll find me a lively corpse.'

A note of panic entered her voice.

'What do you mean by that?'

Leiston's mind was made up. He pulled out another chair and sat down beside her.

'I'll tell you. I've spent the last twenty years following the Colours. I've seen the world and if I'd been free, I could have married a dozen times over. Widows don't last long in a regiment or they go off the strength. Soon, however, I shall be finished soldiering. And when I'm done with it, I shall be looking for somewhere to settle down. Now, if I were a single man, I should marry – for I have a little nest egg. But as I'm not, I shall return here, Mrs. Leiston.'

The woman reeled and he caught her.

'Steady, woman. I'm a fair man, you'll find. And tidy too. You could do with someone to see to the farm by the looks of it.'

'Ralph . . .' she whimpered. 'What about poor dear Ralph?'

'Aye. We shall have to think of something to tell him. But it should not be above the wit of man. I tell you what. You shall say I'm a cousin of your poor dead husband and that I have been abroad most of my life. We shall pretend to wed while he is away.'

'But he is to be an officer.'

'Then we shan't have much difficulty in deceiving him. I've been doing it for twenty years.'

One last furious note of defiance sounded.

'I will not allow this.'

Her nostrils flared and the plump cheeks shook.

Leiston stood up.

'You're a fine looking woman,' he said calmly. 'Despite the fact of being on the wrong side of forty. I'll spend tonight at the Limeburner's, but my kit will be moved in tomorrow.'

The figure in black wilted in defeat.

'I'll need a room for my corporal – see if the bailiff can put him up – and you'd better put me across the landing from your room. We've a lot to talk about before I go back to the depot. That'll be at the weekend. So you'll need to draw extra rations. Now then, where did you say my mother was buried?'

Leiston left the grave by the yew and walked into the church. It seemed much smaller than he remembered it. Everything did, for that matter. He walked slowly up the nave with his shako held in the crook of his arm. Then he saw what he was looking for and crossed to a small chapel. A bust stared back at him from above a coffin-shaped relief set in the wall. The blank marble eyes were as arrogant as ever. They'd even got the hard thin mouth right. Leiston strained to read the inscription in the gloom. Cut into a bronze plaque, freely engraved with a frieze of drums, Colours, laurels and cannon, were the words:

'Sacred to the Memory of General Sir Ephraim Augustus Murdo Mallindine, C.B., Justice of the Peace, who departed this life on October 4, 1849, aged 78. At Vimeira, Busaco, Talavera and Salamanca, and on many famous battlefields he did not flinch in the service of his country. As an administrator in foreign climes he did not spare himself. To this parish he was a benefactor. Sic Transit Gloria Mundi.'

Been at Talavera, had he. Leiston wondered whether Sir Ehpraim had witnessed the 29th's evening battle for the hill. The old devil had seen a deal of blood spilled in his time. Automatically he reached out a hand to a marble epaulette. Dust. He sniffed and wondered what Sir Ephraim would have said if he had lived to see Eldred married to a parson's daughter who rode like a dragoon.

As he passed the ugly cut-stone font on the way out a half hidden door opened and a tall pale man with straggling mutton-chop whiskers appeared.

'Good day . . . er . . . Sergeant. Can I help you? It is not often we get a military man here.'

'Good day to you, sir. No, I've seen what I came to see. In the chapel there . . .'

'Oh, you mean the Mallindine Chapel. Yes, it's a very good likeness, I'm told, although I hardly knew him. I don't think I ever saw him in church. But then he was already old when I came here.'

The vicar put his head on one side and peered reprovingly in the direction of the bust.

'Did you know him, Sergeant?'

'I had some dealings with him years ago. I was just curious.'

'Yes. I see.'

The vicar sounded vaguely disappointed.

'Well, I'd better be going, sir. If you'll excuse me . . .'

'I'm so pleased you saw what you wanted, Sergeant. And it is a good likeness of the general, is it?'

Leiston paused outside the porch to replace his shako.

'They've missed one thing, sir. The scar across the bridge of his nose.'

He adjusted his hat to give it the merest hint of a tilt.

'Sabre slash, I believe,' he added, turning on his heel.

Susannah Leiston stood at the window looking out across the meadow. She could just glimpse the occasional flash of scarlet through the trees as the dog-cart made for the gate. Even with the proof before her eyes she found it difficult to believe the events of the past three days.

'Pardon me, Mum, but what shall I do with this? The sergeant left it in his room.'

The maid held out a sheathed knife with a large bone handle. Engraved on it were the words: 'Taken by Corporal Jasper Baggott, Her Majesty's 29th Foot, at Chilianwala, January 13th, 1849.'

'Shall I send Giles to run across the fields with it?'

The maid waited while her mistress turned the weapon over in her hands.

'I shouldn't bother, Ethel,' she replied. 'He'll be back.' Her voice dropped almost to a whisper as she stared across the fields. 'Oh, the sergeant will be back, all right!'

The furore caused by the disaster at Chilianwala did not last long. The arguments continued only until the blunders of the Crimean War eclipsed it five years later. True, Lord Gough subsequently described the 'bayonets only' order as 'an act of madness' and conceded that it would have been sensible of the 24th to have 'put in a volley or two' before the charge.

True, an obelisk was erected by the British Government, bearing the names of the dead, which the rains did their best to erase each season. Not that it mattered to the dead. They had learned the hard way that soldiering is not all glory. And that what glory there is flourishes but briefly. It took only seconds for the ripples to close over the muddy grave where Private Connelly lies to this day wrapped in the Queen's Colour of the 24th Foot.

REGIMENTS OF THE GRAND ARMY OF THE PUNJAUB

3RD THE KING'S OWN LIGHT DRAGOONS. Raised in 1685 during the Monmouth rebellion they became the 'King's Own' in 1742. The following year they nearly lost their standard when it was seized during heavy fighting at Dettingen. It was being carried to the French rear when Trooper Thomas Brown's horse bolted with him through the enemy ranks. There, although his bridle arm was disabled, Brown cut down the Frenchman, seized the trophy, and charged back to his regiment, jamming the staff of the flag between one leg and the saddle. Although they took part in the Peninsular War, the 3rd developed their great reputation in India. They earned the title 'Mudki Wallahs' for their stubborn behaviour in that battle during the First Sikh War, and the charge of their grey squadron at Chilianwala may well have saved the day. It is interesting to compare that action with El Alamein in 1942 when the 3rd Hussars (they dropped the dragoon title in 1861) charged Rommel's gun line in 'Operation Supercharge'. The regiment amalgamated with the 7th in 1958 to become The Queen's Own Hussars.

9TH LANCERS. Although they were raised as dragoons in 1715, became light dragoons in 1783 and lancers in 1816, the regiment had seen only limited active service (in the Peninsula) before the Sikh Wars. From 1846 onwards, however, they were seldom missing from the battlefields of India and Afghanistan and were in the forefront during the Boer War. During the First World War, after a costly rearguard action at Mons, the regiment did much of its fighting on foot in France until mounted action became possible late in 1918.

At El Alamein in 1942 their tanks fought in the same desperate break-out battle as the 3rd Hussars with whom they were brigaded at Gujrat almost 100 years earlier. The title 9th Queen's Royal Lancers, which they had used for many years, became official in 1920. In 1960 they became part of a joint regiment, the 9th/12th Royal Lancers.

14TH THE KING'S LIGHT DRAGOONS. Raised as dragoons in 1715, they did not receive a number until they became light horse in 1776. In honour of the marriage of the Princess Royal of Prussia to the Duke of York they were given the title of the 14th (Duchess of York's Own) in 1798, and adopted the badge of the Prussian eagle crowned and holding orb and sceptre. This was dropped in 1915 but restored in 1931 as the badge of the 14th/20th King's Hussars. The regiments had amalgamated ten years earlier.

Although they were employed on home service until the Peninsular War, the 14th served as Wellington's workhorses throughout the campaign. They saw no more active service until the Second Sikh War. After the unhappy affair at Chilianwala the regiment went on to become one of the crack units in India, giving outstanding service during the rigorous but little publicised campaign in Central India during the Mutiny. During the First World War they fought in the gruelling Mesopotamian theatre and were in action in Kurdistan as the war ended. In the Second World War they won three battle honours in Italy.

10TH FOOT. Stalwarts from Marlborough's day, when they fought at Schellenburg, Blenheim, Ramillies, Oudenarde and Malplaquet, the 10th did not see spectacular service again until the Sikh Wars when they played an important part in the victory of Sobraon in February 1846. At Multan and Gujrat they continued the struggle which ended in the annexation of the Punjaub. According to legend a soldier of the 10th who looted a jewelled sword hilt at Multan got so tired of being pursued by the East India Company's prize agents that in the end he threw it down a well at Lahore. Despite their more notable service in Egypt at Atbara and Omdurman, in 1898, their Sphinx badge refers to the 10th Foot's service in the Suez expedition of 1801. During the First World War the regiment, which became the Lincolnshire Regiment in 1881, served in France from Mons to the end of hostilities. The 'Royal' title was given for services in the Second World War. They are now merged in the Royal Anglian Regiment.

24TH FOOT. The 1st Battalion was raised in 1688 and fought under Marlborough at Blenheim, Ramillies, Oudenarde and Malplaquet. The 2nd Battalion, raised in 1804, promptly added eight Peninsular battles to the list, before being temporarily disbanded. Within thirty years of the fierce fighting in the Second Sikh War both battalions found themselves involved in the desperate campaign against the Zulus when 555 officers and men were killed at Isandhlwana, the majority of them serving with the 1st. Seven V.C.s were won by the 2nd at Rorke's Drift. Although the 1st Battalion originated in Kent and the 2nd in Warwickshire, they had recruited for some years in Brecon and in 1881 became the 1st and 2nd South Wales Borderers. During the First World War the 1st Battalion played a notable role at Ypres in 1914 holding the line at Gheluvelt Chateau until a charge by the 2nd Worcestershire threw back the Germans. The 2nd Battalion served throughout the war with the crack 29th Division. Both battalions saw severe fighting during the Second World War, the 1st in the desert and the 2nd in Norway and Normandy. In 1969, on amalgamation with the Welch Regiment, they became part of the Royal Regiment of Wales.

29TH FOOT. Wellington described the regiment in 1809 as 'the best in this army' and they went on to live up to their name throughout the Peninsular campaign. Raised in 1689 by a Coldstream Guards colonel – hence the similar badge, a Star with the Garter – the 29th had a varied career, serving under Marlborough at Ramillies, being concerned with the unsavoury riots in Boston in 1770 and supplying sharpshooters for six men o' war at the naval battle known as The Glorious First of June. After the Napoleonic Wars, the 29th went through both Sikh wars with great distinction. In 1881 it became the 1st Battalion the Worcestershire Regiment, the 36th Foot becoming the 2nd Battalion. During the First World War the 1st Worcestershires served in the 8th Division and during the great German offensives in 1918 played a notable part in holding the enemy. In the Second World War the direct descendants of the 29th were overwhelmed at the fall of Tobruk but reformed to take part in the invasion of Europe. The regiment amalgamated with the Sherwood Foresters to become the Worcestershire and Sherwood Foresters Regiment in 1968.

32ND FOOT. With a fighting history going back to 1704, when they took part in the capture of Gibraltar, the regiment can claim to bear some of the most illustrious battle honours on their colours. They lost 350 men, killed and wounded, at Quatre Bras and Waterloo, and after taking a leading role in the Second Sikh War, were the mainstay of the garrison at Lucknow during the Indian Mutiny when they lost 198 men killed alone. As a tribute to their conduct during the 87 days of the siege they were designated light infantry. In 1881 the 32nd and 46th (South Devon) Foot became the 1st and 2nd Battalions of the Duke of Cornwall's Light Infantry. The 1st D.C.L.I. were among the first British troops in action in August 1914 and served in France throughout the First World War. In the Second World War it served in the famous 10th Indian Division, winning fresh honours in the desert and Italy. The Cornwalls merged with Somerset to become the Somerset and Cornwall Light Infantry in 1959 (thus amalgamating two regiments which served in Gibraltar in 1704). In 1968 both were absorbed into the new Light Infantry Division.

60TH RIFLES. Originally raised as the 62nd Foot in 1755 they became the 60th Royal Americans two years later when a corps based on the American Ranger system was required. At first this meant discarding unnecessary and cumbersome equipment and training as light infantry, but in 1797 a battalion was clothed in green and by May, 1815, all eight battalions of the regiment were in dark green uniforms and armed with rifles. The presence of the 60th gave a decided advantage to Wellington during the Peninsular War, Napoleon having forbidden the use of rifles on the ground that they took too long to load. Unlike line regiments the 60th did not carry their battle honours on their Colours but on their Maltese Cross badge. They became the King's Royal Rifle Corps in the 1881 reorganization and are now the 2nd Royal Green Jackets.

61ST FOOT. Although they had seen service earlier in the West Indies, the 61st earned their high reputation under Wellington in the Peninsula. At Talavera they suffered heavily and they had the highest casualties of any regiment at Salamanca. This did not keep them from sharing in the battles through the Pyrenees and the sanguinary clash at Toulouse. After their stout service in the Second Sikh War they proved themselves to be outstanding at Delhi during the Indian Mutiny. In 1881 they became the 2nd Battalion the Gloucestershire Regiment, being linked with the 28th Foot. Ypres was the scene of dogged resistance by the battalion in 1915 and they repeated their achievement at Cassel, also in Flanders, in 1940. The lineal descendants of the 61st were back in France on D Day. Combined with the 1st Battalion they were thus involved in the Imjin River battle in the Korean War. At the time of writing the 28th/61st amalgamation is still in existence as the Gloucestershire Regiment.

1ST BOMBAY EUROPEAN FUSILIERS. A regiment of the East India Company, they took part in a number of campaigns towards the end of the eighteenth century including the storming of Ahmedabad in 1780 and the siege of Seringapatam in 1799. They saw further action against the Mahrattas and in the Persian Gulf. After the Sikh Wars and the Indian Mutiny they became the 103rd (Royal Bombay Fusiliers) Foot. In 1881 they were named the 2nd Royal Dublin Fusiliers. The old 1st Madras European Fusiliers which became the 102nd Foot after the Mutiny, were designated the 1st Royal Dublin Fusiliers. Like the Munsters, the Dublins served with distinction in the First World War and were disbanded in 1922 when the Irish Free State was created.

2ND BENGAL EUROPEAN FUSILIERS. A regiment of the East India Company, they were raised in 1839 and took part in the Afghan War of 1839–42. After service in the Second Sikh War they further distinguished themselves at Delhi during the Indian Mutiny. Absorbed into the Crown forces, they were designated the 104th (Bengal Fusiliers) Foot. In 1881 they were renamed the 2nd Royal Munster Fusiliers. The 101st Foot (raised in 1756 as the 1st Bengal European Fusiliers) became the 1st Royal Munster Fusiliers.

BENGAL HORSE ARTILLERY. Formed in 1800, they saw their first active service under Abercrombie in Egypt the following year and by the time they were merged with the Royal Horse Artillery after the Indian Mutiny consisted of thirteen troops in three brigades. Nicknamed The Red Men by the Afghans, because of their distinctive helmets with horse hair manes, they had their depot at Dum Dum. Modern descendants of the Bengal H.A. include F (Sphinx) Battery, R.H.A., and L (Nery) Battery, R.A.

BENGAL FOOT ARTILLERY. The early companies formed by the East India Company in 1748 suffered in the events leading up to the Black Hole of Calcutta. They were present at Plassey in 1757 and played an important part in all the major Indian campaigns. The presence of bullock or elephant-drawn heavy guns was essential in the siege operations against the massive fortresses of India. After the Mutiny the artillery was taken over by the Crown with other East India Company regiments and a policy of keeping cannon out of the hands of native troops was implemented.

31ST BENGAL NATIVE INFANTRY. As the 2nd Battalion of the 15th Native Infantry they helped to defeat the French threat to India at the beginning of the 19th Century, taking a prominent part in the actions at Delhi and Laswaree in 1803. After their service in the Second Sikh War they won further honours during the Mutiny and became the 2nd Queen's Own Light Infantry. As the 2nd Rajputs they fought in China in 1900, Mesopotamia in the First World War and in Burma during the Second World War.

70TH BENGAL NATIVE INFANTRY. They became the 11th Rajputs after the Indian Mutiny and served in Canton in 1858. The regiment was in Mesopotamia in the First World War, took part in the Afghan War of 1919 and as the 5th Rajputs were overwhelmed after a stubborn fight in Hongkong in the Second World War.

4TH BOMBAY RIFLES. This regiment which acted as sharpshooters at the siege of Multan became the 104th (Wellesley's)

Rifles after the Mutiny. As the 1st Rajputana Rifles they fought in the Middle East in the First World War, returning there with the 4th Indian Division in the Second.

3RD BOMBAY LIGHT INFANTRY. Also members of the Multan force, they had a long tradition of service stretching back to the Mysore campaign of 1789. Becoming the 103rd Mahrattas after the Mutiny, they served in Abyssinia in 1867 and returned there as the 1st Mahrattas with the successful British forces in 1940. They were subsequently involved in severe fighting in the North African campaign.

THE KHALSA.

After the end of the Sikh Wars the British paid the Khalsa a genuine compliment by enlisting its veterans in dozens of infantry regiments. The warriors repaid the trust shown by standing firm during the Indian Mutiny. Four battalions suffered severe casualties at the siege of Delhi. One of the Punjaub's most famous regiments, the Ludhiana Sikhs, later the Royal Sikh Regiment, were the first Indian unit to arrive in France in 1914. Battalions of this and other Sikh regiments, plus Jats and Punjaubi Mussulmans, saw service all over the globe in the two World Wars.

OTHER REGIMENTS MENTIONED IN THE TEXT

13TH FOOT. Raised in 1685 and converted to light infantry in 1822. Granted the cypher P.A. (Prince Albert's) and the monogram 'Jellalabad' for their defence of that place in the Afghan War of 1839–42. They became the Somerset Light Infantry, 1881. Now part of the Light Infantry Division.

44TH FOOT. The 44th lost 22 officers and 645 men during the retreat from Kabul in 1841. They made their last stand at Gandamak. A Waterloo regiment, the 44th became the 1st Essex in 1881, the 56th (West Essex) forming the 2nd Essex. They are now part of the Royal Anglians.

58TH FOOT. One of Wolfe's Canadian regiments, fighting at Louisberg and Quebec, they were originally associated with Rutlandshire but in 1881 became the 2nd Battalion the Northamptonshire Regiment. They are now part of the Royal Anglians.

87TH FOOT. Originally the Prince of Wales's Irish Regiment, when they were raised in 1793, they became the Royal Irish Fusiliers in 1827. In 1881 they took the title of 1st Royal Irish Fusiliers (Princess Victoria's) and were linked with the 89th Foot.

98TH FOOT. Latecomers to the Army List, the regiment was raised in 1824 at Chichester. Sir Colin Campbell, later Lord Clyde, was their commanding officer from 1835 to 1847, leading them during the wars in China. Although they were present in India during the Second Sikh War they were mainly responsible for protecting the Governor-General and the East India Company's treasure chests. They became the 2nd North Staffordshire in 1881 (linked with the 64th Foot).

GLOSSARY

Amballa	Large town in the eastern Punjaub. The British cantonments were established in 1843.
Amritzar	The holy city of the Sikhs. Also famous for its courtesans.
Anna	Small coin – a sixteenth of a rupee.
Babul	Acacia tree.
Bala Hissar	The citadel at Kabul, stormed during the British punitive expedition in 1842.
Batta	A bonus payment by the East India Company paid to soldiers as an active service allowance. The source of much friction.
Bhang	Indian hemp – eaten, smoked or drunk by Sikhs despite religious restrictions.
Blitey (Blighty)	From Belaiti – Europe. Blitey water – soda water.
Budmash	Robber or footpad.
Chapattis	Thin cakes of unleavened bread.
Chupao	Attack.
Dafadar	Sergeant.
Dhai pat	Hit and run.
Dhak	Tree used for making red lacquer
Dhooli	Litter.
Doab	Triangle of land between the converging arms of rivers.
Dogra	Warrior tribe who live in the Punjaub. Dogra regiments served in the Indian Army after the Sikh Wars.
Durbar	Ceremonial meeting.
Durga	Hindu goddess of death, also known as Kali, Bhawani, Parvati. Idol black with four arms.
Engrese	English.
Feringhee	Also English or British.
Ferozeshah	Town in the Punjaub near the site of British victory in First Sikh War.

Gandamak	Scene of massacre of 44th Foot in Afghan War (1841).
Ghari	Light carriage.
Ghat	Riverside steps.
Gurkhas	Hillmen from Nepal. Supplied regiments to Sikhs and British prior to 1848.
Gorah-log	White folk; also 'lords'.
Hindu	India's largest religious sect, usually vegetarian and believing in many gods.
Hindustani	Language of the Hindus (Urdu is the Mohammedan form).
Hodson	Legendary leader of Hodson's Horse (9th Cavalry) who commanded the Guides during the Second Sikh War. Killed at the siege of Delhi.
Indus	Historic waterway of North West India forming the largest of the five rivers of the Punjaub. The others are the Jhelum, Chenab, Ravi and Sutlej.
Jang-i-Lat Sahib	Commander-in-Chief.
Jat	Cattle breeders and farmers in the North West and warrior caste.
Khalsa	'The Pure' – Army of the Sikh nation.
Khalsalji	Those of the Khalsa.
Lahore	Chief city of West Punjaub (West Pakistan) where Kipling edited local paper and spent much of his early life.
Narain!	Hindu expletive or exclamation.
Nickel-jao!	Clear off!
Ooriyas	Farmers and warriors from Orissa.
Palankeen	Form of portable chair, normally carried by eight bearers, often for long journeys across country. Falling out of use by 1848.
Pani	Water.
Pathan	North-West frontier tribesman – Mahommedan.
Pesh-kabz	Sikh dagger.
Pice	Quarter of an anna.
Pulton	Regiment.
Punjaub	Land of the Five Rivers, North-West

	India. (Panj-nad – name sometimes given to united rivers immediately below the final junction where the Chenab meets the Indus.)
Rajput	Warrior and tribal race of Western India – Hindu.
Rattan	Cane or staff.
Resaldar	Major (sometimes Rissaldar).
Resaldar-Major	Colonel.
Rupee	Silver coin.
Saalam	Greetings.
Saddhu	Wandering holy man, sometimes wearing very little.
Saise	Groom.
San sakai	Sikh book of religious prophesies.
Sari	Native female gown.
Sepoy	Native soldier.
Shaitan	Devil.
Sikh	Warrior race following the Granth, or Book of Nanak (1469–1539).
Sirdar	Governor or revenue collector. Sometimes Sardar or Dewan.
Sirkar	Company – Engrese Sirkar, English (East India) Company.
Sobraon	Scene of Gough's victory over Sikhs in 1846.
Sowar	Cavalry trooper.
Shootar sowar	Camel despatch rider.
Subadar	Company commander in native regiment.
Suttee	Hindu practice of burning widows with husbands.
Tatty	Grass woven into blind.
Tatty-wallah	Servant who throws water on tatty.
Tiffin	Lunch.
Tulwar	Heavy curved native sword with single edge.
Wordi-major	Native adjutant.
Zenana	Women's quarters. One of the signs of Sikh unrest was their threat to European women that soon they would all be shut in the Sikh zenanas.

SELECTED BIBLIOGRAPHY

Adams, J., *The South Wales Borderers*, Leo Cooper, 1968.

Angelsey, Earl of, *Sergeant Pearman's Memoirs*, Cape, 1968.

Baird, J. G. A., *Private Letters of the Marquess of Dalhousie*, Blackwood, 1911.

Bajwa, Fauja Singh, *Military System of the Sikhs 1799–1849*, Delhi, 1964.

Bruce, G., *Six Battles for India*, Arthur Barker, 1969.

Daly, H., *Memoirs of Sir Henry Dermot Daly*, Arthur Murray, 1905.

Fortescue, The Hon. J. W., *History of the British Army*, Vol. XII, Macmillan, 1927.

Gale, Gen. Sir Richard, *The Worcestershire Regiment*, Leo Cooper, 1970.

Hughes, Major-Gen. B. P., *The Bengal Horse Artillery, 1800–61*, Arms and Armour Press, 1971.

Khoi, Sita Ram, *Sunset of the Sikh Empire*, Orient Longmans, London.

Maharajan, Jamohan, *Circumstances leading to the annexation of The Punjab*, Allahabad, 1949.

Rait, R. S., *Life and Campaigns of Hugh*, Viscount Gough, London, 1903.

Singh, Kushwant, *A History of the Sikhs*, Princeton University Press, 1966.

The Sikhs, Allen and Unwin, 1953.

Smith, Sir Harry, *Autobiography*, John Murray, 1902.

Smith, Vincent A., *The Oxford History of India*, 1933.

Thackwell, E. J., *The Second Sikh War*, London, 1852.